Summer Love
An LGBTQ Collection

Summer LOVE

An LGBTQ Collection

Edited by Annie Harper

duet an imprint of interlude press

Contents

Foreword

Summer is that "in-between" time when anything can happen. The days are long, long enough to reinvent yourself, to discover who you really are, to find the courage to open yourself to love. When we at Duet set out to publish our first collection of love stories featuring LGBTQ protagonists, we knew immediately that we wanted to set the stories in summer for that very reason.

In compiling this collection, we looked for examples of love that serve as catalysts for awakening to new ideas, new possibilities and new confidence. The stories we chose are about finding love in a range of its manifestations—from first love to the love that heals a broken heart, from platonic love to second chances.

Nine original stories from debut authors make up the *Summer Love* collection. In Rachel Davidson Leigh's "Beautiful Monsters," a campaign volunteer is assigned to assist his high school's Gay Straight Alliance for the Pride Parade, forcing him to face the students he had previously avoided and the truth about himself. Naomi Tajedler's "What the Heart Wants" explores the discovery of attraction and desire through a different lens: a young woman's experience drawing figures in a summer art class.

The sweetness of a love forged in summer is present in three stories: "The Willow Weeps for Us" by Suzey Ingold, in which a young son of a grocer falls for a charming piano teacher on the eve of World War II; "The Most Handsome" by S.J. Martin, a story about a Cape Cod boy, recently out as transgender, who meets and falls in love with a college student visiting for the season; and "My Best Friend," a young gay man's letter to his childhood best friend.

In "The Fire-Eater's Daughter," Amy Stilgenbauer writes about getting another chance for happiness, when a local girl must choose between caring for her mother and running off with the traveling carnival to make a life with the beautiful and mysterious woman who stole her heart. Rachel Blackburn offers insight about a different sort of fresh start in "On the Shore," in which a young woman retreats to her parents' beach house to nurse a broken heart, but instead meets a vivacious girl who helps her find joy again.

Accepting and celebrating who you are and how you are different is explored in Caroline Hanlin's "Something Like Freedom" about a boy who finds a safe space from which to imagine a new future after leaving his conservative parents' home and in "Surface Tension" by Ella J. Ash, a story about a camp counselor who wants one summer where he can fit in without labels, but who ends up having a very different experience when he falls for the out-and-proud "head of canoe instruction."

We are proud that *Summer Love* authors represent a spectrum of sexual and gender identity, as do their characters. Thought-provoking and brave, delightful and sweet, the stories in this collection will move and inspire. That a young reader may see himself or herself in these stories is our mission at Duet. That *all* readers see that love is love, no matter how you identify, is our greatest wish.

—*Annie Harper*

Beautiful Monsters

Rachel Davidson Leigh

C ODY HARDLY FEELS THE FIRST BLOW TO THE BACK OF HIS chair. In the seven weeks since he started volunteering for the Parker campaign, his office-mate Carrie Dodson and her boredom kicks have become his closest friends. Sometimes, when the donors aren't picking up and the office AC dies, she wads up the used call lists and tosses them at the back of his chair, calling out points when she gets him in the head. Today, she works up a good rhythm before he finally pulls out both earbuds and looks back, eyebrows raised.

"Markhausen." Carrie gestures toward his supervisor's office door with one manicured thumb, her big blue eyes blinking under a cloud of bleached-blonde hair. "That's still you, right?"

That's when Cody hears a voice calling from the other side of the door. For a second, he isn't sure what to do. For all the regularity of his presence as a campaign peon, he's spoken maybe five words to the middle-aged dragon lady in charge. To be honest, he's shocked that Judy knows his name. Judy doesn't *do* names.

He stares at the closed door, eyes wide in confusion. "What do I—?"

"I dunno." Carrie looks as surprised as he feels, but considerably less concerned. She glances at Judy's office and shrugs. "I guess you go in."

Cody nods and stands, like a robot in a seventeen-year-old boy's body. There's no way he could have gotten in trouble. A trained monkey could enter this data without breaking a sweat.

He pushes the door ajar with the pads of his fingers and steps inside to find his boss, the unstoppable Judy Gould, nearly buried under stacks of printer paper. He assumes the space at her feet is clear, but he can't see anything except her head over the piles towering on either side of her desk. Until now, she has existed only as a passing blur of angles and three-inch heels, her elbows and fingernails slicing the air like knives, her lipstick the color of congealed blood.

"Cody!" She smiles and waves him in, already scrolling through something on her phone. "I was starting to think that those headphones had done something to your brain. Get yourself in here."

He leaves the door cracked and hesitates before perching on a stack of folders piled atop a metal folding chair He focuses on balancing his weight, which isn't easy when his feet barely hit the floor and his hands are slick with summer sweat. Judy, of course, doesn't notice a thing.

"You're in high school, yes?" she asks, glancing up from her phone. He nods and she barrels on.

"Here's the deal. There's a kid at St. Claire Senior High who's been pestering me for ages about getting the campaign involved in 'youth issues,'" she says with violent air quotes, "and I finally told him that we could 'team up' for a parade on Friday. He brings bodies, we bring campaign signs and we get him off our backs for one more week. I'll even throw in the markers for some artistic involvement."

"So." She stands, and Cody is reminded of a hawk before it dives in for the kill. "Since he's a little shit who can't vote, and you're a little shit who can't vote, I thought it was a match made in budgetary heaven. I know." She grins, reaching for a stack of files in the corner. "Sometimes I outdo myself." Cody wonders if, for Judy, "little shit" is a term of affection.

Judy pulls a piece of paper from the top file and waves it in his direction. "Apparently, his little club meets tomorrow. Go, be nice, and we'll see you next week. Go team!" She raises her fists in mock encouragement, and Cody turns to get out of the office before the walls close in like the trash compactor in *Star Wars*. He has his hand on the doorknob when a chill runs down his back. Judy is laughing. Unless she's literally taking candy from babies, Judy doesn't laugh.

"Oh right," she giggles, and Cody freezes in his tracks. "I hope you like glitter."

Outside the door, he looks down at the paper and almost forgets to keep standing:

ORGANIZATION: ST. CLAIRE SENIOR HIGH GAY STRAIGHT ALLIANCE (GSA)
CONTACT: ANDREAS FURNEAUX
MEET: JULY 26, ST. CLAIRE SENIOR HIGH, RM 124, 11 AM
EVENT: ST. CLAIRE GAY PRIDE PARADE

No. Cody feels the blood drain from his cheeks. *No, no no. Anything but this.* He turns to barge back into Judy's office, but he can't go back in there. What could he possibly say? Instead, he drops back into his chair and stares a hole into the dirty white wall pocked with thumbtacks of campaigns past.

Just out of Cody's peripheral vision, Carrie clears her throat. She gives a wave when he turns. She could pretend that she hadn't heard everything in Judy's office, but there really isn't any point.

"I wouldn't get worked up about a bunch of high school punks, babe. Do you know these kids?" He shakes his head. He doesn't know them. He knows of them. He's been avoiding them for years. "Well, don't worry. Everyone loves a basketball star."

She turns back to her double-wide computer screen and Cody nods. *No. It isn't like that at all.* No one knows him at school. He's fast, so they let him play, but most of the guys on his team don't even know his name. The moment he steps off the court he's just another white boy with blond, wispy hair that won't stay out of his eyes. He's invisible. It's either that or be the runt—the short kid with eyes too big for his face—and given that choice, he'd rather be nothing at all.

Carrie peeks up over her computer to find him still gaping at the wall. "Get a move on, Markhausen. I wouldn't want you to be tired for your big debut!" She grins, and before he can protest he's shuffling toward the front door.

Stepping out of the Parker for Senate northern headquarters in St. Claire, Wisconsin, Cody squints at the mayflies buzzing under Monroe Avenue's only streetlight. Concerned citizens had campaigned for more, but the idea was dismissed as unnecessarily indulgent. The lamp flickers under the pressure of beating wings, and Cody, the proud representative of the Parker campaign, turns to throw up in front of the door.

⚜

THE NEXT MORNING, CODY FINDS HIMSELF WALKING THROUGH the hallways of his empty school. His footsteps echo in long, dull tones. Without air conditioning, the building cooks in its own stale air; the walls sweat like a giant body in the sun and drip condensation into dirty puddles on the floor.

As he walks, Cody rolls a tiny plastic model between his fingers until he can feel the edges cutting into his skin. When he was thirteen, his aunt sent him a model-making kit in a gray box labeled WARMACHINE. He's sure she had no idea what she was doing; she probably walked into the nearest game store and asked what to give a quiet child. Still, she did well. Four years and a hundred models later, he's learned to love the details on a monstrous face. He sculpts wings and paints lips for hours, until his warriors emerge from fields of gray.

The models are meant for a two-person tabletop game, but Cody's never bothered to find someone to play with. Instead he reads about each unearthly face in paperback guidebooks until he knows the characters as well as members of his own family. For years the monsters blurred together, until he found Kaelyssa: Guardian of the Light. In a game full of enthusiastic killers and team players, she is solitary and peaceful. She fights with terrible precision, but her enemies never break her shell. Cody wishes he could pull that peace from the pages of his book and wear it like a winter coat.

Instead, when the world creeps in, he rolls the figure in his hand, or presses it into his leg until he feels the sharp-edged wings against his thigh. On days like today, it hurts just enough to pull him back into his own skin.

Cody hears the meeting before he sees the room. He follows the wordless chatter toward a lit doorway. As he stands, willing the building to fall around his shoulders, a short girl with bushy eyebrows bolts into the classroom. As she enters, the room erupts in greeting. Cody can make out a boy's voice screaming, "Girl, where have you been? I have been *worried.*" Maybe if he sneaks in now, everyone will be paying so much attention to her that they won't notice him come in.

The entire room sees him when he slips inside, but no one seems to care. Cody isn't half as interesting as whatever Bushy-brows is trying to say, and for that he is infinitely grateful.

He drops into a seat at a long table against the leftmost wall and stares at the crowd. This isn't what he expected. He doesn't know what he expected a real group of *those people* to look like up close, but it wasn't this. Even with only twelve or thirteen bodies in the room, they're making enough noise for a mob twice their size. A round boy with short blue hair and domineering hands sits on a table, gesturing to three blonde girls who seem more interested in trading magazines. A boy—or maybe it's a girl—races to lift Bushy-brows in a rib-rattling hug, and they're laughing before her feet hit the floor.

"How could you go without me, you traitor?" Cody stares as a tiny Asian girl with chubby cheeks suddenly wails in existential pain. "I introduced you to Adam Pascal. That was me," she says, jabbing her finger up into the face of a tall, dark-skinned girl whose eyes are rapidly filling with tears. "I showed you the brilliance of his soul, and you couldn't bother to tell me that he would be performing within fifty miles of my body?"

"Maddie—"

"Don't. Just don't." Maddie slams herself into a chair with all the scorn she can muster. "I don't think I know you anymore."

"Mads—"

"Maybe I never did—"

"Oh, come on!" The tall girl drops into a crouch and glares into her friend's face. "It's been years. Literally. I thought you were over *Rent.*"

"Over *Rent?*" The boy on the table turns, aghast, as though she's just implied that it is possible to be over running water.

"Butt out, Terrence."

It's all overwhelming, and Cody feels himself sinking lower and lower in his plastic chair. If he drops under the table and stays there long enough, maybe they'll forget why they decided to meet in the first place and just go home. He pulls a pile of campaign guidelines from his backpack and starts to set them up around his body like a barricade.

Then he hears a dark chuckle from behind the boy called Terrence.

He jerks to attention, and it stops. He flips a packet on parade etiquette right side up, and there it is again—a low laugh that might be directed at him.

Cody leans all the way back in his seat to peek around Terrence and finds a thin white face looking back at him, emphatically unimpressed. From his awkward angle, Cody can just make out the boy who owns the face: long, thin legs crossed on top of the table, long fingers clasped over a thin chest. He tips back in his chair as if he owns the room; Cody wonders if it might not be true. The boy cocks his head at him, but Cody can't stop staring. Somehow, the boy seems to take up more space than his wiry frame should allow. As he leans, the loose ends of his jacket and T-shirt drop away from his body in points as sharp as the lines in his face and his dark, cropped hair.

The boy squints at the papers now piled in front of Cody's face. "I knew it." He nods, and the corners of his lips twitch in the hint of a grin. Leaning forward, eyes hard as cut diamonds, he whispers, "Watch this."

Cody watches. He can't imagine that he has a choice. Slowly, the other boy turns to the group, legs still crossed over the top of the table—and does absolutely nothing. As the seconds tick away, the boy crosses his arms over his chest and cocks his ear toward the group while the noise grows. Cody is suddenly reminded of a chef hovering over a pan, listening for the exact moment when the bacon starts to sizzle.

A minute disappears, and then two, and now Cody can't tell one conversation from the next; the squealing sounds converge until he can't bear to sit still. He opens his mouth to tell this kid exactly where he can shove his little demonstration, just in time to watch the boy toe over a stack of textbooks and send them crashing to the floor. The crash cuts through the room, and suddenly the boy has the entire group's rapt attention. Faces peer from every corner, hands frozen in whatever gesture they'd been making when the pile hit the ground.

Impressive. And from Cody's angle, it almost looked like an accident.

The other boy unfolds his legs and eases to his feet, impassive under the group's gaze. As he stands, he crosses his arms delicately over his chest in a precise show of irritation.

"Good morning ladies, gentlemen and everything in between," he begins. The tall girl tosses a pencil at his head, and he ducks it with ease. "I'm glad to see that you could all join me on this beautiful summer day. We have three days until the glorious crappitude that is the St. Claire Pride Parade, and do we want our presence in the parade to suck, Kaiylee?"

"No," a voice calls from the back, like clockwork.

"No what?"

"No, André, we don't want to make the parade suck any more than it already does."

"That's right. So, in service of that goal—which is what, Maddie?"

"Not sucking."

"Right—I'm going to sit over here with the nice 'man' the Parker campaign has sent over to help us along." Cody hears the implied quotation marks and tries not to scowl into his papers. "We're going to work out the minutiae for the day—"

"The what?" A boy's thin, white hand shoots up from the middle of the pack and the speaker sighs.

"The bullshit, Andrew. For fuck's sake, I keep telling you that books open."

"Fuck you, André."

"Not in this lifetime," he snaps and shifts his focus back to the rest of the group. "So while I'm hashing out boring parking permits with this guy, we're gonna need people figuring out the really important questions. Obviously," he smiles, "I'm talking about what we're going to wear."

"Yes," a tiny girl in the front whispers reverently. "Yes!"

André stoops to pick up a clipboard covered in color swatches from the floor and hands it to the boy sitting on the table. "Terrence, Maddie, Juliet—you're on point. We need something coherent, but not too flamboyant for the St. Claire masses. Unless we're being given campaign T-shirts?" He looks back at Cody and raises an eyebrow at his blank stare. "Let's assume we aren't getting T-shirts. Remember, don't listen to anything Andrew says, and don't let me down."

Cody feels as if he's stepped into some kind of creation ritual without a rulebook. The speech drips sarcasm, and yet no one else seems to notice, or care. Instead, they rush into action as though this André is the second coming of Tim Gunn and they are damn well going to "make it work."

"We have to match!" Maddie squeals to the tall girl who threw the pencil.

"But not exactly, right?" she replies, her dark eyebrows furrowed. "If we all wear the same thing, half of us are going to look like shit."

Terrence is already hunched over a three-ring binder, drawing angular shapes as the rest of the group huddles to contribute opinions.

For a second, André watches, arms still wrapped around his body, mouth pulled into a tight, close-lipped smile. Then he turns, and his smile slips into a line of disdain. "There we go," he says, voice drained, and drops into a chair across the table from Cody. "That should keep them busy for a while. Now, I need to figure out what to do with *you*." He lifts a pencil in two fingers and lets it dangle like a cigarette in a long, elegant holder. Cody is fairly sure that André, if he had his druthers, would be blowing smoke rings between Cody's eyes.

"I—um—" Cody feels his brain stutter and shut off. "I guess we should—" André suddenly focuses his considerable attention on him; his nose is wrinkled as though Cody resembles a particularly unusual insect. "I—I'm Cody and—um—should I call you Andreas?"

"André is fine," he says in a tone that suggests absolutely nothing is fine.

"Okay." Cody stares down at his papers and watches the words swim in front of his eyes. "The campaign has provided guidelines in here about how to—um—to register for the parade and there's something about what we can put on the signs—"

"Are you even old enough to go to this school?" Cody looks up to find André leaning across the table, peering into his face. "Did they send us a middle-schooler?"

"I'm a senior."

"Seriously? I'm a senior. How are you a senior?" André looks genuinely shocked, as if Cody has just told him that he moonlights with the Harlem Globetrotters.

"Seriously. I don't know if you have strong feelings about your posters, but I—I have markers and I think the campaign could provide poster board if you—um—I mean if you don't already have some." Even with the stammer, Cody knows he can play the part of a competent volunteer if this guy will let him. Still, André won't budge. If anything, his eyes keep getting wider. "I could meet with your group tomorrow to make the posters if—if you'd like. What did you do last year?"

"Absolutely fuck all."

Cody feels his expression sour, and André shrugs, continuing: "No, I mean it. We jumped in two days before the event and when we showed up, hardly anyone was there. The entire parade was us, the organizing committee and the drag queens from the Starlight Lounge." André delivers the line like a joke, but he's no longer looking Cody in the eye. "The kids were pissed, but it's not like parades do anything, right? Has any homophobe ever wandered into a shitty little pride parade and suddenly realized the error of his ways? 'Oh shit, I've been wrong all along, these little fairies know how to throw a party.'" André lays his hand over his heart in mock contrition; Cody can't bring himself to laugh. "Anyway, it didn't do a lot for team morale. Thanks for asking."

Cody blanches and looks down at the papers in his hands. "I didn't mean to—"

"But if you're a senior, does that mean you're actually seventeen? You must be one of those wunderkinds who graduate from high school before they hit puberty. Do you already have a contract with NASA?" André asks this last in a low whisper and, when Cody looks up, he gives a smirk that's at once patronizing and utterly bored. Across the table, André carefully crosses one leg over the other and purses his lips as if to say, *Well, dumbass? You gonna answer the question?*

"Really?" Cody's mouth drops open and he dumps the papers onto the desk before he can think about what he's doing. "I'm trying to help you, and you—" He sounds petulant, but he can't seem to stop. "I didn't even want to be here, but I got the job and I don't get why you're riding me so hard, you—you— "

Cody glares down at his scattered papers. It takes one whole breath before he realizes what he's just said. He just—*oh my God*. He looks up in horror to find André leaning back with a wide, self-satisfied grin. "Oh, honey, really? I never ride anyone until after the first date."

"You know I wasn't talking about… that," Cody mutters.

"About what?" André asks, all innocence, and rolls his eyes toward the ceiling. "Oh, don't worry. I won't make you say it. But you should know that it isn't catching. You can't go homo just by acknowledging the pink elephant in the room," he says with a bite. Cody flinches back into his chair. "Now," André says, with a wicked grin, "if you want to go full-on gay, there might be some riding involved, but I'm not sure I'm your guy. If you want, I could ask Andrew. I can't promise anything, but he's pretty desperate. Isn't that right, Andy?" He calls over his shoulder toward the huddle of students still chattering over T-shirt designs, and something in Cody snaps.

"No," he whispers, leaning over the table and poking André in the arm until he turns around. "I really don't get it." André's eyes narrow, but Cody keeps pushing. "I'm here. I'm talking with you about posters and parking, while they're all talking about what? Costumes? I don't get it. I know you don't know me from Adam, but I'm here talking about the 'bullshit,' as you so kindly put it, so what did I do to get on your shit list?"

Cody jerks his head toward the other students and watches as the humor drains from André's face one muscle at a time. He was grinning just a second ago, eyes flashing with humor, but now, under Cody's gaze, André turns to stone. He leans over, elbows pressed into the laminate table, eyes as hard as glass.

"Shit list?" André says in disbelief. "You aren't on my shit list, because I save my shit list for people that matter." He points over his shoulder toward the group, his hand shaking in suppressed rage. "Do you see Kaiylee and Terrence? They both got kicked out of their houses last year, shortly before I got kicked out of mine. She's been sleeping on a blow-up mattress with a friend for the last eight months, and he's been on more couches than he can count. Do you see Maddie? She will never get kicked out of her house, but she'll also never be able to leave. Her mom wants her to take over the family store, which means that she gets to go to college, but she probably won't be able to have an open relationship with another woman until all of her relatives are dead. Some of those kids are depressed, some of them have tried to kill themselves, and even the ones with perfectly wonderful little families are a little fucked up, because it's almost impossible not to be."

André takes a deep, shaky breath and Cody leans back, mouth agape.

"Of course they're talking about clothes and stupid costumes," André continues with bitter emphasis, "because what the hell else should they be talking about? No really, tell me, because this is the place they come to *not* talk about all that other shit. This is where they get to be idiots, like every other teenager on the planet, so they talk about clothes and movies, and I don't get in their way." He sighs and stares down at his own hand as it taps on the edge of the table. "You are not on any of my lists, because—right now—you are standing in their way. I'm sure that you are a perfectly decent sort of person in any other context, but right now—" He breaks off with a swallow and, when he looks up, his eyes shine under the fluorescent lights. "Do you have any idea how much—I spent three months calling your office. That meant three months listening to that woman's voicemail in the stupid hope that someone might notice. I get it. I do. Poor kids don't vote, and the ones without parents might as well be road kill, but fuck it, what else was I supposed to do?"

André pushes himself to his feet, eyes raw, and as much as Cody might want to, he can't look away.

"Cody, I'm *riding you* because right now you're all we've got. I spent three months hoping for some real sign that this campaign gave half a shit about queer kids, and instead I got you."

His words fall like grenades, and Cody sits, helpless to stop them.

André scoops up his backpack from a chair and turns toward the door, his face once again official and distant. "We usually get ready at Warner Park, by the staging area. Be there at five with the poster supplies and I'll make sure they all show up in time for the parade." He nods in a sharp jerk and turns without waiting for Cody's assent.

THREE DAYS LATER, CODY TROMPS ACROSS THE WARNER FIELDS in a haze of fog and sweat. He hasn't been sleeping well, not before the meeting at the school and certainly not after. He keeps wandering into the same memories, reliving them one after another, like a film that won't move past the penultimate scene. It wouldn't be so frustrating if the memories weren't so boring. In every one, he's on the playground by Foster Creek Elementary, across the street from his house. He practically lived on that sand and cement before he started middle school; he could see the swings from his bedroom window. Now, his brain won't stop going back to recess and the crowd of little boys playing smear-the-queer on the open field.

He didn't know what it meant at the time. None of them did. It was just the name for the kid who had to take the ball and run until everyone tackled him and took him down. "The queer" could run anywhere near the school; it was all fair game. But he was always eventually caught, and he always hit the ground coughing and yelling at all the other guys to get off so someone else could take a turn.

Cody was too fast to be the queer. The whole point of the game was the tackle; it wasn't fun if the queer got away, so the other kids never asked and he never offered. Instead, he chased and felt the ground move under his feet. Most of the boys were bigger, so he had to run at full speed into their sides, head down, to bear the impact.

That's what he remembers now: barreling into faceless bodies and watching them crash in a cloud of dust. He can't remember what happened after that. They might have come up laughing. Some might have cried, but he doesn't know. He can't get his mind to move past the rush and sudden crash, jarring his bones as if that nine-year-old is still hidden somewhere inside his seventeen-year-old frame.

He runs. He hits. He falls. And then he's running again, over and over again for days; until last night, when he doused himself with sleeping pills to get a decent night's sleep. This morning, his mom had to shake him and then shake him again to get him out of bed.

As he walks, a black speck emerges in the distance and grows into André, perched on the top of a picnic table, leaning back on his hands, his brown eyes scraping Cody's skin.

André Furneaux might be the first person to make Cody genuinely want to pick a fight, to say something dickish and throw a punch. Whenever he's been able to stop reliving the playground, he's thought about André's eyes, and what he might have to do to make them go dark in irritation. The answer is probably nothing. He just needs to exist to piss André off.

"You made it," André calls, as Cody gets close enough for heckling, "and here it is: only five thirty." He holds up his phone, as though Cody could read it from ten feet away and clucks like a mother hen. "Did you get lost? You didn't actually just move here from an air force base in Russia or anything, right?"

"I walked." Cody dumps his bags on the dry dirt at André's feet and looks up; the figurine pokes his hip in the pocket of his jeans. "The Saturday bus schedule is weird and I didn't factor in the—"

"Oh, stop. I know. I just got here five minutes ago." André snorts and pushes himself off the top of the table, revealing a paper bag filled with streamers and yardsticks. "Are you usually immune to sarcasm?"

"Usually?" Cody asks, mostly to himself. Nothing about this is usual. "Usually, I don't feel quite so necessary. After all, you've only got me." He digs into the nearest bag for the black Sharpie and feels André stiffen. He hadn't meant to throw André's line about being the "only one" back in his face, but now he doesn't want to take it back. He waits for André to tell him to fuck off, but the words never come.

"Huh." Cody peeks up to see André biting his lip and smiling ruefully at the sky. "You know," he says, "I may have overstated that point... for emphasis. I remember saying something about lists." He shrugs, and Cody has the distinct sense that this is the closest André will come to an apology.

"Emphasis," Cody echoes in disbelief.

"Let's go with that. Like you said, you're here," André says, and the corner of his lips twitch as he crouches to reach into his own bag. "Plus, you're not all they have, thank God. There's me, there's Terrence, and Maddie's pretty intense when she wants to be."

"I noticed." Cody risks a tight smile, and something tense between them starts to crackle, like frost breaking under the sun. He searches for a peace offering and jumps on the first stupid thing that comes to mind. "Just so you know," he starts, slowly, "it wasn't just you. Judy—the woman you called— she's awful to everyone. I still remember listening to her answering machine message a million times when I was trying to volunteer. I don't think she ever called back either way. I just showed up at the office and they never made me leave."

"Well, that's just beautiful."

"Isn't it?"

"Truly, democracy in action. I can see the posters now. *Come volunteer for democracy... if you absolutely insist.*" André flexes into an imaginary camera like a disgruntled Rosie the Riveter and looks Cody in the eye. Cody feels his stomach give an almost audible flip. He coughs out a laugh, looks down, and dives into a paper bag in search of supplies.

He holds up a Sharpie without looking back; André takes it and retreats to the picnic table with a piece of poster board and a stencil of the letter G. He sits cross-legged on top of the table while Cody spreads the poster board out onto the pavement and eyes the sign-making materials like a pop quiz.

After a long minute sizing up his poster board, Cody senses eyes on his back and turns to find André watching him. He raises an eyebrow, but André waves, unfazed. "Don't mind me, I've just never seen anyone commune with paper. Is it talking back?"

Cody rolls his eyes and goes back to the poster board. "Not yet."

"You sure? Because I can handle crazy. Some might even call me an expert."

"I'm sure," Cody sighs. "I'll let you know if I start receiving messages from the tree afterlife."

"Oh, *sassy.*" André sounds almost proud. He also sounds closer; his voice hovers just above Cody's shoulder, and his breath skims the back of Cody's neck. "Not bad for a straight boy." Cody flinches, but André barrels on. "You should try that line on Kaiylee. At last year's parade she said *she* could commune with trees."

"Was she one of the ones pissed about last year?" Cody's voice sounds steady, as if he isn't pushing down on a rising wave of bile. The word "straight" has never felt so overwhelmingly wrong, like putting on a parka for the Fourth of July.

Above his head, André stares thoughtfully toward the parade staging area at the end of the park. "No," he answers slowly. "To be totally honest, I was the only one who got my panties in a twist, but if you tell any of them that I just used the word 'panties' in a sentence, I will end you."

"Understood."

"I guess I was just expecting more," André continues, his voice dropping to little more than a murmur. "I don't know why. Most of the folks who live here couldn't spell homosexual with a dictionary in both hands." He gestures toward the four bars and one lonely Lutheran church visible from the park. Walk a few blocks in any direction, and the view wouldn't change. They stare down the street as a man in hunter orange props open the door of the Falcon Bar and starts sweeping out the entrance.

André shakes his head down at the table. "I've been watching too much Logo. Some piece of my brain wanted a movie parade and thought a horde of spectators would materialize out of the woodwork." He laughs up at the sky and as he smiles, he lights up like the sun. All of the sharp angles that seemed ready to cut in the classroom are instantly delicate, ringed in a halo of light. Cody has to look away; he can't imagine that André would want a stranger to see him so vulnerable.

By the time André stops laughing, Cody's back to his poster board, back turned and eyes carefully trained down.

"Well then," André says, peeking over Cody's shoulder at the still-blank canvas, "if this is still a standoff in ten minutes, I'm calling for backup." He waits for a response, but Cody can't find one. The emptiness of the poster board feels insurmountable. All the slogans he can think to write on the poster involve labels he can't attach to himself, and he cannot imagine carrying any of them down the middle of the street.

"Hey," André pokes him in the shoulder with the covered end of his Sharpie. "You're thinking too hard. No one's even going to look at our posters, because we've already established that no one is going to be there. Cody—oh, for fuck's sake. It's like you've never seen a marker in the wild." In a blink, André climbs down onto the ground, turns the poster board ninety degrees and starts scrawling in broad, red strokes. Cody watches as words emerge, the marker seeping through the fibers like blood in the sand.

"There." André sits back to study his work and then turns the poster for Cody's approval. "I got it started for you. It's inelegant, but nobody gives a shit, and I promise that just looking at the word won't make you like boys." He rolls his eyes as he stands and walks back toward the paper bags, and Cody can only stare at the poster.

There it is: G-A-Y in rude red chicken scratch.

It's just a word, but he thinks he might shake out of his skin. "You don't get it," he whispers, before he can stop his mouth.

19

"I already like boys. I've always liked boys and—" He sucks in a breath. "And that's not the *problem.*"

The words rush out in a wave, and when they hit, André finally turns, squinting, confused. Cody knows the minute they sink in: André's face goes lax in shock.

He's never said it out loud. Not in his room, not in the shower, not anywhere outside of his head. It sounds bitter and pathetic. He shouldn't have said it here—not in a pile of dirt, not in front of this tall, beautiful boy who doesn't understand. André inches forward, one hand out in front of his body, but Cody's already gone. As quickly as his mind shut down, it rushes back to life, and he runs.

CODY RUNS FOR WHAT SEEMS LIKE HOURS, FEET PUSHING OFF of the pavement, then the dirt and finally the long grass beyond the park fields. He used to love it here—not the park, but this hazy space where he runs too fast and breathes too hard to make sentences. It's what he does: When his dad's gone quiet or when he can't figure out a color scheme for his models, he runs. The wind picks up the edges of his shirt, and as he falls into a steady rhythm the world melts under his feet.

When he sits for too long, he can almost hear the mental gears grinding in his skull, but when he runs, he can't feel himself think. When the gears in the back of his mind threaten to turn, he runs harder, until his lungs burn and his eyes fill with tears. Maybe if he keeps going, the heat in his lungs will expand and he'll burn away, leaving a smoldering patch on the asphalt to mark his departure. He could just disappear.

He's never wanted anything more in his entire life.

Finally, he runs out of air. His hands drop to his knees and he hunches over the road, coughing into dirt so dry that his breath kicks it up in puffs. He has to go back. He wants to run until he forgets his own name, and all the names that anyone else might want to lay on his back; maybe then he could wake up on foreign soil and create himself anew. But right now he has to go back.

He stands and stares back over his shoulder at the speck in the distance that was André. André, who's been planning. André, who's bringing the whole club to carry signs that Cody couldn't make. André, who's already spent one year wondering what happened to his perfect day. André, who probably popped out of the womb knowing who he was and where he was supposed to be. Before this week, Cody can't remember when he last saw André from any less than a full hallway's distance away. That's when he'd catch a yell or a bleat of laugher from the clump of bodies up ahead, and find another way to class. For years, Juliet, Terrence, Maddie and the rest were just *that group* he didn't name, like a species too foreign for safe identification But still, even from a hundred feet away, André reeked of confidence. Cody might not have known his name or been able to pick out his face in a lineup, but it was obvious that *that boy*, with his crowd of loud, bizarre friends, was at home in his own skin.

Cody sucks in a ragged breath and starts running back toward the picnic table and all the art supplies he couldn't bring himself to use. It's too late for the posters, at least for the ones that didn't come from the campaign, but he'll 'fess up and apologize to everyone until he runs out of ways to say that this year's mess was all his fault. *I'm sorry I was too weak. I'm sorry I had a meltdown over poster board. I'm sorry. I'm sorry. I'm sorry.* André won't make it easy on him. Whatever uneasy truce they formed back there will be gone, but Cody can't say that he deserves anything less.

As soon as he can see the picnic table, Cody knows that he's been running too long. The empty clearing now holds at least ten teenagers, all dressed in the campaign's white and blue.

Terrence hands out rainbow handkerchiefs from a white trash bag, while André's sparring partner, Andrew, shoves new arrivals in André's direction. At the picnic table, Maddie and Juliet, the girls who'd been arguing about Adam Pascal back in the classroom, have mended fences; at least he thinks they have. But he doesn't remember Juliet, the tall black girl, being quite so *bald*. Maddie, the little raging one, sits on the picnic table bench, while Juliet sits on the table itself, leaning over and doing something serious with her friend's hair. They haven't seen him yet. He could still turn around and disappear into the park. For a second, he entertains the thought of just leaving all of them to celebrate the parade in peace, but then the huddle shifts and Cody finds himself looking directly into André's upturned gaze.

He can't make out André's expression, but it can't be good. There he is; André Furneaux, self-appointed champion of gay misfits, and Cody can't even deal with markers. As he gets within shouting distance, André starts walking toward him; when he gets within a few feet he holds up one hand. Cody stops in his tracks and feels his stomach jump into his throat. *No.* André doesn't even want him to come back. He'd been prepared for anger, but the rejection aches like an open wound. He turns to walk back into the park, his hand twisting the figurine in his pocket, when he hears André quietly say his name.

"Cody? Are you—?" André squints, eyebrows furrowed, and Cody's jaw drops in shock. André wants to know if he's okay. He's worried about whether or not the wimp who ran out on him is okay. Cody almost laughs. He'd never considered that André might care.

"I—" He starts and then realizes that he has no idea how he's doing. Still, he nods and André slowly lowers his hand to twitch at his side.

"Well," André says slowly, "I didn't think you were coming back."

"Yeah, neither did I." Cody shrugs and stares down at André's feet. "Surprise?" he tries, waving his splayed hands near his waist.

André doesn't smile. If anything, his face falls. His eyes drop to the ground. "You know," he says, "I've got plenty of idiots here to wave signs and be publicly stupid if you want to sit it out. I know you didn't really choose all of this." He waves back toward the students getting ready for the parade and finally catches Cody's eye. "You don't have to—"

"No." Cody replies, louder and more quickly than either of them expected. He shoves his hands in his pockets, but doesn't look away. "I mean, I'm—I want to be here. Besides," he raises an eyebrow and tries to smile, "if I go, you guys are probably gonna walk the wrong way on the parade route."

For a second, André just stares, squinting into Cody's face as if unsure whether to laugh. He cocks his head and Cody does his best to look certain. Something in his face must pass muster, because André breaks into a smile tinged with pride and beckons Cody to follow him into the crowd.

As he turns toward the group, André mutters Cody's line under his breath in disbelief. "The wrong way on the parade route... Jesus, I wouldn't let that happen, and if I did you wouldn't be the one to stop it," he calls over his shoulder.

"Who then?" Cody scoffs, right behind him. "Terrence?"

"*Please.* It would be Maddie, if anyone." André turns to face Cody and walks backward toward the tables. "Terrence and Andrew would walk us all into Lake Superior if someone didn't tell them to turn at the shore. We'd be knee-deep in water and—"

"Hi, Terrence." Cody raises a hand at the blue-haired boy physically blocking their path, and André turns with a guilty smirk.

"Glad to see you could join the party," Terrence deadpans, pressing a rainbow bandana into André's hand. André grabs a second bandana out of the bag, stuffs one in each of his back pockets and then goes in for a third.

"Cody was checking out the parade route," André replies, in a smooth lie. "It turns out we're still walking six blocks through absolutely nothing and then calling it a day." Terrence laughs, and, as he turns away, André presses a handkerchief into Cody's hand. "Use it wisely," he whispers into Cody's ear. "You're one of us now."

One of us. He's never been part of an "us." Cody stares down at the lines on the handkerchief and then at the two patches of color on the back of André's jeans as he walks toward the arriving cars.

Cody expects panic, but it doesn't come. Maybe he isn't ready to be Gay with a capital G, but if "us" can mean being one of these idiots, then maybe he's ready to have people of his own. As he watches the sharp sway of André's hips, the heat rising up his neck doesn't feel like fear. It feels like… clarity, as though the run put everything in perspective, and now he can't stop seeing André in crisp, dazzling color.

Someone presses a sign into his hand and guides him toward the parade staging area with the rest of the crew. Once again, he can't hear himself think over the din, but it's different now. At the meeting, and for years before that in the hallways, he felt like an invader locked out by a wall of sound, and now he's somehow wandered inside.

In their parade spot, next to a sad little flag stuck in the ground, parade-master Maddie tries yelling for quiet. She jumps up and down, waving her arms, but the noise grows, magnified by the echo between the pavement and the brick of the bar walls. She stamps her foot and Terrence takes it as a sign and stoops to let the tiny girl clamber onto his back. By the time she manages to get her head above the crowd, they're all watching.

"Thank you, Terrence," she calls. "I've never felt so dignified." The group giggles, and she glares from her dizzying height. "To the rest of you idiots, I want to see enthusiasm out there. Smile your asses off. Chant like you've never chanted before, because there might only be three people, but we are gonna give them a show! There's always the news crews, and we make a fabulous report!" A cheer rises from the little group, and Maddie's jaw twitches as she tries not to smile.

"Unfurl the banner!" she bellows, and out it comes, a plastic screen-printed monstrosity, long enough to require four carriers. "Banner holders to the front, everyone else to your stations. Signs in hand!" They hustle into place, and she smiles like a general at a military tattoo. "At the moment, you don't make me want to throw up. Well done. Let's move out!"

"Sir, yes sir!" Juliet calls back, and they're on the move, a crowd of weirdos putting one foot in front of the other.

They might be one of ten groups in a parade for almost no one, but from Cody's spot in the middle of the chaos, it's hard to care. For one thing, people, actual people, dot the sidewalks and smile as the parade walks by. When he tosses Tootsie Rolls into the street, children race out to scoop them up before dashing back to their parents on the curb. They look giddy, less because of the candy, Cody guesses, and more because they get to run into the road without looking both ways. No cars, no stop signs, just candy. One boy darts out and hurries back as though the magic that's turned the world upside down might dissipate at any second, and Cody knows how he feels. He's standing in the middle of the street, screaming at the top of his lungs, and so far no one's telling him to stop. In fact, Maddie keeps telling him to use his diaphragm.

She marches backward in front of the banner, calling out chants at will. Juliet laughs after every chant, and for the first time Cody recognizes the call and response that once sent him scrambling for another path to class. *Heeeey,* he'd hear from down the hall, *We're lookin' too good for Calc II. Am I right? Of course I'm right.* Then Juliet would laugh, and he'd run the other way. Out here, it's just Maddie and Juliet doing what they do, and Cody finds himself laughing along.

"I say sexy, you say bitches. Sexy!"

"Bitches!"

"SEXY!"

"BITCHES!"

Mostly, they all shout to themselves until the second block, when drag performers in sequins and peach lipstick fill the sidewalk outside the Starlight Lounge and start chanting back.

Cody's head spins in the heat, and sweat trickles down the back of his shirt under the late afternoon sun. He can't wrap his mind around everything—not the sound, not the jostling bodies, and definitely not the hand at his elbow when he almost falls over his own feet. It's too much at once, and so he marches along in choppy patches of sensation and light.

Terrence spins Andrew East Coast Swing-style as they turn the corner onto Quentin Avenue, whirling to the beat of the band two blocks away.

They trail behind an all-female motorcycle gang, and one of the ladies invites Maddie to jump on the back of her bike; Maddie spends the rest of the parade grinning, dangling from the back of a 1997 Honda Valkyrie.

When they run out of children to feed, they unwrap the candy and throw it at each other. What doesn't drop gets eaten, and they ride the sugar high like toddlers.

The sun reflects from the stop signs like fragments of broken glass—

And then there's André.

He's everywhere: signaling to Terrence, passing instructions up the line, ordering Maddie to get her ass off the motorcycle. He's constantly at the edge of Cody's vision, but never looks him in the eye until the parade ends and Juliet pulls lipstick out of her bag. In the reflection of a car window, she writes "Parker for Senate" on her forehead and suddenly they're all writing on each other's faces in "Impatient Pink" and "Burgundy Wine." Cody turns from watching Andrew's steady hand to find André leaning against the hood of the car, one eyebrow raised and a lipstick tube in the palm of his hand.

"I don't know if it's your color. Would you like to find out?" he smiles.

Cody nods, but he doesn't consider how close someone must be to paint words on his skin. André's face hovers inches from his cheek; his eyes are focused in concentration, and when his breath skims Cody's ear, goose bumps roll down Cody's neck in waves. He tries to stare at the ground and stay calm, but then André carefully places his thumb and forefinger on Cody's cheek to hold him in place, and he forgets how to breathe until André steps back to examine his work.

"You're passable," he shrugs, tossing the lipstick on to Kaiylee, "and I resisted drawing a penis."

Cody frowns as the lipstick disappears into the crowd. "Don't you want a turn?" It's not that he wants a chance to steady André's face; it only seems fair.

"Absolutely not." André taps his shoulder and points toward a cluster of microphones and blazers down the street. "See those cameras? They're headed this way, and I'd be willing to bet that at some point they are going to want a statement from the leader of these hooligans. While you look super enthusiastic, I don't want to go on local television wearing lipstick that isn't on my lips."

"Lips are still an option," Cody shoots back, and stops himself before he can think about rubbing a smear of color into André's bottom lip.

"Of course they are," André snorts, crossing his arms over his chest. "And so is streaking through the parade route, but my pants are staying on."

"The lipstick might play better on the local news." Cody shrugs and holds onto the car for dear life. Now the André in his mind isn't wearing pants. He is, however, still wearing lipstick and a smirk that looks suspiciously like the one creeping across André's face in real life.

"Now that you mention it, maybe my interview could use a little spice." André glances down at his own body, and Cody feels himself flush a vibrant red. "I might be a stick with legs, but I'd like to think I'd be memorable."

"Right up until you got arrested for indecent exposure." Cody swallows.

"It might be worth it." André squints up at the sky and his smirk bursts into a grin. "We didn't get campaign press for the parade, so a little nudity might do the trick. I can see tomorrow's headline: 'Local Boy Bares All for Queer-Loving Candidate.'" He trails his splayed hands through the air in a high arc, as if he could make the words appear in lights. "See? Memorable."

He glances over at Cody, and that's his cue, but Cody can't think of his line. He can only think about the hint of collarbone visible over the dip of André's shirt collar and how both lines must continue under the fabric, so he doesn't say anything. Instead, he kicks the gravel at his feet and tries not to imagine the soft skin at André's waist or how the sharp points of his hips might feel under the tips of Cody's fingers.

André would be horrified if he knew what was going through Cody's mind. He'd either be sick or die of laughter, but Cody thinks either one might be better than the sudden silence. He looks up, when he trusts himself, just in time to watch André's face fall.

"Huh. I just killed that dead." He's still smiling, but the light doesn't touch his eyes. "My apologies for making you uncomfortable." In the heavy quiet, the last hints of his smile fade into a hard, brittle line. "Maybe we should schedule a trip to an art museum so that you can see an ass in a controlled environment, hmm? Is that what you need to keep your brain from exploding at the very suggestion of naked men? Or maybe it's just me." He takes a deep breath as his eyes turn to glass. "Maybe you'd be fine talking about someone else's ass, but the thought that I have a body under here somewhere gives you hives." He wraps his arms tighter around himself and breathes a humorless laugh. "It's okay, you wouldn't be the first. Is the idea of me streaking making you throw up in your mouth?"

In his head, Cody can't stop protesting. *No. That isn't it.* That isn't what he means at all—but none of the words make it to his mouth. He can't even make his body move, until André turns to go and he chokes out a strangled, "Wait."

"Oh, it speaks." André retorts, but he turns, arms still crossed over his chest.

"It speaks," Cody murmurs. "It doesn't speak very well, but let me say three things before you tell me to fuck off." He waits for André's shrug and rambles on, eyes trained on the ground. "First, you don't need to be naked or wearing lipstick to be memorable. You just are. I don't think you could help it if you tried. Second, that headline would end the campaign instantly, and third," he looks up into André's eyes and slips into a shaky smile, "if you were naked, I would be okay as long as you weren't running in the other direction."

André takes a sudden step back. At first Cody thinks he's running away, but then he sees the shaking hands: André's stunned. He opens his mouth as if to speak and then closes it again without saying a word. Cody desperately wants to stare back at the ground, to make sure that gravel is right where he left it, but he forces himself to look up into André's dumbfounded gaze. He fights through the blood pumping in his ears, as André's eyes grow wide.

"I—I don't—" André tries, one hand reaching to rub at the back of his neck. Just as his eyes start to melt into something warm, a loud bleat of a laugh echoes at Cody's back. They both turn to find the sound, and Cody remembers that they aren't alone.

In the last five minutes, Barbara Ryans, a petite blonde reporter with an equally blond cameraman, has set up shop by their group. In front of the camera, Maddie and Juliet are having the time of their lives, apparently working out a comedy routine on local television.

Ryans looks overwhelmed. "Ladies," she trills in an anxious flutter, "you said that you planned outfits for the group? How did you decide on this look?" She gestures toward Juliet's midsection as if conjuring an army of coordinated torsos, and Maddie takes the opportunity to steal the mic.

"Barbara, I was in charge of the 'look,' so to speak, but I am not responsible for that," she says, pointing at Juliet's head.

"My hair?"

"Your lack of hair," Maddie snorts, poking at Juliet's skull. "I still can't believe your parents let you shave your head the night before a gay pride parade."

"Let me?" Juliet giggles and strikes a pose for the camera. "My mom shaved my head herself, and now she's waiting to take pictures of me with the drag queens. She thinks I look cute—like a young Grace Jones."

"Are you kidding me?" Maddie says, deadpan. "What's wrong with your family that they think Grace Jones is *cute*?" She pivots as if to make the reporter answer the question, and André waves to catch Cody's attention.

"I—I should probably save Barbara," he stutters, still ragged around the edges. He hesitates, but Cody waves him on.

"Go," Cody says, jerking his head toward the reporter. "I'm right behind you."

Maddie takes his usurpation in stride, handing over the microphone and stepping back to allow their "fearless leader" to answer the next question for the camera. André still seems off, but Cody can't imagine anyone else would notice.

Nor would they notice how the sun sets behind the bars on Quentin Avenue, casting a ring of light around buildings that have no business looking so beautiful. They wouldn't notice the faint dusting of confetti on the grass, or the echoes of the lone trumpet he hears now that the rest of the band has gone home. They wouldn't be able to see anything that matters. Most of all, he just told a boy—a stunning, confusing boy—that he would quite like to see him naked, and the world hasn't come tumbling down.

Cody doesn't realize how far he's drifted from the interview until he feels André stiffen at his side.

"Could you repeat the question?" André asks, in a monotone.

Barbara smiles, showing off every one of her tiny white teeth. "Of course! Since we got to learn all about that young lady's parents, could you tell us about your family? Are they here today?"

She tips the microphone back into André's face with careless ease, as though she's just asked about his favorite color. Perhaps, in her mind, she did; but André looks quietly terrified. As he blinks into the camera, Cody can see him mentally flipping past all the ways in which he cannot answer her question. Before Cody's brain has time to talk to his body, he lays his hand lightly on André's elbow and steps forward into the light.

AN HOUR LATER, THE DAY SLOWLY FADES INTO TWILIGHT. From where they sit, on the front steps of Foster Creek Elementary, Cody can just find the moon peeking out over his house across the street. It reflects from the metal jungle gym and the trees, casting striped lines of light across the dark grass and the black pool of pavement between the school and the deserted road. In the wind, the lines ripple with the trees until he can almost imagine the parking lot as an immense lake of murky water standing between his seat and his bedroom across the way. While they've been sitting on this stoop, the concrete has grown cold under his legs and the palms of his hands, but he isn't ready to go inside. His parents are in there, wondering where he's gone and waiting for the news to start at exactly nine thirty-five.

No one watches the local news anymore. It's become a joke, all weather reports and puff pieces. No one watches the local news—except his parents, and his aunts and his cousins in Minocqua. They'll be hanging on every word, and it would be just his luck if they all had their ancient DVRs at the ready.

At the time, the words hadn't really seemed meaningful. When he started speaking into the microphone, it was just one more riff in the symphony of sensation on Quentin Avenue. André was frozen and someone needed to say something, so Cody spoke.

He'd pivoted from the family question. "Of course," he explained, as the campaign representative, "the Parker campaign is immensely grateful for families like Juliet's and for volunteers like those in the St. Claire GSA for giving their time and their energy to a candidate who will stand up for their rights. It's very inspiring." He nodded and Barbara nodded back, as if they'd all become friends.

"So inspiring! And from young people too," she cooed. "So, Mr. Markhausen, do you have any personal investment in the parade today, or is it just another day at the office?"

Cody felt a weight land on his arm and turned to see André's eyes focused on him. André was ready to jump back into the interview to save Cody from an idiotic question, but for reasons Cody couldn't fathom, he didn't let himself be saved. He imagined stepping back. He imagined saying, *No, these are not my people*, and in that fraction of a second he realized that he didn't have a choice.

"I am here, first and foremost, to represent the campaign." He smiled tightly. "But personally, it's nice knowing that there are organizations in St. Claire that support people like me." He didn't elaborate and Barbara didn't ask. In seconds, she switched to the next interviewee, and Cody stood frozen as the rest of the world moved on without him.

Cody can't remember what happened from one moment to the next, after that. At some point, everyone else must have gone home. He must have said goodbye and walked all the way to the school, but he can't remember anything after "people like me." It's all a blur of numb movement... or, numb movement and André. When he found himself sitting on the steps, staring out at the blacktop, André was there too, sitting one step up on Cody's right and staring out into the same empty space.

Cody's home is right there, but he can't go inside. He isn't ready. Reality is in there, in the form of his parents, and he isn't ready to face them and whatever new version of his life just emerged on camera. He's so scared he can't see straight and he can't put his reasons into words. When he looks at André's face, his own pathetic terror turns his stomach.

"Where are you sleeping?" he asks, and watches André jump at the sound. He'd jump too; he has no idea how long they've been sitting here, staring across the street at his front door.

André cocks his head and stares. "At the moment?"

"No," Cody shakes his head. Words are hard. "Where are you sleeping tonight? Once you finally get rid of me, where are you going?"

"Oh. That." André hunches over his own knees and fiddles with an errant thread on his hem. "My aunt's couch, probably. I've been there for the last month. What does that have to do with—?"

"Nothing." Cody cuts him off and looks away, at the ground, at the playground, anywhere but at the face of a boy who has no business comforting him. "It's just—" he starts. "I don't know what's wrong with me. Your parents literally kicked you out of the house. You're couch-surfing before you're old enough to vote, like a living, breathing, after school special, and I don't know why I can't just stand up and go home. You know what's going to happen in my house tomorrow morning? My mom's going to make me a Pop-Tart. No matter how much they want me to be *someone else*, I know that I won't have to go sleep on somebody's couch."

"Pop-Tarts are crap. You know that, right?" André nudges Cody's shoulder with his bent knee, and when Cody looks back, he finds a smile at the corners of André's lips.

Cody scoops up a handful of gravel and scowls as he tosses it out into the darkness. "Yeah, but she makes them because she thinks I like them. That's the whole point." He resists telling André to stop laughing at his righteous sulk.

"I thought the whole point was to eat food that isn't made of plastic."

"André." He sounds like a whiny child, even in his own head, but it's only because he can't get his thoughts to sit still. He sighs and feels André's knee back against his side. "I don't know what's going to happen. Maybe *that's* the point. I—I don't think they're going to get mad, but—"

He thinks back over seventeen years of mornings, afternoons and nights—seventeen years when his parents just knew that someday he'd get married, or at least take some poor girl to prom. That was never in question. His mom's still going to want to know about the usual shit, but there's going to be this entirely new *thing* in the mix. It feels as if he's just thrown a bomb into his bedroom window, and now he has to wait and see if it's packed with phosgene or laughing gas.

"They might be disappointed, but—but I think this *thing* is going to be bigger than that. It's going to be everywhere."

André sighs behind his back. "It really is."

Cody cracks a smile. "You could have lied to me."

"Have we met?" André replies, smirking at Cody's halfhearted glare. "Unless your folks secretly love *the gays*, it's gonna be weird for a while. My aunt tries, when she has time, but then she remembers why I'm on her couch in the first place and it's awkward as hell."

"Ugh, God." Cody drops his head into his hands with a groan. "I'm sorry. I didn't mean to—of course you have to deal with that shit too." He keeps making it worse. Someone needs to tape his mouth shut before he completely alienates the only person who—

"Hey," André scoots down a step, and they're sitting shoulder to shoulder on the cold concrete. "You wanna just run away?"

"What?"

André shrugs. "Go. Leave. We could say screw it to the awkward. Screw the couch and the Pop-Tarts and just go."

"Screw the Pop-Tarts?" Cody echoes.

"Why not?" André waves his hand into the darkness. "Let's go to Chicago right now. Your folks wouldn't be able to find you for a while. And, let's be honest, my aunt wouldn't even try. I don't have anything to put in an apartment, but we could probably get one. I'm persuasive."

"I think you mean annoying." Cody laughs. "Do you have a couple hundred dollars hidden in those pants?" Poverty wouldn't stop Cody from going, but André doesn't need to know that.

André pats his pockets. "Sadly no, but come on," he prods, poking Cody in the shoulder. "It'll be an adventure. If we're going to run away from home, we might as well start robbing banks and forging artwork in our spare time. Voilà, rent money."

As André gestures over the blacktop, Cody can't help but see the apartment, like a movie projected into the darkness. It's a dump. They can't afford anything better than a hole in a crappy wall. Their imaginary sofa is covered in mystery stains, and André has his feet up on some excuse for a table—but it is beautiful. In his fantasy, a beam of light casts shadows across their floor, and even the empty pizza box feels like home.

"I can paint," he offers quietly, and André's smirk stretches into a grin.

"Of course you can!" André pops up and strides into the open darkness. "You can be the artist who makes replicas of the

Mona Lisa, and I'll be the clever man who sells your creations to idiots and thieves. Yes! Not to brag, but I think this may be my birthright. It was meant to be." He turns with a flourish, eyes lit with possibility, and Cody, elbows on his knees and chin in his hands, looks up into the fantasy flickering in André's eyes. Right now, with the stars at his back, André could convince him to buy the moon and a case to put it in.

"You're not really going to get me out of here, are you?" Cody asks after a pause.

André ducks his head in silent laughter. "Not a chance in hell. I have work tomorrow, and I'm not tanking my record for any handsome face." Cody's ears heat up. Handsome, he said, as though the adjective made sense. Not cute, but *handsome*.

"I was this close, though. You almost had me," Cody says lightly, and André's gaze shifts up in surprise.

"Did I?" he asks. Even though André's smile says he's kidding, his eyes actually want to know. He stares at Cody's face, and for a second the question hangs in the air like an open invitation. Cody's not sure who turns away first, but he finally breaks the silence as he looks toward his own bedroom window.

"I'm sure that if you ever decided to run off to Chicago, you'd have plenty of boys ready to drop everything for your life of crime." Cody's voice is intentionally glib, but he's surprised when André laughs—and keeps laughing.

"Oh, you're serious!" he grins. "Where do you think I'd find all these boys who date boys, under the floorboards? St. Claire doesn't have community theater, all of the clubs are twenty-one plus, and I've known everyone in the GSA since we were five." André walks out into the concrete waters until Cody can't find his face in the darkness. "I'd ask where you were hiding, but I think it's known as the closet." His tone lands like a gentle poke, and Cody feels the heat rise under his collar.

"So you've never—?" The thought that André, with his legs and his smile, hasn't been with anyone, feels as foreign as their fantasy apartment.

"Nope," André shakes his head. "I'd ask about you, but it seems unnecessary— not because you couldn't," he clarifies at Cody's flinch. "You just haven't gotten there yet."

And now it's Cody's turn to laugh. *Hasn't gotten there yet?* He's a mess. In the last week he's thrown up outside a campaign office, had a panic attack over a poster and accidentally come out on broadcast television—in front of a McDonald's. Cody says this last bit out loud, and André rolls his eyes.

"There are less dramatic ways to make an entrance." André nods, making his way back to the stoop and settling onto a lower step, so that he has to look up, just slightly, to see Cody's eyes. "You know what happened when I came out? I spent weeks talking to myself before bed. I didn't know who the fuck I was, so I just kept talking until I started to make sense. It turns out I was still basically the same asshole I was before I came out, but it took a lot of words before I could be sure."

Cody bites his lip, but doesn't look away. "Talking, huh?"

André shrugs. "Yup, I still do it sometimes, when the world refuses to listen to my infinite wisdom." He raises his fingers to dangle his imaginary cigarette holder and props his elbow on his knee. "That's the world's loss and my pillow's gain."

"I think I can do you one better," Cody responds, and starts digging in his pocket. This is a really bad idea, but as soon as he imagines André alone on his aunt's couch, talking to a pillow, he knows he doesn't have a choice. "I told you that I can paint, but I didn't say what." André cocks his head as Cody fishes his figurine out of his pocket and holds her in the palm of his hand. "I paint models—for fun. They're supposed to be for a game with other people, but I don't really play. I just paint. This one—her name's Kaelyssa and she's supposed to be a warrior, but I think she might also be a pretty good listener."

Cody bites his lip as André stares in open-mouthed confusion at the model in Cody's hand. For a long, silent minute, Cody's sure that he's gone way too far. He's never shown his models to anyone. And now, he's just given this boy a homemade doll with plastic boobs. He wants to sink into the concrete, until André abruptly stands and offers his hand.

"Can I see it under the light?" He gestures toward the street-lamp burning by the playground, and Cody lets himself be pulled to his feet. Under the lamp, the light falls around their bodies like a glowing shield. André cups his hands under Cody's and carefully raises the figurine into the light. "There she is," he smiles and leans in until Cody's staring at the top of his head. "Did you really make her on your own?"

"Yeah," Cody breathes, but he can't focus on a toy, not with André's warm hands around his, not with the tips of André's thumbs drawing circles along his fingers. André might not know that he's doing it, but right now that tiny motion feels more important than any painting Cody's ever done.

"I can't keep her," André says, "but if I could borrow her, I… her eyes do look nurturing, in a psychotic sort of way."

Cody laughs. "She grows on you." He needs his hands back if he's going to hand her over or remember how to breathe, but André isn't pulling away.

"If I'm going to borrow her, though, I will need to give her back sometime."

Cody's brow furrows. "That is the definition, but if you want to hold onto her—"

"No," André cuts in. "I mean—" He licks his lips, and the question in his eyes looks almost like fear. "Is there a time when you might want me to come over... here, and give her back?" He finishes breathlessly.

"Yes," Cody squeaks and then, more quietly, "tomorrow's fine... if you want."

André takes an unsteady breath, and a grin slowly spreads across his face. "Tomorrow, huh?" He raises an eyebrow, and Cody ducks his head.

"She might miss me," he mutters, scowling down at their hands. André laughs low in his throat, as if he's sharing a secret, and Cody finally understands why people think laughter is so gut-wrenchingly sexy. He would do anything to make André keep laughing, just like that, forever.

"And what if I need her again, some other night? What if her therapy services are required?"

"Then," Cody answers, "we'll need to set up some kind of shared custody."

"Because she might miss you?"

"Exactly." Cody nods, and sucks in a breath as André leans until his jaw grazes the side of Cody's cheek.

"She might not be the only one," André whispers and slowly presses his lips to the taut skin at Cody's temple. Heat blossoms from the spot in waves, spiraling through Cody's body and pooling deep in his stomach.

As André's lips leave his skin, Cody lets out a soft gasp. It echoes in the silence, and no part of him cares. His face is red and his ankles are feeding mosquitoes, but this lamplight is just short of heaven. "I should really go," he says, biting his lip. "Are you—tomorrow?"

"Yeah." André steps back and nods, one hand rubbing at the flush creeping up his neck. He delicately plucks the model out of Cody's open hand and turns her over between his fingers, using her little armored hand to wave goodbye. "I'll see you," he smiles, and as he walks away, disappearing between the streetlights, Cody knows that he will. André is going to show up at his door, and Cody's going to be there to let him in.

As Cody walks toward his front door, he thinks about Kaelyssa and how solitude isn't the end of her story. In the guidebooks, she has three lives sparked by three great moments of change and, in her last incarnation, she joins a team. She finds warriors whose powers rival her own, and together they take on the demons at the gate. He'd never paid much attention to that last piece, but now he feels it pushing him up the steps and past the broken screen door. He doesn't enter alone; he has an army at his back and they're painted in "Burgundy Wine." His army might be loud and small, but they're his and he's theirs. He walks toward the light still shining in the kitchen, his shoes echoing against the tile, and for the first time all night, he's breathing fine. ✦

The Willow Weeps for Us

Suzey Ingold

HIS MOTHER HAS ALWAYS JOKED THAT HE IS THE ENGLISH rose of the family; his fair skin has never taken well to the intense bouts of summer sun that occasionally grace their part of England. She finds his freckles endearing, not to mention the way the tips of his ears and the rise of his cheekbones turn pink. Jack finds all this tiresome and looks forward to September, when the leaves begin to dull and turn crisp around the edges once more, and the sun will wane with them.

The same cannot be said for Tom, the once scrawny cat who somehow came to be adopted into the Harrison family when Jack was a child—he takes to basking in the sun during these warm months with a quiet enthusiasm. Today as he rises for work, Jack finds Tom splayed across the windowsill with the sun bouncing off patches where his fur is thinner. With his old age, Tom's fur is beginning to grow in mere tufts in some places compared to his otherwise sleek coat.

Jack scratches behind Tom's ears gently, and the cat shifts and purrs in his slumber. Tom cracks an eye open and regards Jack with a lazy gaze; a single green eye meets Jack's hazel ones.

"It's all right for you," Jack comments. "You can lie there all day and not have to worry about turning the color of a tomato."

He can already hear his mother's voice floating up from downstairs reminding him not to be late.

"Not that the boss will mind, I suppose," Kathryn teases as he comes downstairs. Her hand comes up instinctively to straighten the collar of his shirt.

He sighs, but makes no move to bat her hand away. His father will have been at the shop since shortly after dawn, savoring the quiet of the early morning before the town becomes busy—which it will be by the time Jack arrives.

Kathryn suggests breakfast, but Jack declines and simply pinches a freshly baked roll, plants a kiss on her cheek and makes for the door. He likes to take his time on his walk into town, to dawdle along the dirt track that runs between the trees. It's cooler beneath the branches, too: sunlight flickers between the leaves and casts patterns against the ground. The soles of his shoes are starting to wear from the rough tree roots that edge the path, but he cannot afford to get a new pair.

The Harrison family's small grocery has been quiet in recent weeks; vegetable patches have sprung up in the gardens behind people's houses, new allotments farther back, and many find it more economically viable these days to tend their own greens rather than buy them, old habits be damned.

Though he is twenty-one, Jack's parents still look on him as a child—as they do his sister, who is younger than him by six years. They make vague, threadbare excuses about the changes rippling slowly beneath the surface of their community, as if neither he nor Eliza hears the radio as it relays the news during dinner; as if they don't know of the impending threat from the continent.

Jack sighs, idly kicking fallen branches from his way as he nears the end of the path, and crosses over the stream, a tributary of the River Cam, by means of a small bridge. He has seen this stream rage loudly over the rocks after a heavy rain; now it is shallow, barely trickling. It has been some time since it last rained.

The shop is quiet. He finds Mrs. Aitken, an elderly neighbor, eyeing a crate of tomatoes with a critical frown. She doesn't respond to his greeting as he fastens the green apron at the small of his back, but she's been losing her hearing for years, so Jack doesn't take offense. The uniform is just a formality, since, for the most part, Jack's responsibilities remain within the confines of the storage room at the back. His father's is the face the local customers know, and that's what keeps the Harrison family in business.

The back room is a mess. Jack's father is many things—a great businessman among them—but organization is not his strong suit. Jack remembers stacking boxes back here as early as age six; Kathryn looked on in amusement as he tugged tirelessly at crates too large for his small stature to bear.

Jack hears voices out front, and the bell over the door jingles. He shifts a fresh crate of apples over his left shoulder and pushes the door open with his foot. His father is talking jovially with a young man. Jack faces his father's broad back: the elder Harrison would be the last to admit it, but Jack can see that he is beginning to age. His hair is fading into a silvery gray; his shoulders show a tiredness that Jack knows didn't used to be there. The stranger, in contrast, radiates youth, from his stance to his laugh, his vibrant eyes and the dark hair neatly swept back over his head. Jack's mother would adore for Jack to have that kind of hair rather than the persistently fluffy chestnut curls that grow wildly on his head. This man looks sophisticated and handsome, down to his neatly pressed shirt and fitted trousers. Jack feels like a little boy in comparison, with his shirt large over his wiry frame and traces of earth beneath his fingernails.

"Just the boy we need," his father declares as the closing thud of the door to the back room interrupts his greetings with the stranger. Jack looks up. "Jack will sort you out," his father adds. He claps the man on the shoulder and moves to attend to Mrs. Aitken, who has finally selected some tomatoes.

Jack puts down the crate. The stranger's gaze follows the movement, and a small smile plays on his lips when Jack straightens. "Apples, is it? That you're after?" For want of something to do with his hands, Jack fumbles for a brown paper bag. There's a reason he usually works out of the range of the public eye.

The man's smile remains friendly, however, with no hint of the condescension Jack is used to.

"I suppose so," the man responds and tucks one ankle behind the other. "About a pound should be fine."

Jack nods. The intensity of the man's gaze makes it difficult to look away. He feels the tips of his ears heat up as he weighs out the apples and puts them into the bag. The man smells clean and fresh; his scent is intoxicating over the earthy aroma of the shop.

"Anything else?" Jack asks, swinging the bag over itself to twist the ends into tight knots.

"Any recommendations?" the man asks in turn, plucking a strawberry from the opposite shelf and biting the flesh from the stalk. His tongue chases the juice, and he hands the green remains to Jack with a lopsided grin. "Don't want to make a mess," he shrugs and gestures to the crate. "A pound of those, too."

Jack supposes that this highhandedness should irk him somewhat; nevertheless, the man doesn't seem arrogant.

"I didn't know Mr. Harrison had a son," the stranger comments as Jack weighs the second bag. "Jack, is it?"

Jack nods absentmindedly, paying little attention to the handfuls of strawberries he places into the bag.

"Well, nice meeting you, Jack." The man smiles again as he pays for the fruit. "Apologies for the strawberry stealing."

Jack watches him go with the strawberry stalk still tucked into his fist. It's only once the door swings shut that it occurs to Jack: he never learned the man's name.

HIS MOTHER IS NOT A WOMAN OF MANY RULES, EXCEPT THAT dinner must always be a full family affair. This pulls Jack and his father back from the shop each evening and gets them clean, presentable and seated by seven o'clock. The radio is left on in the background these days, though Jack tries his best to tune out the talk of attacks and invasion.

His father had not served in the Great War; lingering health problems from his childhood caused him to fail his medical examination. He had taken his own father's place running the grocery at age eighteen when Jack's grandfather enlisted instead. The position should have been temporary, but ultimately became permanent.

Jack has known little of war, beyond children's idle chatter and games in the schoolyard. But with each passing day, it becomes more likely that war is a reality Jack will have to discover for himself.

"Richard stopped by today," his father tells the table, once the food has been served and grace said.

Kathryn laughs. "I take it the allotment isn't proving as fruitful as he'd hoped?"

"Potatoes are coming on well; not much to be said for the rest. Not quite the green fingers type, as he put it."

She titters, and her cheeks flush as she reaches up to smooth an imaginary stray strand of light brown hair. Jack assumes they must be talking about the same man as his strawberry thief—Richard. "Who needs green fingers when he puts them to far better use as it is?"

A chunk of carrot lodges in Jack's throat; eyebrows are raised in his direction as he coughs violently.

Attention is drawn from his coughing fit and heated face, however, when his sister, Eliza, taps her fork on the edge of her plate with an excited grin and asks, "Richard who teaches piano?" Their parents nod in affirmation. "He teaches Jane and Lillian. Apparently he's dreamy," she coos, flicking a sidelong glance at Jack. He steadfastly ignores her gaze and stares down at his plate, his appetite lost.

"Hmm? And what did you think of him, Jack? You two seemed to be getting along rather well." His father looks at him expectantly. The subtext is clear: *A friend could do you some good.* "Jack? Is he dreamy?" His father guffaws.

Jack sighs and props his head on one hand, even though he knows his mother will scowl at him for having his elbow on the dinner table. "Oh, yes. He's a catch," he responds dryly.

Conversation dies down after that, and the focus turns to the quiet monotone of the radio announcer. Jack ignores it, instead noting the strawberry juice stain that clings to the side of his thumbnail.

ELIZA CATCHES HIS ARM AS HE RETIRES TO HIS BEDROOM after dinner. She's got an inquisitive look in her green eyes, one Jack knows far too well. He remembers it from as far back as Eliza's childhood, when she stole knick-knacks from his room for sport. Her curls, lighter in color than his and verging on blonde at this time of year, spring free from the clips shoved haphazardly into them and frame her face, making it look round.

She grins at him, revealing the small gap between her front two teeth that makes her look so cheeky.

Jack sighs. He's halfway through *A Tale of Two Cities*, the third in his stack of the Dickens collection inherited from the grandfather he did know and he's eager to get back to it. "So?" Eliza probes, her voice low even though their parents are well out of earshot. "What's he really like? Richard?"

Richard. "Odd," Jack replies honestly. He can't deny that the man has remained on his mind for the better part of the afternoon. Flashes of their brief encounter keep coming back to him: Richard's smile, almost mischievous in hindsight; his long, elegant fingers—piano-playing fingers—plucking the strawberry from the crate; his figure disappearing out the door.

"Odd," Eliza echoes, quirking an eyebrow. "You two ought to get on well, then."

Jack doesn't expect to see Richard again, even though the local community isn't vast by any stretch of the imagination. Perhaps this is a mechanism of self-defense, something to prevent his mind from whirling off into a flurry of possibilities about a man he barely knows. He wouldn't admit it to his parents—maybe not even to Eliza—but loneliness hits him hard, and often. They have let him know that they suspect it, but he brushes off their concern, eager to prove to them as much as to the rest of the world that he is capable of being alone.

TODAY IS AN ONION DAY, UNFORTUNATELY, AND JACK SPENDS it elbow deep in the vegetable, stacking crates. His father has been persistently humming a Coleman Hawkins number all morning, merrily driving Jack around the bend with the dancing saxophone melody. The older Harrison would say it is a tune for a summer's day with the sun shining, as it is now, but Jack never much enjoyed jazz.

He thinks, instead, of how Eliza glanced at him yesterday across the dinner table. As if she knew something, perhaps. Eliza has known about Jack since she stumbled across her older brother sharing kisses with Billy from down the road. It was five years ago now, in the lane that runs behind their houses, on a July evening after dusk. Somehow, her ten-year-old mind had carefully wrapped around the understanding that their parents ought not to know a thing about the encounter. Eliza remains Jack's only confidante. Billy was sent to a boarding school in Wales that autumn, and Jack never heard from him again. It was not romance so much as comfort: the sense of relief that he was different, perhaps, but nevertheless not alone.

The bell above the door jingles around midday, pulling Jack from his thoughts—though not his father from his whistling, unfortunately—and Richard enters the shop with a sheaf of papers beneath one arm. Jack's gaze catches the markings on the pages. He recognizes it as sheet music, though he's never played an instrument.

"Morning, Mister Harrison," Richard calls, while his feet head toward Jack.

"Morning, Richard." To Jack's surprise, his father seems unperturbed that his son, rather than he, is this customer's first point of contact.

Jack wonders if his father has ever stopped to consider the possibility of him one day taking over the shop.

"Morning, Jack."

Jack notes Richard's neatly buttoned shirt and the way it contrasts with a trace of stubble on his jaw. "Afternoon, I think, by now." He pauses. "More strawberries? Or something different?" He proffers one of the formidable onions.

Richard laughs, tucking the papers more firmly under his arm. "No, no. I'm just here to settle a debt. It seems I underpaid you yesterday." He pulls a few shillings from the depths of his pocket. "I paid for a pound, but it must have been closer to a pound and a quarter."

Jack wills the red flush to remain absent from his cheekbones, for the mistake was his, not Richard's. His own distraction is the cause for Richard's return visit. "Oh, no. Please. Consider it a gesture of goodwill. For your struggling greens."

Richard's cheeks glow red now, which makes a smile tug at the corner of Jack's mouth. "Well, thank you. That's very generous of you. Perhaps I can repay you with a cup of tea some afternoon."

Richard doesn't linger today, nor does he buy anything. It's a pattern that seems to mark the day, for they receive little business. Jack's father dismisses him by midafternoon, saying there's little point in him spending any more time unnecessarily shuttered away from the beautiful sunshine.

Jack considers walking to the bookshop (the Dickens is starting to prove a little tiring), but he finds himself strolling in the direction of the river instead, past a cluster of houses. He's not been down this way often; there's been no reason to.

He hears the ping of a bicycle bell behind him and moves closer to the curb, out of the way.

"Jack!" The bell pings again. "Fortunate that I've run into you— it just occurred to me that I've been terribly rude. I haven't even introduced myself." It's Richard, his feet standing still on the pedals as he slows to Jack's pace. "Richard Booth."

Jack just smiles in response, figuring that "I know" would sound as daft out loud as it does in his head.

"Where are you headed?"

Jack shrugs, fitting the pace of his footsteps to the steady roll of the bicycle. "Nowhere in particular."

"Lovely afternoon for it." The bicycle chain clicks softly. "Have you considered my offer? A cup of tea? I live only a little way down the road."

Jack has no good reason to refuse Richard's persistence, except perhaps for the nerves that line his stomach at the thought of spending time alone with the man. Jack has taught himself to keep his feelings contained, be they lust, desire or affection, ever since Billy. Richard makes that lesson seem hazy, and that frightens Jack. It reminds him too much of how he felt when Billy left: confused, with no one around who could possibly understand or answer the questions that remained.

"I don't see why not," Jack replies finally with a little more spring in his step as he keeps pace at Richard's side. "If you're sure I won't impose."

"Why would I offer if I thought you'd be an imposition?" Richard grins and pushes his feet down onto the pedals with more force, and the bicycle picks up speed. "Don't fall behind!"

As Richard shoots ahead of him, Jack stutters and starts running: his feet pound against the road; his long legs bring him back to Richard's side in no time. Richard is laughing somewhat breathlessly, and the sound is infectious. Jack's stomach hurts by the time Richard pulls up by the side of the curb.

"There you are! Your sense of time is getting worse in your old age, Rich," a young woman calls. She is sitting on a low bench outside what Jack presumes must be Richard's house. Cupping a hand over her eyes to shield them from the sun, she stands and smooths her long, elegant burgundy skirt. "And who's this?"

Jack swallows and glances at Richard. He feels like a child told off for playing in places he shouldn't—the woman's voice could be his mother's.

"Julie, meet Jack. He's the Harrisons' eldest, from down at the greengrocer." Richard walks his bicycle up the path and kisses Julie's cheek. "Jack, my girl, Julie Clark."

Jack smiles through his teeth; his eyes flicker between the two of them. Richard murmurs apologies for his tardiness; a second kiss lands closer to the corner of Julie's mouth. Jack hovers on the balls of his feet. "I didn't mean to interrupt your date. Perhaps I'll drop by another time."

Julie replies. "Nonsense! Join us, please."

She ushers him in with a beaming smile, her arm slipping through Richard's with a practiced ease that makes Jack's stomach churn. He gets the distinct sense that he is now an intruder on Richard's personal life, but he doesn't wish to be rude when both Richard and Julie seem so persistent in urging him to join them.

The house is quaint, lined with heirlooms and the odd photograph. Jack lingers by a photo on the bookshelf of a young man and a woman with a toddler in her arms. The little boy has a wide, toothy grin. Jack isn't sure how he recognizes the child as Richard, but he does.

Richard nods toward the picture. "This was their house." Jack notes the use of the past tense, but he doesn't want to ask.

Richard prepares the tea while Julie shows Jack the vegetable patch with an amused twinkle in her eye. Many of the leaves are withered and limp. Then Richard comes to stand in the doorway and watches them silently. Jack frowns and gently touches a tomato leaf. "Have you remembered to give them water?"

Richard bites his lip. "Oh."

Jack picks up the discarded and apparently unused watering can and fills it from the outdoor tap while Julie cackles with glee.

TEA IS A LOUD AFFAIR: JULIE HAS A LARGE AND BOISTEROUS personality; her laughter is so exuberant, it fills the room; her shoulders shake with it, and her fair hair falls into her eyes. Jack has no wish to compete with her, so he remains quiet; his fingers trace over the patterns on the teacup. Julie speaks enough for the three of them, with her hands as much as with her voice, although Richard interjects observations of his own.

"Oh, stop! You're horrible, I'm not going on one of those rickety boats!" Julie bats at Richard's arm, though she is laughing still. She shakes her head more firmly and then props her chin on her hand and shifts her blue-eyed gaze across the table. "Take Jack instead."

Jack raises his eyes from the table and looks at each of them in turn.

"All right," Richard agrees, leaning back in his chair and looking over at him. "What do you say, Jack? Care to join me on a punting expedition? I have yet to explore the river by boat and it's just eating me up inside." He punctuates the statement with a smack of his hand on the table. The teacups rattle on their saucers.

Punting down the river is something Jack has been doing with his sister since he was a teenager; they take turns poling. It's a perfect activity for a summer's day.

"You've never been?" Jack repeats, blinking. "Well, that just won't do. An inability to grow vegetables is one thing—but this is deplorable." For a moment, Jack forgets Julie's presence—perhaps due to her sudden unnatural quiet.

"Ah, a true connoisseur." Richard nods approvingly.

Julie claps her hands, clearly keen not to be forgotten in the making of plans. "I'll make you boys some provisions."

⁜

SATURDAY DAWNS CRISP AND BRIGHT. DEWDROPS CLING TO individual blades of grass and catch the bare skin at Jack's ankles where he's rolled up his trouser legs. His mother had eyed him suspiciously as he left; his explanation was rather vague, only "plans to spend the day with a friend." It's likely that Jack is too early, but he figures that the riverbank is as good a place as any to pass some time before his companion arrives.

It's quiet, which he supposes is unsurprising for this time of the morning. He settles onto the grassy bank, kicks his legs out in front of him and takes the apple his mother insisted on sending with him from his handkerchief. He'd been sure he would feel nervous, more bubbling and butterflies at the pit of his stomach; but an unexpected sense of calm washes over him at the prospect of spending his day with Richard.

Jack doesn't wait long before footsteps sound behind him, jogging down the sloped bank. "You're early," he comments, as Richard helps him to his feet.

"So are you." Richard's fingers close around Jack's wrist and he tugs Jack toward the boats. "I hope you weren't waiting long."

Jack shakes his head, memorizing the press of Richard's thumb against the tree of veins on the inside of his wrist. "No, not long. Not long at all."

Jack quickly learns that, while Richard may have many fine attributes, the upper body strength needed to pull the heavy wooden boat down from the bank and into the water is not one of them. He, however, has many years of practice, and gently eases Richard out of the way before hauling the boat smoothly down to the river in one swift pull. Richard clears his throat as if embarrassed, rubs his hands together and sets to work gathering their supplies to take onboard.

"The trick is to stop the heavy end digging into the grass on the way down," Jack whispers conspiratorially, and the laugh he gets in response warms his chest with pride. He finds he is growing addicted to the way Richard looks at him—not as the child he has grown tired of people considering him to be, but as a man. His equal. Richard hands him the pole. Jack is already in the boat, one foot still planted on the grassy bank to keep it anchored.

"So, comparatively, how difficult is the actual punting?"

Jack helps Richard into the punt before pushing them off the bank. He toes off his shoes and socks and waits for Richard to follow suit, by which time the boat begins to drift into the center of the river. "Don't be discouraged if it seems tough at first. Just try not to lose the pole in the river."

Richard grumbles under his breath, something that sounds like "near impossible, then," but resolutely reaches for the pole and gestures for Jack to sit in the opposite end of the boat.

Jack does as he's told, biting back the suggestion that perhaps he take the first leg to show Richard the basics—he gets the impression that the other man has a stubbornness about him Jack would be unlikely to break through. Instead, he settles against the worn cushion, folds his legs under himself and carefully watches Richard's movements.

"Wrap your hands firmly around the center of the pole," Jack instructs gently, but with enough authority to indicate that he knows what he's talking about. "Slide it up through your hands as quickly as you can and then plunge the end somewhere on this side." Jack gestures to the left side of the boat.

Richard lifts the heavy pole barely an inch, and it makes a dull thunk as it sinks right back into the same position. Jack tuts playfully under his breath, and Richard rolls his shoulders back, ready to try again. "In my defense," he begins as he raises the pole—far more effectively this time around—"I am far more accustomed to being the teacher than the student. And, I momentarily forgot the context of my instructions."

By the time Jack interprets Richard's meaning and his cheeks flare with heat, Richard has managed to land the pole in the correct position.

"What now?" he asks, his bare toes wriggling against the wood as he keeps himself balanced.

"Drag. Drag the boat along," Jack stammers. A splash of water hits his cheek. Richard looks far too pleased with himself for having mastered the art of doing that much with the pole, if nothing else.

"Relax," Richard murmurs and although he makes it sound as if he means, "in relation to the boat," Jack can't help but think that he means it in some wider context, too.

They weave their way down the river—not quickly, by any standard, but there is no urgency in the day. Richard fumbles with the pole more often than not; sometimes they don't move so much as float aimlessly. But no one else is on the river and so they can only collide with the banks, which they bounce off of more than once with a kind of repetitive, albeit unintentional, determination.

For a while, Richard talks of his allotment and the house that begs for repairs he doesn't know how to do, and—very briefly—of Julie, too. After that, they travel in comfortable silence as Jack sips his mother's homemade apple juice from a glass bottle and Richard focuses on steering the boat in a moderately straight line down the river.

"Uh-oh," Richard says suddenly, drawing Jack's gaze away from the butterfly he'd been watching skitter over the edge of the grassy bank.

"Uh-oh?" Jack echoes, raising an eyebrow. Richard's knuckles are white where he clings to the pole. Jack doesn't need to ask; he can tell from the pole's angle that it is stuck in the mud of the riverbed.

"All right," Jack sighs and carefully climbs to his feet. "Time for me to take over, then."

Richard looks somewhat sheepish as they cross in the middle of the boat, and on impulse Jack reaches for his forearm and squeezes it firmly in reassurance.

The pole is fairly easily retrieved with a bit of jiggling this way and that. Jack emits a small grunt as it bobs up. He watches the water sliding down the pole and falling onto his arms as he raises it.

They pass under a bridge, forcing Jack to duck so he doesn't hit his head, and he feels cooler for a moment. The boat glides out from under the bridge and Jack doesn't have time to get the pole back into the water and steer them clear of the overhanging trees before they're under one.

Richard bursts into laughter as the branches of the weeping willow tickle their sides and envelop the boat almost entirely. One end of the punt digs into the bank and they grind to a halt. Jack sighs and pushes his hair back from his forehead.

"This seems as good a place as any to picnic," Richard points out, then moves the provisions into the center of the boat and encourages Jack to secure the pole in the riverbed and join him.

Jack's contribution consists, unsurprisingly, of fruit; its juices run from the small crates he'd packed it in. "Yesterday's leftovers," Jack explains, extracting an overripe strawberry as evidence. "No longer fit for sale, but in my opinion the sweetest." He pops the fruit into his mouth, and the light red berry stain remains, coating the tip of his thumb and forefinger.

Richard, on the other hand, has made an array of sandwiches—or more likely, Julie has, although Richard neither confirms nor denies the probability—and presents them, neatly arranged, along with a few cakes wrapped in an embroidered handkerchief. It is pleasantly cool beneath the tree—an appropriate place to have stopped, if only by chance. The branches hang lower at Jack's end, however, and tickle at the top of his head; Richard seems to find this particularly amusing. Jack finally gives up and moves to the space the older man has preemptively cleared next to him.

Jack feels pleasantly content as he settles there, with his leg resting idly beside Richard's. He can't eat any more—ever the sweet tooth, he has gorged himself on perhaps one too many cakes—but he can't help but watch from the corner of his eye as Richard bites the end of a particularly shrunken strawberry before tossing the rotten end toward the bank.

It occurs to Jack that this man, this man whom he doesn't even know well, who has small leaves and other foliage clinging to the back of his shirt and the ghost of stubble on his jaw—it occurs to Jack that he wants to kiss him. Perhaps more than he's ever wanted to kiss anyone in his life. Twenty-one years have led up to this kiss that he now craves.

Richard seems to feel his gaze, for he turns his head, and suddenly their proximity is highlighted. Jack can feel the heat of Richard's breath over his lips, and it sucks all the air out of his lungs. He feels almost lightheaded by the time Richard's hand comes up to rest on his jaw and his thumb grazes the bone. It's as if he's coaxing Jack to him, pulling him closer on an invisible, utterly unbreakable thread.

The tip of Richard's nose bumps against Jack's, and Jack's eyes flutter closed. Richard seems to take this as consent; there is no hesitation in the press of his lips on Jack's, a firm and relentless pressure. Jack can finally breathe again. His hand falls to Richard's thigh—for something to cling to, above all else—and Richard in turn tightens his hold on Jack's face. Richard's tongue grazes Jack's lower lip and Jack tastes the sweet tang of strawberry underlined with sharper hints of currant.

Jack pulls back just as Richard rears forward to deepen the kiss and their foreheads bump gently. Almost in unison, they breathe out and into a laugh. "I'm sorry," Jack murmurs.

"Don't apologize," Richard responds quickly, biting his lip as if trying to contain a wide grin. "As long as I can do that again."

Jack wants to yell, to shout the flurry of fiery feelings rushing through his bloodstream. There is no outside world anymore; there are no people; there is no Julie, nor any fear or worry. There is only the pair of them, and this moment. Jack finds himself laughing, the light in his eyes glowing as much as the flush on his cheeks. "I'd tip you out of the boat if you didn't."

They linger under the willow; the faintest ripple of the wind is all that flutters through to them from the outside world. They share kisses and memorize the press of palm to palm and how their fingers lace together. Jack learns that Richard smells inexplicably of wood smoke at the crook of his neck and that three freckles form a small triangle just above his collarbone.

Other punts go past now and again, accompanied by the cries and laughter of the people in them, who are struggling with their own heavy boats. They must see the tail end of Jack and Richard's boat protruding from under the tree, and yet no one disturbs their sanctuary beneath the leaves.

The sun is low in the sky by the time they pull into the main channel of the river once more, and the two men fall silent, as if unsure what they may say to one another now that they have resumed their places in the outside world. Jack wishes for nothing more than to take Richard's hand in his own again; he sits alone in some emptiness now, as Richard steers them back toward the bank from which they departed. He fears they will forget every moment shared beneath the tree, as if it never happened. Even worse, he fears remembering, because that could hurt him more.

But then he looks up, and Richard is smiling at him, and the only thing Jack seems unable to remember is his anxiety.

JACK IS HOME IN TIME FOR DINNER, WHICH SEEMS TO SURPRISE Kathryn, as if she had been expecting him far later in the evening. It's clear she's pleased, though; as she brings hot dishes to the table, she asks questions that Jack answers selectively. She presses his cheek in a gesture of affection, her hand warm from the plates. There's a hint of a smile on her lips before she pulls away, unties her apron and sets it over the back of her chair. He notices Eliza listening from the doorway, her quick and calculating mind no doubt reading into the silences where their mother does not. For a fleeting moment, Jack wonders what might happen if he told the truth. Would his mother cry? Would his father run him from the house in anger? Would Eliza support him still, or would she turn her back too?

They switch on the radio, and all talk of the day's excursion is abandoned. The tone of the news has shifted in the past few days, with reports now focused on the how and what and when of Britain's defensive action.

"The British government is beginning to look more seriously into plans for putting together the armed forces necessary to go to war, should the time come. It is expected that the numbers go far beyond that which the country currently has in its reserves, thus likely turning the emphasis to immediate enlistment."

Cutlery remains untouched on plates, save for Jack's. He keeps his head slightly bowed, and the prongs of his fork tap his plate as he eats. He knows that his family is observing him, waiting for him to say something, anything, about his uncertain future. He is the only man in the family eligible to be sent to the front if war breaks out. And it is with him that the Harrison name rests.

Jack lifts his head only when he is finished. His family's plates are still untouched, and the pity and concern mapping their faces is enough to make his stomach churn. A frown knits his father's graying eyebrows.

"May I be excused? It's been a long day, I'm quite tired," Jack says.

His mother does not utter a word, merely nods and allows him to rise from the table.

Jack tries to think back to his afternoon with Richard, to relive every brush of fingers and fevered kiss, but other thoughts keep intervening. Richard will be expected to enlist, too. He doesn't know if that makes it better or worse. If they were to end up out there together, would Richard hold him if he were frightened, kiss him if he were wounded, soothe him to sleep? Would they dare risk it? Could others be trusted to turn a blind eye in such circumstances?

Jack sits perfectly still on his bed with his knees tucked up to his chest as this whirlwind of thoughts circulates, faster and faster, blurring together and falling apart at the seams. Tom nudges at his toes but slinks away when he receives no response. Jack hears a roaring in his ears, and his skin feels hot and cold all at once. He barely registers the knock on the door and breaks free from his cycle of worried thought only when his sister enters the room. "I don't want to talk about it, Liza."

62

She slips into the room and shuts the door behind her, pouting. "Don't be a spoilsport. I've been just dying to hear about your date since you walked through the door."

Jack feels as though a warm breeze has just washed over his shoulders, and the untarnished memories of his day with Richard return. He smiles and pats the space next to him. "He's even dreamier than you could imagine."

Eliza grins.

JACK SPENDS LESS AND LESS TIME AT THE SHOP, BUT FOR ONE reason or another, his father doesn't complain. Maybe he's trying to adjust to running the business by himself again, if—when— Jack has to leave. Or maybe he pities him, wants him to spend whatever time he has left just being a twenty-one-year old in the summertime. Whatever the motive, Jack doesn't question it but revels in the luxury of spending his mornings ambling down by the river, slowly making his way toward Richard's house in time for him to return from giving his morning lesson. The basket on his bicycle is always stuffed with sheet music, lines and dots and squiggles that are all but incomprehensible to Jack.

Richard has tried more than once now to sit Jack down at the piano and teach him where to place his hands and how to press the keys; he has tried to guide Jack's fingers through a basic jingle. But Jack fumbles, and gets frustrated, and, in truth, has no interest in learning how to play. He would far rather just watch Richard.

They pass many an afternoon with Richard playing melodies at the piano while Jack lies on the floor, hands folded over his torso, and just listens. Richard can convey a million feelings and thoughts in the music and, when playing, often falls uncharacteristically quiet and allows the notes to speak on his behalf.

"Do you think it'll be different one day?" Jack asks one overcast Wednesday afternoon, as gray clouds gather thick in the sky. His eyes trace the faded marks and cracks on the ceiling, ones he's surprised he hasn't memorized by now. Richard continues to play something Jack can't place—but then, he doesn't know much about music. Jack leans on his elbows and looks at Richard's profile, at his head bent slightly in concentration. "Do you imagine that one day I might be able to walk down the street holding your hand, just as you might hold Julie's?"

Richard doesn't say anything, but the music shifts, its tone lightening into something almost jovial from its previous reflection of outside elements. Jack sighs and lies back down, a smile playing on his lips. "Mm. I hope so, too."

If Julie notices anything, she doesn't comment, but treats Jack with all the fondness of an older sister. She has a habit of walking into Richard's house unexpected and unannounced, sometimes bearing home-baked goods—more than enough for all three of them. She feigns surprise, but it seems she is less and less nonplussed to find Jack there.

One day she enters so quietly—altogether unlike her—that they do not hear her approach until the door to the living room clicks open. The book between them is innocent enough; Jack has been reading Richard some of his favorites from the John Keats collection he brought over this morning. As the afternoon has ticked by, concentration has wandered somewhat, and had they heard Julie so much as a moment later—

Even now as she stands poised and silent in the doorway, she must see where their ankles touch, where Richard's shirt collar gapes, must notice the flush of Jack's lips, as deep as the color in his cheeks. "I brought scones," she announces. "Richard, dig out some jam, won't you?"

If Jack lets himself believe that she knows nothing, he only feels guiltier. He doesn't discuss this with Richard, doesn't want to push more weight onto him.

Eliza tries to discourage him from this attitude. "I've never known you to be selfish, Jack. I think you have every right to be that way for a change." She pauses, avoiding his gaze. "Especially now."

Jack doesn't relish the idea of being selfish, but he understands Eliza's concerns. In the newscasts the word "enlistment" has changed to "conscription," and his age is the peak of the most-wanted bracket. Every day he wonders if today will begin his uncertain future, but every day nothing happens. Even then, relief does not quite sink into his bones. Richard says he dislikes the idea of inevitability, firmly maintaining his "if, not when" stance in all discourse. Jack smiles sadly: if or when, he doesn't suppose he has much choice.

"I suppose not," Richard says and sighs. "But it's nice to believe that one might."

ON MONDAY, SEPTEMBER FOURTH, 1939, THE DAY AFTER WAR is declared, Jack receives a letter. He fears marching orders but, rather, it is an invitation to a dance being held by the local church. They're calling it a sendoff, but they mean farewell: one last chance for the girls to dance with their toy soldiers, before they begin to play a game they can't possibly know how to win. The invitation is unsigned, but Jack suspects that it is Julie's doing. His mother leaves him no choice about his attendance—he finds a shirt and his father's tie laid out on his bed before dinner.

Kathryn plucks a flower from the rosebush outside the house as he leaves, snapping off the thorns before giving it to him. "For whichever young lady it is that you've been spending all this time with." She smiles encouragingly.

He twirls the rose between his fingers as he walks, and the evening sun makes its petals glow.

The church door is propped open when he arrives, and the band has started. Jack hears chatter and laughter, not the somber sounds of a subdued affair that he had feared. His feet freeze to the top step.

"Psst!" Richard's head pops up from the greenery at the side of the church. He offers a wide grin and his hand, to help Jack down to his level.

"This is from my mother." Jack holds out the rose, its stem a little bent from where he's fiddled with it on the walk.

Richard chuckles and tucks it into his shirt pocket as best he can. "If I didn't know better, I'd think your mother rather liked me," he teases, taking Jack's other hand, too.

They stand there together and Jack wonders whether this will be the last memory he will hold of this man, who has come to mean so much—if this moment of seclusion is for their own farewell, away from the eyes of others who would not understand.

"Julie will be missing you," Jack murmurs, nodding toward the church. Prolonging the inevitable isn't going to help, Jack knows that much.

"No, she won't be." Richard clears his throat. "I believe she came with her cousin. He's been in training since April—he's to be an officer." Richard pauses, but Jack waits for him to continue in his own time. "She came to me yesterday. After the announcement. She wanted to part on good terms, no matter the outcome. To say that she understood I could never give her my heart the way she wanted me to." He smiles. "And she wanted me to send you her best wishes and her love."

Jack can't help but laugh softly, for he should have known that Julie would be too smart not to see and understand, just as Eliza has always done. Acceptance is a kind of love that Jack is pleased Richard, too, gets to experience—not least when it gives them tonight, together.

He pauses in thought, frowning. "We can't go in."

"No. We can't," Richard agrees, and then grins just a little too widely. He tugs on Jack's hand, and the two of them round the back of the church.

The church casts a shadow over a wide field, which is secluded from the road and not visible from inside. The band can be heard; the music is accompanied in a softer tone by the voices of their peers. The latter wane as they walk farther out, but the music remains, almost unaltered by distance.

Richard lets go of Jack's hands, takes a step back, and gives a small bow. "May I have this dance, Mr. Harrison?"

Jack glances back toward the church; the proximity makes him nervous. But when he turns back to Richard and sees the hope in his eyes, he cannot understand his own fears. He may die tomorrow or in a year. He may return to England in full health and die an old man. But he will never have this night again.

Jack steps forward into Richard's arms and places his head on Richard's shoulder as a strong hand fits into the small of his back. They link their other hands together, and their feet sink into the unkempt grass. Crickets chirp nearby, but that and all other sounds are temporarily muted as a plane rushes overhead, flying south over the peaceful evening where Jack, oblivious, dances in his lover's arms.

The Fire-Eater's Daughter

Amy Stilgenbauer

FRIED FOOD. THE AIR REEKED OF IT.

Fried hot dogs.

Fried mushrooms.

Platefuls of fried dough smothered in powdered sugar.

The onslaught smelled like a delicious poison, and Ruth wanted to lap up every moment.

She paused, breathing deeply. Only a year before, these smells had made her queasy. Then, they had brought to mind her utter failure: a misplaced F-sharp and a few nervous wording wobbles during the "Star Spangled Banner." The missteps not only lost her the title of Miss First Town Days 1954 and a tidy sum of scholarship money, but led to more than one of the judges suggesting that she wasn't quite American enough. Thinking about their words, so casually thrown about, still made Ruth grind her teeth. She was American. She ironed her dark spiral curls daily back then, forcing them straight, just like all the other girls at her high school, and she didn't speak with even a hint of an accent. Of course, her mother barely spoke a hint of English, but Ruth had been the one judged that day, not her mother. The deep fried cream stick she ate before the judging had been meant to prove them wrong, so it probably went without saying that she threw it up all over the second-place girl.

None of that mattered now. This year, the smells brought a different picture to her mind: mischievous grey eyes, calloused-but-tender skin a shade of deep olive, crimson lips and eyebrows plucked into a precise arch. Constance Lambrinos, the fire-eater's daughter.

Constance had appeared like a miracle seconds after the pageant. More than anything, Ruth had wanted to escape. The instant the also-ran girls had been sent from the stage, she had broken into a run, trying to put as much distance as possible between the crowd and herself. But the running hadn't lasted long. She had never been able to sustain speed over distance, and it had been all over when her left heel snapped, sending her flying forward into the waiting arms of the angel outside the sideshow.

"Look what I caught!" Constance had announced, her voice a rich alto, like dark chocolate. And the lips that spoke those words... Ruth hadn't been able to respond. She had been so awestruck by Constance's voice, her beauty, her sturdy arms gripping her shoulders.

Yes, a year ago, the festival meant humiliation and defeat. This year, it promised the greatest possible joy.

Deliberately trying to keep her pace slow, Ruth made her way past the fried food vendors and the men hawking games of chance. "Try your luck, pretty lady?" they called out, but to her, their words were only a pleasant buzz that meant Constance was near once again. All winter, she had dreamed of her face, desperately hoping that, when this day came, Constance would remember their connection. Her hopes were buoyed by the occasional letter, but still a nagging, insecure voice whispered that a girl like Constance had surely found someone else. The two had shared a magical week, filled with long talks about their hopes and dreams and the holding of hands. But, despite the rose-colored haze that had settled over her memories, Ruth couldn't be sure.

The sideshow tent, with its bold red and black striped canvas, was set back from much of the hustle and bustle of the festival's main fairway. But it still attracted a crowd. Women with their short summer bobs and pastel parasols gasped as a barely-dressed man walked by carrying a massive snake on his equally massive shoulders. A young girl with a long reddish beard drew japes and snickers from a gaggle of teenagers. Ruth felt a twinge in her stomach at the sight and hurried on, eyes searching each face for the fire-eater and his daughter.

She saw him at the end of the row. A crowd gathered, watching the rail thin man tilt his head back and swallow the burning torch. He removed it from his mouth extinguished, then, without warning, opened his mouth, issuing a flame that relit the torch. The onlookers burst into hysterical applause. They begged for an encore. He merely laughed, breathing perfect smoke rings as he did so.

"Ruth?" A sultry voice behind her beckoned. It couldn't have been any louder than a whisper, but that heavy alto sound carried. For a moment, all activity stopped. There was only Ruth and the sound of Constance's voice. Slowly, terrified that, if she moved too fast, the illusion would shatter and the voice would be gone, Ruth turned. There stood Constance. For a moment, she looked almost identical to Ruth's memory. Gradually, the magic passed, and Ruth found herself able to see more subtle changes: a small burn scar on her cheek, a new, hopeful light in her eyes. A small part of Ruth had expected that seeing changes in Constance would upset her, but the opposite was true. These changes meant Constance was real and not concocted by her imagination.

"Constance," Ruth whispered. She felt a lightness, as though she could float away. "Is it really you?"

"Of course it's me. Who else would it be?" Smiling, she took Ruth by the hand, keeping her steady and on the ground.

"I was afraid—"

"Don't be." Still holding her hand, Constance led Ruth from the tent toward the fairway.

Ruth was enthralled by Constance's hands. They were heavily calloused from years of carnival setups and teardowns, but somehow still tender and soft. Absently, she rubbed at one of the callouses with her thumb.

Constance stopped and looked back at her with a smile. Ruth hoped she would say something like, "I missed you," but her only words were, "Are you hungry?"

Trying not to be disappointed, Ruth nodded.

They wove through the crowded fairway until they reached Constance's chosen destination: a French fry vendor. Ruth had to laugh. Of all the deep-fried items on offer, Constance had chosen the common potato. "French fries?" She asked.

"Papa's friends with the vendor. Trust me... " She gestured something Ruth didn't understand and received a giant tub from the woman running the cart. Then she proceeded to dose the willowy sticks with vinegar.

Ruth took one hesitantly, unsure of the vinegar, but, when she popped it into her mouth, she felt a rush of heat and flavor: tangy, salty, savory and somehow also sweet. Only Constance could make potatoes exotic. "That is good."

"I told you to trust me."

"Does she put magic in them?"

Constance tsk-tsked and shook her head. "If she did, it would be a secret, now wouldn't it?"

Ruth took a few more of the fries as Constance glanced around looking for a suitable place to sit. There were so many things Ruth wanted to ask her. How had her past year been? What new and exciting (or old and familiar) places had she seen? Her life seemed so mysterious, so glamorous. Ruth had lived in New Philadelphia since she was two years old and could remember little else. Constance, however, began the questioning.

"What have you been up to, Ruth?" she asked. The look of genuine interest on her face made Ruth shiver.

"Nothing, really," she replied, taking more fries.

Constance raised a skeptical eyebrow. "Nothing? You've been in stasis since last July?"

"No, but—"

"Good. I do worry about this town. It seems like, every time we come here, it's stayed exactly the same."

"It's not that bad, is it?"

Constance scanned the area; her eyes worked like radar trying to pinpoint an exact location. "Those geese!" She cried out, pointing toward a gaggle near the lake. "I could have sworn those same geese were there last year."

"All geese look the same," Ruth replied with a laugh.

"Not to me." She tapped her right temple. "I have the eye. I can tell these sorts of things."

Ruth didn't know whether to laugh at that or not. "Maybe they like coming to the festival," she suggested instead, daring to go on only in a meek, embarrassed tone. "Maybe they only get to see one special other goose each year here... a special goose that puts vinegar on its bread scraps."

A faint blush crept over Constance's face. She smiled at Ruth, but there was a hint of sadness in her smile. Ruth didn't like to see that, but she didn't know what to say.

"Would you like to ride the Ferris wheel?" Constance asked.

Ruth nodded. "Let's finish the fries first?"

"Yes... we know how delicate your stomach can be."

AS THE BRIGHT ORANGE FERRIS WHEEL CAGE DOOR SNAPPED shut, Constance squeezed Ruth's hand. "I've seen a lot of Ferris wheels in my life," she said, her eyes growing distant. "But this one is my favorite. I think I like it because it has these cages." She placed her free hand on the wire mesh window. "It makes me certain I won't fall out."

"It makes me feel trapped," Ruth said, looking at the floor of the car.

Constance smiled wryly, but said nothing else. She simply squeezed Ruth's hand once again as the car lurched higher.

When they reached the top, the car stopped, allowing riders to enjoy the view. Below, the festival seemed to be populated by tiny dolls rushing in and out of booths and tents. The band setting up at the amphitheater looked like fairies carrying miniature instruments. Beyond lay the town of New Philadelphia, its buildings all arranged in neat rows, looking just as small, if not smaller. Ruth felt her stomach spasm. At first she thought it was due to panic, a newly developed claustrophobia, but then she recognized it: an urge, a need, to do something.

"Constance," she whispered, her voice so quiet and nervous she was momentarily worried Constance didn't hear it. When the other young woman turned, Ruth kissed her.

Constance returned the kiss with an immediate, almost desperate enthusiasm. Her mouth felt warm, like the still smoldering coals of a long-burning fire, but there was a sweetness, a tang and even a savory quality as well. The taste, the sensation, spread through Ruth's body, filling her again with such an overjoyed lightness that she knew instinctively she must cling to Constance or risk floating to the top of the car. Constance clung back as if she knew this fact as well, pressing her hand into the small of Ruth's back, not allowing the smallest space between their two bodies. Her other hand found its way into Ruth's hair, entwining there, not allowing their lips to separate until time stopped and they breathed as one.

The car lurched into motion, breaking the spell, and the pair parted reluctantly. Ruth could not pull her eyes from Constance. Her face seemed to have a magnet behind it and Ruth's attention could go nowhere else. Neither spoke. They sat, stone-faced, hands almost touching.

The car made another circuit. It had barely gone halfway up, when once again, they seized one another. The kiss was more fevered. Ruth felt as though the warm smoldering in Constance had turned to a frenzied flame. It intoxicated her and she responded in kind: kissing harder, pressing closer, grasping tighter. She felt her blood racing through her veins. It felt hot, burning like Constance, and every cell begged for it to never end. When they finally reached the top once more, Ruth thought that should she spontaneously combust, it would an appropriate end to her life.

They separated again on the descent. This time it was Constance who would not look away. She locked Ruth in such an intense gaze that Ruth found it hard to keep a blush from overtaking her face. When they left the car, Ruth had to stare at her shoes lest she turn a poodle-skirt shade of pink.

"Did you do some kind of magic on me?" Constance asked as the two ventured up the hill and into a patch of trees away from the bustling festival below.

"Me?" Ruth laughed. "No. I'm not the one that can do magic."

Constance laughed as well. "You think I can do magic?"

"Well…"

After turning away for a brief second, Constance turned back, appearing to have produced a tiny flame at the end of her pinky finger. "I can do this, but it's only a trick." She touched the flame to her lips and it was gone. "You, on the other hand, you have me spellbound."

Ruth didn't know what to say. She had been hoping since the previous year that Constance's feelings mirrored her own, and here was her confirmation, but her mouth was a desert, devoid of words. "How—?"

"It's just a trick," Constance replied. "Papa shows me all kinds of tricks. It's all about being able to handle pain really—"

"No, I…" Ruth shook her head. The fire performance was impressive, but she didn't want to talk about that. She didn't know the words for what she wanted to talk about, though, or where to begin. "How have you been… since last year?" she asked instead.

"Traveling," Constance replied breezily. When Ruth did not respond, she went on. "We spent most of the winter in Florida. It's a whole other world down there, Ruth. You wouldn't believe…"

Ruth tried to stop herself, but her eyes suddenly welled up with tears. She squeezed her eyes shut, a last ditch effort to fight the droplets back. But Constance saw.

"Your cat eyes are running," she said.

"Sorry…" Ruth wiped her eyes, trying to brush the tears away, but only smeared the makeup.

"Don't... don't..." Constance took a handkerchief out of her pocket and gently dabbed at Ruth's eyes. "What's wrong?"

"I want to go with you," Ruth found herself saying before she even realized it was what she wanted. "I want to travel with you, see everything, instead of waiting for you to come back."

"Ruth—"

"I don't want to just go to secretarial school and hold my breath waiting for the summer."

"I want that too, but Ruth... I..."

Ruth took a deep breath and turned away. She sat on a small rock and smoothed her skirt in a slow, deliberate way. It calmed her. "You have others in other towns. I know... I understand."

Constance's eyes widened, then clouded over. "Where would you get an idea like that?"

"Isn't that how it works? I mean... you're only in a given town for—and you're so—"

"Damn, Ruth. You really think that?"

Ruth shook her head. She didn't know what she thought anymore. All she knew was that Constance coming back had been her only thought for the past year. She couldn't imagine a world in which scores of other people didn't feel the same way.

"I wish you could come too, Ruth. I thought about you every day... but this life isn't for you."

"Why not?"

"Ruth..." She gestured around at the small town festival.

It all looked perfectly fine to Ruth, who watched Constance with a puzzled expression. "You think I'm boring? Like my town that doesn't change... or... what?"

She thought about her hometown; how the same man had been mayor her entire life, and how the grocer's had a plaque proudly proclaiming that the store had been run by the same family since the 1840s. There were similar plaques at the bank, the newspaper office and even the school. Maybe everything in her town did stay the same. But then, didn't that mean that she didn't belong there? After all, she certainly felt changed.

"No. It's not that at all, Ruth. Listen..." She seemed to be searching for words, so Ruth waited, growing more uncomfortable with each passing second. All she wanted was to be with Constance for more than the brief time the festival allowed them. It didn't seem all that much to ask. "Carnival folk... we're different. That's why we're here in the first place. That's why we start."

Still, Ruth didn't understand. "I can learn to do something—"

"I wish it were that simple."

Ruth felt a strange anger, an urge to rage back at Constance's rejection, growing inside her. She didn't like it and tried smoothing her skirts again to rid her brain of the thought. It didn't work. The words began spilling out unbidden. "How are we supposed to be together if we can only see each other one week a year? Do you care about that?"

Constance sat on the wall next to her, taking her hands to still them. "I don't want to think about that right now—"

"When do you want to think about it?" Ruth could feel the heat of the fresh tears flowing down her cheeks.

"I just want to enjoy our time together. How are we supposed to do that while mourning the time we don't have?" Constance took out her handkerchief again, but Ruth wrenched away.

"How am I supposed to enjoy our time when you tell me I'm not *different* enough to be with you?"

"That's not what I meant."

But Ruth was not finished. Shouting now, she stood up and paced, unable to look back at the young woman watching her with such a confused and concerned expression. "You really think I'm not different, Constance? You think I'm like all of them down there? Well, let me tell you something then. My mother and I, we came from Poland when I was two years old and NOT ONCE, not even for a day, have those people down there let me forget exactly how *different* I am." She took a long deep breath, trying once again to calm herself. "You and your Tata ran away from something because you were different; well, so did we, and I still am, Constance. I am still different. Am I not allowed to run away again? Not even to be with the person I love?"

Constance looked shocked. She sat watching Ruth for a long moment, making Ruth, who didn't know if she was angry or simply absorbing the information, very uncomfortable.

"That was too much. I'm sorry... my temper..." Ruth trailed off as Constance jumped up and kissed her.

IN THE FRONT WINDOW OF THE LITTLE APARTMENT OFF FRONT Street, the lamp still glowed dimly. Ruth could see the curtain had been pulled back to watch who might be coming or going, but at some time during the evening, it had begun to shift back into place. To Ruth, these were all very clear signs her mother had tried to wait up, but had fallen asleep. She was probably still in the chair by the window.

Taking great care not to make a sound, Ruth made her way up the outer stairs, unlocked the door and slipped inside. There she found her mother, exactly where she had expected her: slumped over, fast asleep in the rocking chair next to the window. Ruth felt a pang in her heart when she considered her mother, far too thin and frail, looking at least a decade older than her true age. Gently, trying her best not to disturb her, Ruth picked up the quilt that had pooled at her mother's feet and draped it over her shoulders. "*A gute nakht, mamele,*" she whispered in Yiddish before kissing her cheek.

As she slipped into the bedroom, Ruth's mind reeled, filling with second thoughts. Her mother was so helpless. If she left her mother here alone, who would look after her? Who would talk to the utility company and make sure the water stayed on? Who would work with her on her English? Who would make sure she fed herself? She was so helpless, and the thought sent a wave of guilt over Ruth, who had to sit down on the bed until it abated. She felt so ashamed. How could she have forgotten about her mother? When the thought occurred to her to leave, it had felt so natural, so perfectly right, but now she was torn. If she ran away with Constance, her mother would be all alone. If she stayed, she knew she would regret it, every day.

"Ruth?" Her mother's voice called from the bedroom doorway. Ruth brushed at her eyes before turning to face her. In the doorway stood Hannah Pasternak, petite and pale as ever. Her thinning black hair fell down to her shoulders; her nighttime head wrap had fallen off sometime during her fitful sleep. The tiny woman had wrapped the blanket around her shoulders and looked for a moment as though she carried more bulk.

Ruth stood up quickly and started forward to help her toward the bed. "Mama! I didn't mean to wake you."

"Nonsense. I was waiting for you to get home." She eschewed her daughter's assistance, tottered across the floor on her own and sat down, then motioned for Ruth to join her. "I want to hear all about the festival."

Ruth sat down obediently, but shook her head at the thought of telling her mother about the day. "You don't want to hear a—"

"Of course I do. You were very excited this morning. Dancing around here like a princess on the way to a ball." As she took Ruth's hand, a knowing expression passed across her mother's face. Ruth wondered exactly how much she knew or thought she knew. "What's his name?"

"I—"

"Don't be tight-lipped with your mother, Ruth. I remember acting very similarly about your father."

Ruth's blush intensified to a very deep crimson, almost the same color as the lipstick Constance wore. "I'm not trying to be tight-lipped. It's just—"

"Ah, you think I won't approve." Ruth was further taken aback by the look on her mother's face. It was almost playful. She had never once seen her mother wear this expression, and it was unsettling.

"Mama, listen to me. There is no—"

"It would have to be someone who worked for the festival. I haven't seen you out with anyone since you graduated." She shook her head somberly. "You spend far too much time taking care of me—I don't make arrangements for you like I should. It can be hard to meet people in this town. Perhaps we should have gone elsewhere years ago. Somewhere more open."

Ruth squeezed her mother's hand. "Mama. You don't need to worry about me. I'm fine."

"You're my daughter. Worry about you is what I do."

The pair sat in silence for a long while. Ruth watching her mother. Her mother watching her. Initially Ruth's plan had been to come home, pack and be gone before she was noticed, but now that was impossible. She couldn't go tonight. She didn't know if she could go at all. Worst of all, Constance would probably be very understanding. Ruth didn't want to see her calm look as she nodded and said something like, "Of course, well, it's probably for the best."

Part of her wanted to tell her mother everything, but at the same time, a nagging doubt stayed her.

She continued to watch her mother's face, searching her eyes for some sign, some indication that she knew more than she was letting on. What she saw were loving, determined eyes; eyes that had already given up more than their fair share of her own hopes and dreams to keep her daughter safe, to give her a good life. Eyes that carried a heavy history of leaving her home and family. Eyes that struggled still to find meaning in the world around her. Ruth wanted to be the one to give her what she needed now. She wanted that more than anything, more even than Constance's fiery kisses. She couldn't bear to give her mother any further sorrow by leaving.

"Mama," she began, about to say something about secretarial school, when another idea came to her. It was a gamble, perhaps too much of a gamble, but she knew deep down that she had to try. "Mama, her name is Constance."

"Constance." Her mother seemed to roll the name around in her mouth as she said it, tasting every letter, prodding to see if they had nutrients and substance. "Constance—"

"She's a fire performer," Ruth said, uncertain how to proceed with her plan and already doubting herself. "Well, a fire performer in training. Her father is a fire performer—"

"So, she does work for the carnival?" Ruth waited for the disapproval, but her mother's face was a mask.

"Yes."

"Fire performance… that sounds dangerous."

"It's splendid. You should see." Ruth took a deep breath. It was now or never. "Perhaps, you could come tomorrow?"

"Constance," her mother said once again, still sampling the letters. "Yes. I think I would like that very much."

THE NEXT MORNING, RUTH COULD NOT EAT HER BREAKFAST. Her stomach churned at the thought of her foolish actions the night before.

Her mother, however, seemed oddly chipper as she took Ruth's untouched bowl of oatmeal. She even smiled when she asked, "What's the matter, Ruth? Are you ill?"

Ruth wanted to ask her mother the same question. "No, Mama, I..." She trailed off, her stomach churning again and feeling worse than it had on the Miss First Town Days podium.

"When are we going to the festival then?"

Any hope that she had forgotten about their discussion vanished. Ruth felt her ears begin to ring in tandem with the empty lurch in her gut.

"I don't know, Mama, maybe—" But she knew there was no getting out of it, and she couldn't put it off. If she wanted the plan to work, it was now or never. "When do you think you'll be ready?"

Her mother grinned, a rare gem of a smile. "I'm ready now."

Ruth took a deep breath and nodded.

A moment later, Ruth's mother was wrapped in a shawl, even though the newspaper said it would be almost ninety degrees that day. Ruth tried to hide her trembling nerves, lest her mother offer her a shawl, too.

As they maneuvered along the fairway, Ruth refused to so much as glance from side to side. She could no longer hear the vendors and barely took notice of the fried food smells that had so intoxicated her the day before. She had one goal: to get this over with as soon as possible. Then she would know, once and for all, what to do.

The crowd at the sideshow tent was much as it had been the day before. Ruth watched her mother's face, looking for any sign of disapproval, disgust or worse, but nothing of the sort appeared. She seemed to be taking it all in without comment or change in expression. Ruth couldn't imagine what might be going through her mind as they watched a woman bite the head off a live rat. She looked up at her mother's eyes, trying to study her face, but her expression was blank.

"I suppose you expect me to be sick?" she asked Ruth, as the woman disappeared behind a screen. "How little you know me, Ruth. I have seen far more disturbing things in my life than rats."

Ruth didn't know what to say.

The fire-eater stepped up next. He carried two thin flaming torches, which he spun wildly between his fingers, sending the flames whirling into long arms. Ruth could see the blank expression on her mother's face shift a little and hoped that had more to do with awe than anything else. She glanced around, searching for Constance, but she was nowhere to be seen.

The crowd gasped. Ruth turned back; her eyes went wide as soon as she saw Constance, who was dressed in billowing white pants that matched her father's. Hers were cinched tightly just above her hips with a metallic belt that seemed to be made of bells. Instead of a replica of her father's loose tunic top, Constance wore one that was very tight and left her midriff exposed. Ruth found it hard not to stare.

She strolled up to her father and took one of his torches. In perfect unison, the two tilted their heads back and swallowed the still-burning flames. A moment later, they spit the flames back out. As usual for his act, the fire-eater relit his torch, but his daughter used her fire to light a hula hoop.

Ruth bit her lip, terrified. She knew Constance was talented, magical even, but this was something she had never seen. Her heart pounding all the while, she watched Constance rotate the flaming hoop around her hips. The crowd cheered wildly. Ruth's mother took her hand and squeezed it tightly.

"*Krasavitse!*" her mother whispered.

"She's incredible," Ruth replied, agreeing. She too thought Constance a great beauty.

WHEN RUTH FINALLY FOUND CONSTANCE AFTER HER performance, she didn't look like someone who had just been dancing with flames around her body. Ruth knew that she would have been sweating up a nervous storm herself, but Constance appeared almost serene, and there wasn't a single singe on the pristine white costume.

Suddenly, her demeanor changed. The serenity vanished as her eyes widened and she raced toward Ruth. "I thought you had changed your mind!" she exclaimed, embracing her. "When you didn't come—"

"I..." Ruth found herself unable to explain as Constance pressed her lips to hers. They were warmer than ever. Part of Ruth assumed they must have absorbed some of the fire.

Her mother's light cough interrupted them. "You must be Constance," she said easily in accented English. Ruth felt as if the floor had fallen out from under her.

Constance, a faint blush still on her cheeks, nodded slowly. "I am—"

"And I am Hannah. Ruth's mother."

Constance looked to Ruth immediately. Her eyes and nose wrinkled into a confused, concerned expression. Ruth didn't like the situation at all. She suddenly felt as though she had betrayed Constance by bringing her mother here. That hadn't been her intention.

"I want her to come with us," Ruth said quickly.

"Come with us?" Constance said, her voice crackling like kindling as she did so.

Ruth's heart hurt. This wasn't what she wanted. "She needs this," she pleaded. "Not... for the same reasons... but... I can't leave her. Not here. Not alone. Not in this town. Not after everything."

"Ruth... I thought we talked about this—"

"We did," Ruth stood firm, and it surprised her.

"Young lady," Ruth's mother interjected, her voice revealing none of the surprise Ruth was certain she must have felt. "I know you see before you a frail old woman wearing a shawl in July, but I can assure you, there is more to me than meets the eye."

A quizzical expression passed over Constance's face. "Ma'am?"

"When I was a little girl, I often dreamed of the trapeze, or the high wire, or even, oh this is going to sound quite silly, training cats..."

Try as she may, Ruth couldn't imagine her delicate mother on the trapeze. Once she had dropped a glass when her hands went numb; surely hanging in the air was out of the question. Constance knew none of this, though. Ruth had spoken very little with her about her mother. When she glanced over at her, she saw an amused, yet impressed, expression. Ruth appreciated it. Something about the look on Constance's face said she saw her mother as worthy of respect just as Ruth did.

"Cats?" Constance asked, her eyes sparkling.

Ruth's mother laughed, nodding. "I had several growing up. I taught them to stand and shake on command."

"Your mother has magic too!" Constance said. Ruth wasn't sure if she was teasing or being serious.

The thought that this all might have been a mistake still nagged at Ruth's mind. She looked from Constance to her mother and back again, unsure what was happening or what to do about it. A sort of understanding seemed to have passed between the two most important women of Ruth's life, but she, herself, did not seem to be privy to it.

Her mother approached and placed both hands firmly and solidly on Constance's shoulders. "Take care of my little girl."

"Mama?" Ruth asked, still not understanding.

Turning to her daughter now, Ruth's mother smiled: a sad, but hopeful, smile. "This is your adventure, Ruth. You're young. Go and take it."

"No," she said, shaking her head. "You could train cats."

Her mother laughed. "Ruth—Go. Live."

"Not without you."

Taking a deep breath and pulling her daughter into a close hug, she whispered. "I'm not half so weak as you think I am. I will make it, little one. I want you to do the same."

Ruth pulled away, tears in her eyes. Her mother touched her cheek. "I suppose I did all right by you after all." She took Ruth's hand and placed it in Constance's. "Go. Live."

Constance and Ruth looked at one another. Warm tears were leaking out of Ruth's eyes. Tears she didn't understand. Joy or sadness, she wasn't sure. Constance touched her face, about to wipe the tears away, and then Ruth knew: They were tears for all that had been and all that was about to be. 🐿

Surface Tension

Ella J. Ash

L OGAN JUMPS INTO THE COOL LAKE WATER. THE SUN IS
setting—blues and oranges and pinks—and the icy water
startles his body. He's here for his first night of pre-camp in the
Catskills at Camp Sandy Hills, a traditional summer camp with
a creative arts flair. He did not make that up—that's what it says
on the sign. When he saw it, he knew he wasn't in Allentown
anymore. In fact, he's as far from Allentown as he can get until
he leaves for San Francisco after he graduates from high school
next year. It's perfect: Everyone at the camp dances and sings
and comes from places that are distinctly not Backwardville,
Pennsylvania.

Not only that, but he's swim staff, the football team of summer
camp. No one will bat an eye at him. And yeah, he's gay. Even
though he gets taunted at school based on assumptions, he's only
told his best friend, Sarah Silverberg. He is so looking forward
to a summer as just one of the swim guys.

Logan knows he's an enigma. As goes the cliché, he likes musical theater, singing and fashion. But he's also athletic, a swimmer
and a straight-A student, despite his disdain for high school:
he wants to get out of Cowtown and is totally uninterested in
teenage dramas—girls buying boyfriends Hallmark cards to

celebrate three-week anniversaries only to break up four days later. It is a real-life sitcom of ordinariness, a place he simply does not belong. It's no wonder he doesn't fit in.

But this summer, he will have a taste of escape. He's anonymous in a place where he can appreciate theater without sticking out. It's going to be bliss. The water curls around his body, the stars are bright in the sky, and the air is summer-night cool.

PRE-CAMP TRAINING SESSIONS ARE LESS THAN ENTHRALLING. Fire safety and equipment storage are only so gripping, and the food so far has been… well, what do you call hotdogs baked into a cheese soufflé? Yeah, no surprises there. But Sarah's with him at camp and the other staff are nice, fun even. Logan shares a cabin with the other male swim staff: a relaxed blond guy named Stuart Keele, whose biggest flaw appears to be a penchant for parading around in a towel while speaking Klingon; an oafish, kindhearted guy named Matt Smith; and a dancer named Kevin Shyam, who, Logan secretly acknowledges to himself, has the best six-pack he's ever seen. He doesn't usually let himself think such thoughts, but some things are impossible not to notice.

So far, these guys are certainly less offensive than many of the other people he's had the displeasure of encountering in high school. Even though it's summer camp, they haven't batted an eye at his coordinated duvet and throw. How is he supposed to feel at home without a throw pillow or two? The cabin itself is clean but entirely basic—bunk beds and small cots, itchy yellow wool blankets and green rafters above. Logan's bit of flair didn't stop the swim guys from inviting him to play volleyball with them against the other staff last night, so he figures it's okay.

Logan's not used to being an asset in a team sport, but he was. He's tall and broad and apparently can spike a ball right in front of the short, athletic head of canoe instruction—a spike that won the game. Pats on the back, high fives—he's definitely not in Allentown anymore. Even the hot canoe guy—Dave, Logan thinks his name was—turned to him with a smile and a wink and said, "Next time, I think I want you on my team, freshman." Cocky.

⚜

"Hey Logan, wanna come throw the ball around with us?" Stuart is holding his mitt as he and Matt head out the cabin door.

"No thanks. Baseball isn't really my thing." Logan sighs and he takes out his novel. Few things are less appealing than standing in the beating sun, waiting for a hard, small object to be thrown at his face. Besides, he is about to solve the mystery in the latest Mary Higgins Clark novel.

"All right. Suit yourself. Matt, will you grab Dave, meet me at the baseball diamond? He's in the cabin beside the waterfront."

"On my way." Matt stops at the door; a goofy grin creeps over his face. "The female swim staff should be just about finished with their workout, right? Lucky bastard in that cabin—"

Stuart shrugs. "Dude, don't think Dave really cares about girls in swimsuits."

"Yeah, totally. That's probably why they put him there. Lucky bastard," Matt repeats. "Head of his section *and* near the hot girls."

"Wait, what?" The question is out of Logan's mouth before he catches himself.

"Dave's into dudes," Stuart answers. He seems pleased with himself. Logan looks from Stuart to Matt, trying to figure out if he's more surprised by the information or their nonchalance about it.

"He is?" Logan can feel his face flush.

"Yeah, why? You've got a problem with that? Not cool, dude." Stuart shakes his head as he walks out the door behind Matt.

Logan bites his lip as he picks up his book. He feels dizzy. *What exactly just happened?*

AT DINNER, MATT SITS AT LOGAN'S TABLE WITH A TRAY OF chicken nuggets and fries and not a green vegetable in sight. He is followed first by Stuart and then Dave, who puts down his tray and excuses himself to talk to the camp director.

Stuart, sitting across from Logan, looks at him sternly. "Dave's my best friend, Logan. If you're not okay with the gay thing, then—"

Logan can't help it; he lets out a high-pitched "ha!" and, "I feel like I'm in the Twilight Zone," before quickly excusing himself to use the washroom. When he returns, composure regained, Dave is seated across from Matt and beside Stuart, Logan turns to Stuart and whispers, "Don't worry about it, okay?"

After experiencing a dinner with David Westin—*Dave*—gay Dave, out Dave, head of canoe instruction, everybody's best friend Dave—Logan can only conclude that this guy is perfect, and in the most infuriating way. Yes, he is a good-looking guy; Logan can appreciate that without being raunchy . He is on the short side, but has a nice body: strong legs, dark curly hair and, yes, really quite striking brown eyes that, impossibly, seem to twinkle. Logan is not sure what rose-colored world Dave comes from, but he clearly hasn't had to struggle much. It's kind of nauseating. And he's so nice, to, like, everyone.

"Do you sing, Logan?" Dave asks.

"I'm at creative arts camp. What do you think?"

"That's great. I'm organizing a staff Sing-Off for the evening program. Hope you'll join us."

"Dave, you totally won that game for us!" Stuart is effusive.

Dave shakes his head. "No, guys. It was a team effort. Seriously."

"I'll clear the table and get the dessert tray. First brownie for the new guy?" Dave grins at Logan.

Dave is the outtest boy Logan has ever met. And, camp veteran; athlete by day, performer by night; every camper's crush, every staff member's confidant. He's only Logan's age, but he's in charge of his section. And also, it seems, proudly and nonchalantly gay. Not a hint of a scratch on him. Honestly, Logan's not sure it could get more irritating.

AFTER DINNER, LOGAN DROPS SARAH OFF AT HER CABIN; Stuart and Dave are talking outside of what he guesses is Dave's cabin—a solo staff cabin, because he's section head. *Yippee.* As he debates approaching them to walk back to his cabin with Stuart, he overhears his name. And he can't help it; he sneaks behind a tree to listen. Who wouldn't?

"You know, man, I think Logan, the new guy, he might be uncomfortable with the gay thing." Stuart's voice is all genuine concern and Logan bites his tongue to keep from laughing out loud.

"Logan? You mean Mr. Of-Course-I-Can-Sing, with the sass and the searing blue eyes and the incredible swimmer's build?"

Dave sighs and smirks at Stuart. Logan's eyes bug out. He's pretty sure that was a compliment. About *his body.* Though Logan is almost beach-boy handsome—blue eyes, thick auburn hair, athletic build—he's never been a stud. There was always too much swish in his swagger, even if he can outswim all the jocks who refuse to let him forget it.

"Oh no, dude. Don't tell me you're—no, dude. He was really weird when I told him you're gay."

"Really?" Dave looks more amused more than perturbed. "What did he say?"

"He was just really surprised and, like, I don't know—when I told him that if he's not okay with it, that you're my dude—" Dave smiles affectionately. Stuart is a sweetheart, if not the sharpest knife in the drawer. "He gave me the weirdest look and said that he feels like he's in the Twilight Zone."

"He did, did he? Where's he from again? Hick town, Pennsylvania, right?"

"I think so, why?"

"I mean, I don't really know. But I kind of think—already thought—and now maybe really think that he actually—"

"What?"

"You know, plays for *my* team." Dave shrugs. Like it's no biggie. Man, Stuart is clueless. And apparently Dave, well, isn't.

"No way." Stuart is clearly surprised. Dave just nods. "No man. I know you think he's hot and all. But—"

"Mmm, he is." And with that, Dave walks into his cabin.

It's the evening before the campers arrive, the evening of the Dave-led staff Sing-Off. In other words, karaoke, and you choose a duet partner to "battle" with. There's no real point, Logan muses, other than an excuse to sing, but okay. He and Sarah have an excellent duet planned, if he does say so himself. "Popular" from *Wicked* does have the perfect self-deprecatingly humorous tone to suit his summer of bliss and fitting in. Last night he had in a not-ironic discussion about the best musical theater productions with three straight guys, and no one gave a hint of being fazed. So what if Tony from *West Side Story* or Danny Zuko from *Grease* are their dream roles? At least they know the songs.

"And it's Sing-Off time!" Dave croons into the mic. His minions respond with rousing *whoops* and *woohoos* and Logan has to admit the energy is infectious. Dave and Stuart start off the night with a well-rehearsed rendition of "Summer of '69." *They're pretty good.* Dave has an undeniably magnetic stage presence; even without his bum-shaking, which Logan is absolutely not letting himself notice.

"Look at his body, Logan. He can move!" Sarah whispers.

"You have such a one-track mind."

"Like you don't."

"I don't," Logan says. He doesn't, not really . He'd never let himself.

"So who is going to help me do the next duet?" Dave then sing-songs the terrible, terrible Beatles' song pun: "Won't you please, please help me... Logan?"

He did not just—he did. Ignoring his red cheeks, Sarah pushes him toward the stage to sing a duet with Everybody-Loves-Dave.

"How about some classic Temptations?" Dave says. And before he has a chance to voice objection, Logan finds himself center stage, mic in hand, singing "Under the Boardwalk" with a guy. A guy who seems not to feel one ounce of concern about singing an undeniably flirty duet with him in front of the entire staff.

Logan can rise to the occasion—and he does. He is certainly not going to undermine an opportunity to perform, and he can easily pull off a little Temptations. And from the sound of the applause as the song ends, he—fine, *they*—sounded great. But that doesn't mean he wanted to be there.

Once the applause dies down and his adrenaline high ebbs as he steps off the stage, he's shaking.

Sarah tries to get his attention. "Logan, it's your turn to choose a partner."

"I need to get some air," he says. "Dave can go again." He frowns as he walks into the cool night air.

"He's not feeling well," Sarah covers for him as he walks out, and a minute later the music starts again with an unquestionably Sarah version of "A Heart Full of Love," paired with a voice that sounds like Matt's.

Logan's heart slows down as the cool breeze hits his skin. He's not even sure what he feels, except overwhelmed. He leans against a tree on the way back to his cabin and takes a few breaths. The still beauty of the leafy, tree-lined path calms him slightly. And then he hears footsteps coming toward him in the otherwise perfectly quiet night.

Dave. Of course. Logan faces him..

Dave walks toward him. "Logan?"

"What *was* that?"

"What?" Dave looks genuinely concerned.

"Why did you ask me to sing that duet?"

"Because you said you liked to sing," Dave answers. Of course he'd come up with *that. Of course.*

"Are you trying to make things more difficult for me?"

"Excuse me, *what*?" A flash of irritation moves across Dave's face.

"Where I come from, two boys get beaten up for singing a duet together. Or rather, two boys just don't do that."

"Yeah, where I come from too."

Oh. "Really?"

"Yes, really. But this isn't *that* place."

"So you're just assuming that I'm gay, that I would want to do something like that?" Logan's not sure why he says that. Why he puts Dave on the defensive. But apparently raw emotion doesn't always make sense.

"Logan, I could have sung that duet with Stuart. No one cares."

Logan has to admit, at least to himself, that this may be true. "You could have," Logan agrees, relaxing slightly. "He has the biggest guy crush on you I've ever seen." Logan rolls his eyes and Dave chuckles.

"True."

"God, you're cocky." Logan's eyes roll again, but playfully . "And it's The Drifters, by the way. The Temptations covered *their* song."

"Impressive." Dave nods and continues, "And yeah, okay? It has more than crossed my mind that you might be gay. But if you're not? Fine, okay. Unless you're a raging homophobe, oh well, and on we go."

"Of course I'm gay. It's kind of obvious, isn't it?" It's a relief to say it.

"I guess, but whatever. It's musical theater camp. Nothing's obvious."

"Touché."

Logan feels the beat between them and then somehow they both giggle.

"This is just supposed to be my 'Summer of Un-gay,'" Logan reveals, and Dave's eyebrows rise.

"What is 'un-gay'?"

"You know, gay-irrelevant. Like you said, it's musical theater camp—a place where I can actually be anonymous, not stick out. I've waited seventeen years to blend in," Logan says, "and then you go and—"

"Blow your cover?"

"Kind of, yeah."

"Hmm."

"What?"

"I think I'd waited fifteen years—when I first came to camp—to actually *be* gay. To be out. To not have to pretend I was swooning over the cheerleader instead of the basketball player. I'm always so invisible at home." Dave shrugs, but there is sadness in his eyes.

"And here you're not."

"No."

"And you assumed that because *you're* out that *I'd* want to sing a flirty duet with another guy."

"I wasn't really *assuming* anything. I just—I don't know—felt like singing a duet with you."

"You *felt* like it?"

"Everyone else flirts all the time. It's innocent. It's fun. And then you were there, so I took my chances." Dave sighs. He looks slightly defeated. "I may be good at a lot of things—yes, cocky, I know—but I guess flirting isn't one of them."

Logan looks at him. He doesn't know how to react. Un-gay is definitely not working very well, because he is suddenly feeling very, very gay. He bites his lip.

"Seriously, Logan, I'm sorry it made you uncomfortable. That was the last thing I wanted. From now on, it's all business." Dave smiles and makes an "aye aye, captain" gesture. It's ridiculous. And somehow Logan still sees flirty. *Dammit.* "I will sing with Stuart and you will be anonymous Logan, The Very Un-Gay," Dave teases warmly.

"Okay."

"Okay." Dave nods and looks him straight in the eyes. "So I'll see you tomorrow, Logan." He pats Logan on the arm and walks away; Logan's eyes follow. Dave takes about six steps, then hesitates and turns around. "But, Logan—"

"Mmm?"

"I liked singing a duet with a cute guy," Dave says, "so let me know if you change your mind."

And then Dave is gone and he's anonymous Logan again, as requested.

The only problem is that being anonymous is not nearly as much fun as being cute.

⚜

THE CAMPERS ARRIVE THE NEXT DAY, AND WITH THEM THE anticipated chaos. Not being a cabin counselor has its advantages, in this time of the newly homesick, but the swim staff administer every camper's swim test. Which means standing on the docks, baking in the sun and testing kids for two days straight.

"All right, group B, out of the water. You're done." Stuart claps his hands at the end of their second day, turns to Logan and says, "And man, *I* am done. I'm stripping this off and jumping in."

"I second that idea." Sarah passes behind them with Dave at her side.

"Exactly. What's the point of swim staff if not to prance around in speedos all day?" Dave says and winks at Stuart.

Sarah smiles. "He said it, not me."

Logan's heart races; he anticipates that Dave will pull him into the conversation, say something casual like, "Right, Logan?" But it never comes. Stuart pulls his shirt off and over his head, makes his not very convincing suggestive eyes at Dave and dives into the water.

꧁

AT STAFF SNACK THE NEXT EVENING, LOGAN SITS WITH MATT, Stuart, Kevin and another canoe staff guy, Jake. They are engaged in the most stereotypical of conversations.

"My ex-girlfriend definitely said boxers," Matt says.

"No way, man. Briefs are classic," Kevin pipes in. *He would think so; he has the body for them.*

Jake shrugs. "Depends on the goal of the moment. Boxers for sleep, briefs for the *ladies*." Kevin high fives him, Matt looks sheepish.

"I don't know, guys..."

Oh God, that's Dave coming over.

Suddenly four eager faces turn to Dave. *Of course, the gay boy must have the answer to man's greatest mystery.* "In my opinion, only a few guys can pull off the brief. I say, boxer briefs—perfect on my ex. And I like them best for comfort."

"Diplomatic even in your underwear choices," Logan says under his breath but just loudly enough to be heard. He didn't really mean to enter this conversation, but something about watching four straight guys, doe-eyed over Dave talking about his ex-boyfriend's assets, just brings out the sass.

Logan has just opened himself up to a myriad of potential topics he does not want to talk about—sex, relationships, his underwear preferences. Too many cans of worms here, and he's just handed Dave the can opener.

But Dave doesn't bite.

"Hey, we can't all have Stuart's six-pack," Dave says, bouncing the conversation away from Logan. Casually. Because that's what Logan asked him to do.

Logan is still feeling inexplicably grumbly when Sarah and Matt walk up. "I was just telling Matt that we have some killer duets to share at the talent show," she brags, grabbing his arm.

"Yes, Sarah. We better get practicing," Logan says, hoping his sarcasm isn't too biting. "Talent show is like the second-to-last night of camp, after all."

"Oh as if you don't like to be perfectly prepared," Sarah rolls her eyes at him and walks off with a wave. He's feeling leftover irritation about Dave and his underwear. He knows he has no reason to be irritated, the opposite, actually. Dave is doing exactly what Logan asked him to do. And it seems that this has only made Dave more infuriating.

"Can I ask you something?" Matt says, breaking the quiet as they amble back to their cabin.

"Sure?"

"You and Sarah know each other from home, right?"

"Yeah." Logan sighs. "I know I was hard on her just now. But we're actually very close."

"But you're not...?" Matt doesn't finish the sentence. Oh. *Ohhh.* Matt wants to know if he and Sarah are an item. This is getting ridiculous. If Matt is presenting the opportunity, he'll take it.

Logan shrugs. "I'm gay, Matt. So *no*, we're *not.* Not like that."

"Yes!" Matt fist bumps the air and looks so pleased. "I mean, not about the gay thing. Not that there's anything—of course, I mean... I just think Sarah's cute, okay?"

Logan exhales, relieved. Matt isn't batting an eyelash at his big reveal. "Oh! Ha! You do? I mean, that's great. You should go for it."

"I should?"

"I try at all costs to avoid talking to Sarah about dating, Matt, but I do think she might..." Logan does try not to talk to Sarah about her crushes, because that inevitably leads to her trying to talk to him about his crushes, or lack of crushes, which he definitely does not want to talk about. Or think about. But he figures a little encouragement is okay, because Matt is far less likely to try to engage him in a conversation about Dave's perky butt... which Logan definitely hasn't noticed.

"Oh, cool. Really? Cool." Matt nods and smiles. "I mean, I kind of figured you might be gay, but Dave always says never to make assumptions—"

"Especially at creative arts camp," Logan adds and Matt hums his agreement.

"So, is it, like, a secret?"

"No, not really. Just kind of irrelevant."

"Okay." Matt appears to be deep in thought. "But like, what if you think someone is cute?"

"Ha!" Logan laughs. "That stuff doesn't happen to gay kids in high school, Matt. We stay irrelevant until college."

Matt stops as he opens the door to their cabin. "Okay. But this isn't high school. It's creative arts camp, remember? Never assume anything." He punches him on the shoulder and smirks before walking inside.

"Ow," Logan mumbles to himself. *Damn him.*

Logan does manage to come out to the rest of his staff cabin that night. He doesn't want to be in the closet. He just wants his sexuality to be irrelevant—and amazingly, it actually might be just that. So amidst a heated argument about whether the navy slacks look nerdy or perfect with the red and navy plaid shirt, he slips in that they should let the gay guy in the room choose. So what if it's a stereotype? It's one he happens to embrace. And while he's pretty sure that Stuart and Kevin share a look behind his back, no one flinches, and he's almost positive the look was a smile.

⁂

FRIDAY NIGHT, FIVE DAYS INTO THE FIRST WEEK AND JUST after the first banquet, Logan opts out of the evening staff softball game. The dinner was almost flawless for a camp meal; the turkey was a little rubbery, but the apple pie was good, and they had sparkling, non-alcoholic cider. Also, the dining hall disco décor—complete with mirror balls created by the fine arts campers—was a nice touch. Still, he craves quiet, so he sets out for a walk along the waterfront.

The camp is beautiful and, while he's never considered himself the outdoorsy type, he can appreciate the wonder of a clear sky full of stars, the scent of evergreen trees and a quiet lake. Logan has to admit that, since coming out to his co-staff, he feels relieved. He can be gay-irrelevant without being closeted, and the easy conversation gives him the relaxed feeling that is so impossibly elusive in Allentown.

As he approaches the boating area, a short walk from the swimming docks along a dirt path, he hears crickets and the quiet sound of shifting water. He expects to be alone, with the campers in bed and the staff at softball or in cabins, but notices one lone canoe in the distance. He stands on the shore and watches Dave dip the paddle into the water, his arms flexing easily, his hair mussed and curlier than he wears it during the day. The breeze is warm, but Logan gets goose bumps when Dave makes eye contact.

"Logan," Dave projects across the water as he starts paddling over. "No softball for you?"

Logan shrugs. "Not really my thing."

"Guess we had the same idea. Care to join me?" Dave offers as he paddles close to the shore.

Logan wants to. He knows he wants to. It's beautiful on the lake. "I'll get a paddle." Logan walks to the shed. The goose bumps are back and he's shivering, but the circumstance is random and not a big deal—not to him, not to Dave. It would have been more awkward to decline the invitation. Though Logan gives Dave a hard time, he likes Dave, admires his easy out-ness, his manners, his kindness, even his ridiculous ego. And while the romance of a canoe ride on a silent lake at sunset isn't lost on him, Dave's relaxed nonchalance toward him removes any hint of *that* possibility. So what if un-gay was his own request? Dave has completely embraced it.

Logan leaves his sandals on the beach, rolls his pants up to his knees and wades out a few steps before he climbs into the front of the canoe. He dips his paddle in the water as Dave starts to steer them away.

The conversation is easy. "So how was the first week of new swimmers?"

"Well, let's see… daily complaints that the water's too cold; fifteen-year-old boys who think they're God's gift to sports, but can barely swim two laps; and kids who enjoy singing a medley from *The Sound of Music* while treading water. So I guess, all in all, it evens out."

Dave chuckles. "I prefer a *Rent* medley for canoe trips."

"Of course," Logan agrees. "Oh but, there's the junior girls. They don't want to get their hair wet." Dave laughs, splashing Logan gently with the paddle. Logan splashes back. "Don't even think about it. I definitely appreciate the importance of flawless hair—"

"Of course."

"But perhaps one should style and coif *after* swim lessons. I just threaten them with ten minutes of treading water and they jump right in."

Dave talks about this and that but stays safely away from anything too personal. Because that's what *Logan* wanted. But they're on a lake and alone, and the reality is that Logan doesn't have many gay friends. In fact, he doesn't have *any* gay friends. And the idea of actually having someone to talk to makes the temptation too great not to take the risk.

Logan rips off the Band-Aid. "So tell me about your boxer-briefs-loving ex-boyfriend." He blushes but gets it out. No segue. Subtlety isn't his forte at the best of times and certainly not when bringing up nerve-wracking, forbidden topics with out and proud Dave.

"You want to know about Colin?" Dave seems surprised.

"I just asked, didn't I?"

Logan turns quickly to look at Dave. He has a sheepish grin on his face; Dave raises his eyebrows but continues. "Okay. Well, we met at the beginning of my junior year last year when I transferred to Smithson—"

"Smithson Academy? As in Lancaster?"

"Pennsylvania boys represent." Dave fist-bumps the air.

"God you weren't kidding when you said that you were from a place where two boys don't sing together."

"No, I wasn't." Dave is earnest. "That's why I go to Smithson Academy, actually. I got bullied at my public school after the only other out gay guy and I started eating lunch together. Not even a boyfriend. I had been waiting so long to be out, but it was safer to be invisible."

"I had no idea, Dave. I'm so sorry." Logan turns to make sure Dave can see his eyes.

"Anyway, I found this summer camp and transferred to Smithson Academy, where they're serious about no bullying in exchange for a lot of your parents' money. The rest is history." Dave sighs.

"And you met a *guy*?" Logan prompts. Because how does a gay kid in high school in Pennsylvania get a boyfriend? Like, what are the odds?

"Yeah. I mean, I think it's more accurate to say he met me. Colin isn't subtle, and when he found out I was gay, well—" Dave pauses. "We were making out in the backseat of his car the next weekend."

"Oh." Logan feels his heart fall into his stomach. He has heard plenty of stories about the backseats of cars. So what if it's never been him? He's always been prepared to wait until college. Maybe he's just jealous. He looks down, dips his paddle.

"Too much? Sorry." Dave seems to sense his unease. Which of course only increases it.

"No. No. I'm not *that* innocent." *Sometimes I feel like I am.*

"No—I didn't mean—I mean. 'Summer of Un-gay?'" *Oh. That again.*

"It's okay, Dave. We're kind of alone, if you hadn't noticed. And I asked," Logan says. "But he's your *ex*-boyfriend?" He asks this against his better judgment; somehow, he wants to be sure.

"Yeah. I mean, we dated for about six months. He was my first—my only—" This time, Dave lets the pause linger. Saying more would be TMI, and Logan really doesn't want to know the details. "But I think we're better off as friends. He's lots of fun to take to a gay bar—Oh my God, I should tell you this story. This one night he took us to The Stonewall in Allentown—"

The Stonewall? Dave has been out to the gay bar in my city? Logan's mind is racing.

"And there was a drag queen pageant that night. When we almost didn't get in, because I didn't have a fake ID, he told them I was Madam Kentucky, the award-winning queen, but my

costume was inside. The bouncer scowled at me but let us in."
Dave laughs and Logan finds himself enjoying the low chuckle
behind him, the shared secrets.

"Oh my God." Logan can't help but giggle, despite his sweaty
palms and the way his heart races at the image of clean-cut Dave
in Allentown's gay bar. "Madam Kentucky."

"Yeah, but anyway—" Dave seems to have accepted the permission, because he's babbling. Less sophisticated. It's cute. *No
it's not.* "I guess Colin's not very—umm—romantic?" Dave tries.
"Cheesy, right?"

"No, not at all." Logan's voice is too breathy. He needs to figure
out how to turn that off.

"So, I just wasn't feeling *it*—don't even know what *it* really is,"
Dave admits. He's bashful. Despite gay bars and first times and
Colin and duets, he seems just as naive as Logan.

"Me neither," Logan adds. A charged quiet falls between them.
They are on their way back to the shore, and Logan senses that,
when they get back, it might get awkward. But he doesn't want
it to be. Not now. His mind races as he tries to figure out how
to gracefully exit the tension between them. And then a paddle
splashes on the water and droplets land all over his back. He
whips around. "What the—?"

Dave maneuvers the canoe onto the sand. "Gotcha." He's grinning like the Cheshire Cat.

Logan steps out of the canoe, rolling his eyes. "At least you
didn't get my hair."

"I wouldn't dare."

They're quiet again as they hoist the canoe to its rafters and
put away their paddles.

"Thank you, Logan Hart, for a lovely evening canoe ride."

Logan bites back his natural sarcasm in the face of sincerity.
Especially sincerity from a sparkly-eyed gay boy who seems at

least willing to be his friend. "Thank you," Logan says, his voice breathy, "for taking me, I mean."

Dave just smiles as they walk along the path back to the main camp. Their arms brush. Logan gets goose bumps. Summer breeze again.

⟡

SATURDAY EVENINGS AT CAMP ARE SOCIALS. ; "SOCIAL" IS AN esoteric camp word for what the rest of the world calls "dances," and which includes: music, mocktails and awkward eleven-year-olds having their first slow dances with six feet between them. If Logan were eleven, he would certainly have stayed home. Which is exactly where the camper standing by the drinks table, Justin Chen, looks as though he wants to be: anywhere but here.

Justin is in Logan's junior boys' swim class. He isn't a bad swimmer; he's completely capable, just uninterested. He's here for the musical theater program—he's clear about his priorities—but he also seems to enjoy cooking and craft shack if you press him. He is not here for outdoor sports, and that includes swimming. He is basically a mini version of Logan, complete with impeccable style for an eleven-year-old.

Logan, however, learned early on that being a good swimmer, the best swimmer, was a way to even the playing field. For one hour, three times a week, Logan Hart was the best at a sport. Only Justin doesn't seem to want to be. He almost revels in his difference. And given his non-swim-class high school experience. Logan gets that too.

Logan walks over to Justin and hands him a strawberry daiquiri mocktail. "Dances aren't really my thing either. The secret is to enjoy the fruity drinks anyway" He smiles.

Justin shrugs. "Thanks. It's also an opportunity to showcase the latest summer fashions, not that anyone cares."

"Oh, I care. I can spot good Comme Des Garcons knockoff jeans when I see them."

Justin smiles. "I'm impressed, for swim staff." God this kid is sassy.

"Justin, come dance with us!" Logan recognizes one of the junior girls beckoning him. *Leanne.*

"Go on," Logan says. He gestures toward the group of girls. "They look like fun."

"I'm just not into it." Justin looks sad and Logan's heart clenches.

"I wasn't either." Suddenly Dave is beside him, looking warmly at Justin, who looks up at him with a start.

"You?" Justin looks skeptical and Logan can't say he blames him. Dave is pretty much the boy next door. He moves easily from football to canoe to musical theater; it's hard to imagine him *othered*. And yet...

"Yeah. I was a gay kid in small town Pennsylvania." Dave just says it, as if he's talking about the weather. "School dances, not my favorite thing."

"Same for me, Justin," Logan says, because he knows the kind of impact it would have made on him to know someone else like him was out there, someone who had at least survived most of high school. Out of the corner of his eye, he sees Dave raise his eyebrow at him before nodding nonchalantly at Justin.

"So don't worry about it, okay? You're not alone," Dave says, punching Justin gently on the shoulder. Justin gives him the best judgmental side-eye he can, but Logan sees a tiny smile.

"Justin!" Leanne demands.

"I gotta go," Justin says, slightly relieved. "But uh, thanks." He says it quickly, before he's engulfed by a group of enthusiastic girls. Logan doesn't get a chance to tell him that friends like Leanne can actually be a saving grace. But he imagines Justin will figure that out for himself.

Dave looks at Logan as he sips his Shirley Temple. "So what prompted that?"

"I'm gay too, Dave." *Honestly.*

"I know, Logan." Dave looks at him to continue.

"Something about a mini version of myself," he replies.

"Ahh." Dave nods. "Nothing like a Justin to rise up against the 'Summer of Un-gay.'"

Dave's trying to be cute, but it annoys Logan anyway. "Enough, okay?" His tone is slightly more biting than he means it to be.

"Enough what?" Dave is still staring directly at him, and now is smirking.

"I've told the swim guys, I just told Justin, you know—like, whatever. Un-gay doesn't work for me apparently. So you can stop pretending—"

"Pretending what?" Dave looks as if he's daring him.

Logan rolls his eyes. "It's fine. I'm out, okay?"

Dave shrugs. "Okay. So now if I'm asking you to pass the waffles at breakfast, I can say, 'Hey, gay Logan, waffles please? Would you like some boys with that?'"

Logan folds his arms across his chest. "You know exactly what I mean."

"No, seriously, Logan. It's not like anything's really different on my end."

"I guess not." But Logan feels uncertain, because somehow he's sort of hoping it will be.

"Unless of course it means I'm allowed to sing duets with you again." Dave smiles, still challenging him. And yeah, *this* is what he means. Not the duet, the dialogue.

"Uh uh, no, I don't think so."

"Oh, I think so. You know me. It's kind of my thing. And singing with a talented, cute guy. *Swoon*." Dave lifts his voice and bats his eyelashes. He's kidding around. But also not. Logan bites his lip but lets the blush run through him. He savors it this time. Dave looks at him as if assessing something. "I think you just gave me permission to flirt, Logan Hart."

"You do need practice."

"I do," Dave agrees in a tone that's somewhere between sincerity and flirtatiousness. How does he do that? "And I always perfect my art."

⚜

AGAIN, DAVE IS TRUE TO HIS WORD. ALTHOUGH HE'S sometimes a bit over the top—like the time he walked along the swim beach as he was toweling off and called out, "By the way, you could totally pull off briefs"—he's usually pretty sweet and subtle. It's this thing that is just between them. Logan has never had anything like it before. And he loves it. It's like a game—sometimes, literally.

The first time, Logan definitely wins. The Monday night evening program is Capture the Flag, Campers and staff take turns running around with a T-shirt hanging out of their shorts, waiting for a lust- or revenge-crazed camper from a different team to pull it out and send them to jail. Logan, on the Blue Team, doesn't at all mind going there when Dave is the Green Team's jail guard.

Dave watches in amusement as the senior camper who caught him escorts Logan into the jail circle. Logan is now in the company of three younger campers who are waiting for someone to incite a jailbreak; alas, he is but a prisoner.

111

"Got a good one for you." Green Team senior boy looks proud to deliver a prize swim staff prisoner.

"He *is* a good one," Dave replies, his amused eyes on Logan. Logan looks straight back. The senior says, "Later, Captain," and runs off, but Logan is too occupied by the staring contest to be certain that he heard him right.

"Hi, Logan." Dave circles him outside the jail, smiling.

"Hi, Dave." Logan follows Dave with his eyes.

"Bummer you got caught."

"Oh, like you don't love having me as your prisoner." Logan continues to stare, and runs his fingers along his neck.

"Oh, I do," Dave says, holding Logan's gaze. "My lucky day." Logan is sure this is an attempt to be suggestive without scaring the campers. Dave is as close to the prisoners' circle as he can get without stepping inside, and Logan is as close to Dave as he can get without stepping out.

"You shouldn't get used to it."

"Oh no?" Dave waggles his eyebrows. It's silly but adorable, and Logan just wants to laugh but keeps the glare going.

"No," Logan insists, "I magically distract the guards until someone is able to—"

"Jailbreak!" A Blue Team senior girl flies in from behind the bushes, screaming the command, and Logan and the others are off before Dave wakes from his Logan-induced daze.

Logan had seen her coming and kept Dave's eye contact. He *totally* wins.

THEN THERE ARE THE QUIETER MOMENTS. LOGAN DISMISSES the junior boys' swim class just as Dave comes strolling along the dock one afternoon.

"Hey," Dave says, smiling.

"Hey."

"That's Justin's class, right?" Dave motions at the boys now on the beach with their towels.

Logan sighs. "Yeah. I wouldn't say he's suddenly embracing his athletic side, but he is jumping in with the rest of them and more than keeping up," Logan says with pride.

"It's sweet the way you're looking out for him," Dave says with a smile.

"Yes, well, gotta look out for one of our own, right?" Logan smiles back. "Not that Justin is for sure—I mean—I shouldn't assume or—"

Dave giggles and places his warm hand on Logan's arm, somehow giving him goose bumps. "Don't worry about it. And I make assumptions too. Remember our mistimed duet? Your gaydar is safe with me." *He's ridiculous.*

"I feel like it's time for a secret tribal handshake or something," Logan says under his breath, shaking his head. Dave pauses. He looks as if he's plotting. "That was a *joke*, Dave."

"Oh come on, it'd be fun," Dave says, grinning from ear to ear. "A secret *homosexual* code." Even when he's being sarcastic, Dave's exuberance shines through. Logan gives Dave the best judgmental glare he can muster while still grinning.

THEY'RE FINISHING DESSERT THE FOLLOWING FRIDAY EVENING when Dave asks Logan to skip the staff weekly evening softball game again in favor of a canoe ride.

"It's an excuse to not play softball," Dave tries.

And while Logan always does exactly what he wants—which would never be softball—he's in. And he absolutely does not spend an extra thirty minutes making sure he looks like an eleven on a scale of one to ten, with an appropriately casual outfit:

khaki capris and a tight red T-shirt with three buttons open at the top. Canoe–appropriate. He can wade without soaking the bottoms of his pants. So what if the T-shirt hugs his chest just enough to emphasize his pecs? Side effect.

Dave is waiting by the canoe, bouncing on his toes in navy blue shorts and a tight, white, collared button-down shirt with a navy-and-white polka dot handkerchief in its pocket. He *accessorized*. But Dave likes fashion—so what if he dressed up? It's probably not meaningful, though Logan admits to himself that he appreciates a guy who dresses to impress. *He* dresses to impress. And he's sure they'd both do it even if they happened to be canoeing with Stuart or Sarah.

"Hey." Dave's eyes sparkle in the moonlight as he watches Logan approach, and Logan's stomach does a pleasant swoop.

"Hey." They lead the canoe into the water and hop in with Dave at the stern, Logan in the front. They chitchat as they paddle away into the nighttime nothingness and the camp becomes more remote, the sky more starry. Logan wills that his hands not sweat and that the conversation be as easy and as real as last time, but they do and it isn't. He's nervous, which is not impressive at all. He rambles too long about the trials and tribulations of teaching swimming with confidence to pubescent girls. At a pause in the conversation, Dave slows down the canoe and ships his paddle.

"Dave?" Logan looks over his shoulder at Dave. Dave breathes out heavily as he looks at Logan. He bites his lower lip.

"So, I am really not good at this," Dave starts out of nowhere. "For one, I want to have a conversation with you, but I bring you out in a canoe where I'm staring at your back."

Dave has a point. Logan takes his own paddle out of the water and carefully turns around.

"Easy fix."

"Okay," Dave starts again, "I feel like maybe I've taken this permission to flirt thing too far."

"Oh." Logan's heart falls while he tries to keep his face neutral. He doesn't know what he expected—probably just a canoe ride and nice conversation—but this feels like rejection. Like what a breakup conversation would feel like, even though he's never had a breakup and there isn't anything to break. He says, "Okay," because what else is he going to say? If Dave doesn't want to flirt, he shouldn't flirt.

"Aren't you going to ask why?"

"No. I'm actually more curious about why you'd bring me all the way out here to tell me that instead of just, you know, not flirting. It isn't a requirement. It's really quite simple. Like if you don't think I'm cute, you know, don't tell me I'm cute." Logan's voice cracks despite his desire to stay cool.

"No. No—" Dave bites his lip.

"I'm glad you find this funny."

"Logan, I think you're cute." Dave looks straight at him, his brown eyes shine in contrast to the black night. "I think you're gorgeous, actually."

"Oh." Logan feels as if he's on that ride at Six Flags that loops you around twice in one direction and then suddenly jerks and flips you backward in the other.

"I really am bad at this—"

"At what?"

"So, like, since you abandoned the 'Summer of Un-gay,' since we've had this flirty thing going on," Dave says, his eyelashes fluttering as he smiles, "I feel like it's just this habit, this thing we do. And it isn't what I really want."

Rejection again? "Honestly, Dave, just spit it out, 'cause you're giving me whiplash here."

"Logan, I like you."

115

"I like you too, Dave. I think we've established that already."
Logan knows he's being difficult, but his heart is beating rapidly
and he can't really let himself believe what Dave appears to be
saying. This stuff isn't supposed to happen to him. And not with
a smart, kind, confident and very out guy, *before* his senior year
of high school.

"No. I mean, I *like* you." Dave looks at him directly before
shaking his head and looking down shyly. Fidgety, he takes his
paddle and dips it into the still lake. The surface tension breaks.
He looks at Logan again, his eyes vulnerable, and Logan stares,
his mouth slightly open, a nervous grin twitching at its edges.
He's shaking. "You're not saying anything."

"Oh." Logan's heart is louder than his voice. "I like you
too. *Like* you." Logan finds his voice somehow, and the con-
fession falls from him, natural and obvious. "I just haven't
known what to do with it. But flirting is fun, so that's what I
went with."

"It *is* fun. I just don't want that to be all this is. I want… this,"
Dave says, gesturing between them, "to be… more."

"Me too." Logan takes a deep breath and finds his courage.
"So….what happens next?" He can hardly believe he is being
such a fishing minx, but apparently this is not his "Summer of
Un-gay."

Dave looks down at the canoe. "Here's where you see that I
am *really* bad at this, because I was trying to be all romantic
on a lake and under the stars but I'm sitting way too far away
to hold your hand, let alone be all caught up in the moment
and kiss you."

"Kiss me?" Logan feels his blood rush through him. "Now?"

Dave blinks back at him, a little incredulous. "Yeah, I mean,
if you want to. That's kind of the point, isn't it?"

"I guess it is." Logan breathes out.

"May I?" Dave walks carefully across the canoe to sit on the little bar directly behind Logan's front seat.

Logan giggles as the boat rocks. "Just don't tip us, okay?"

"Guess that would ruin the moment," Dave says as he perches on the bar. His knees touch Logan's. They look at each other, but Dave doesn't kiss him. Instead, he reaches down and picks up Logan's hand and slowly interlaces their fingers, one by one. Logan watches. It's ridiculously romantic. They smile at each other. Logan giggles again; he's nervous, shaking. It's perfect.

"So when did this dawn on you, Dave Westin?"

"Taking you out on a canoe ride to talk about this?" Dave looks sheepish. "After our last canoe ride?"

"You've been planning this all week?"

"Well, once I had permission to think of you as 'gay Logan'—so I guess that would be after the social." Dave squeezes his hand and shifts closer to him. "Though you asking me about Colin gave me some hope that you weren't really sexuality-free." They smile at each other.

Logan wants this moment. So he takes it. He closes the distance between them and kisses Dave softly. Dave grins into the kiss before pulling away with a wet pop. Their eyes are inches apart and Dave has the warmest, crinkliest smile. Logan is pretty sure he is crinkling right back.

"That was nice." Dave beams, inches from Logan's face.

"Nice? Is that all?"

"Mmmm? Yeah. We can do better." Dave's gaze flicks to Logan's lips, sending a jolt of electricity down his spine.

Dave places his hands on Logan's shoulders and does his best to hold him firmly while balanced on a canoe seat. And this time Dave *kisses* him. Really kisses him. His lips are firm and searching, and Logan figures this is a very good use for Dave's show-offy ways. But as Dave leans forward to pull him closer, the boat tilts sharply to the side, and they pull apart to grab tightly to its edges. "Smooth," Dave mutters.

"Yeah." Logan chuckles, attempting to get his racing heart back under control. "Maybe we should paddle back to shore and continue?" Logan tries to sound sultry but is certain it comes out more like Miss Piggy than Jessica Rabbit.

"Yeah," Dave agrees. He maneuvers very carefully to the back of the canoe and they paddle toward shore.

They're comfortably quiet as they wade back onto the beach and hoist the canoe to its rafters. They reach the shed and put away the paddles, and it isn't until Dave shuts the door and clicks the lock that the silence begins to feel heavy.

Dave looks at Logan and blushes. Then he looks down and reaches for Logan's hand.

Logan breaks the too-full silence. "Where to?"

"I don't know." Dave shrugs but pulls Logan forward. "Thought we could stop by the shore, just a bit away from the storage sheds. Ambience, you know?"

"Yeah, okay." And then they are by the water's edge, holding hands and facing each other, and Logan is fairly certain that they are going to kiss again.

"You have goose bumps," Dave muses as he runs his free index finger along Logan's arm. Which only makes them worse.

"Well, I'm nervous," Logan challenges.

"Yeah, me too," Dave confesses, blushing again.

"You don't have to indulge me, Dave."

"You don't think I'm nervous? Aren't I the one who just bared my heart to you?"

"Aren't I the one who's never done this before?"

"Well, now you're going to assess my skills without the threat of capsizing distracting you from scathing judgment," Dave teases as he takes a step closer.

"*Judgment*, honestly. I don't have any basis for comparison." Despite the goose bumps and the nerves, Logan gives in, places his arms tentatively on Dave's shoulders and lets himself fall. Dave's lips are soft and sure, and he kisses with his whole body, his arm behind Logan's back, pressing them together.

From the moment he noticed Dave's stage presence, Logan was captivated by how physical he is—on a stage, when he swims, in a canoe, when he dances. And now he feels it when they kiss. It's sexy—not a vague concept like the fantasy of 1D's Liam Payne shirtless is sexy, but a real-life, not-a-kid-anymore sexy that Logan feels all over his body. His heart races, and he is breathless, but who needs breathing when there is kissing? Kissing is incredible.

"This is amazing," Dave says during a pause, and Logan chases his mouth again. Kissing *Dave* is incredible.

When staff curfew has them half-running, panting and giggling, back to their cabins, they end the date with a silly smack of the lips outside Dave's cabin and promises of *Let's do this again* and *I want this* and *Yes.* Then Logan is left to jog to his own cabin, compose himself and practice the art of nonchalance as he enters his den of swim boys. He's not suspect. No one would ever expect that he had been making out with the dapper head of canoe beneath the evening stars.

Least of all himself.

LOGAN HAS TO ADMIT THAT SOME OF HIS DEEPLY HELD BELIEFS have been challenged since Dave duetted into his life three weeks ago. Dave's mere existence during Logan's blissful summer escape had already caused cognitive dissonance and apparently rendered his summer of gay-irrelevance impossible. And just when he thought he had achieved what he must admit was a happy equilibrium of being out but not defined by gay, not "the gay kid," he finds his fiercely independent, *high school romance is beneath me* self consumed by thoughts of starlit canoe rides and making out and wanting and wanting and wanting. He wants to play it cool, maintain his composure, but he also wants to sing from the rooftops. And trying to process all of his own emotions is only further complicated by the fact that the object of his desire is Dave Westin.

The thing about trying to figure out whatever your tenuous relationship is with Dave Westin is that *everybody* loves Dave Westin. Somehow, Dave manages to navigate that elusive space of talented-dorky-cool and make everyone—gender, age and sexuality totally immaterial—swoon. Picture it: Dave leading a canoe trip. He teaches, he's patient, he's supportive. *Great stroke, Hayley! You told me you couldn't canoe, Jonah!* He builds the campfire and remembers the marshmallows, and, when the kids are asleep, he plays guitar for the staff, taking requests and bursting into spontaneous harmonies. And the thing about Dave being *that* guy, is that *that* guy's love life is a hot topic. Everybody loves Dave, so *everybody* wants to know who Dave loves. Or likes. Or makes out with by the water's edge. Or whatever. Logan's crazy about him, he definitely is. But honestly, Dave Westin can be exhausting. And this is particularly true when Logan has absolutely no idea exactly what is going on.

Somehow, though, Logan manages what he considers to be three triumphs: maintaining a casual openness, sustaining his independence and yes, making out with the really quite beautiful head of canoe when nobody else is looking.

Unsurprisingly, Logan had limited sleep the night of the canoe ride, a reasonable sacrifice to the adrenaline racing through his body and the feeling of Dave's stubble still tingling around his mouth. His game face is apparently so flawless that the guys accepted his almost-late–for-curfew arrival back at the cabin with barely a shrug, no questions asked, leaving him to stare at the ceiling for most of the night, inwardly smiling from ear to ear. The amount of stir he doesn't cause is almost disappointing despite his disdain for his own secret desire to sing it from the rooftops.

But morning arrives without fanfare or a Goodyear blimp proclaiming that he was kissing Dave Westin by the lake, and Logan is up, perfectly dressed and walking casually to the dining hall with Matt as if nothing has changed. Dave will join them for breakfast and pass the waffles, and perhaps that is the best approach. Nothing happened. Everything is the same. Fever dream.

And that *is* how it starts. Logan sits down with the swim guys as usual. Dave and Jake walk over as usual, carrying the breakfast tray. It's not waffles, though. It's French toast. The boys grumble out their usual morning pleasantries and Dave greets everyone with a little more sunshine and sits down. Dave's eyes linger on Logan's for just a beat longer. Logan detects an extra smile. But he can't be sure. Dave sits across from him, as he often does, and the chitchat at the table can only be described as ordinary. Logan so wants to be cool about this—everybody has hook ups at camp—but he finds that, despite his stoic game face, he is buzzed and he doesn't know what to do with it. So he says very little.

Then Dave's foot knocks Logan's under the table and Dave rests his calf against Logan's leg. It is the tiniest of movements. It could have happened by accident yesterday. But today it's not an accident. Especially not given the way Dave is crinkle-smiling at him right now.

And if Dave can't stop grinning and is looking at him like that, then he figures it's okay for him to be a little bit buzzed.

"Why did Stuart ask *me* before lunch if you were meeting us here?" Logan asks as they walk into the dining hall later. "Aren't you the inseparable twosome?"

Dave looks at Logan, his eyebrows raised in a slightly sheepish *come on* face. "He asked *you* because I told him." Dave shrugs.

"You *told* him? That we spent the evening making out instead of being social participants in the staff softball game?"

Dave laughs, "Not exactly. I think it was more like I told him that I've liked you for a while and told you last night and that we're hopefully going to try things out?" *God, why does Dave have to be so sensible?* "Unless I'm way off base, here?" Dave suddenly goes from cool as a cucumber to vulnerable.

"Mmm," Logan hums, "I think that's pretty accurate." He runs his finger along Dave's arm. This time, *Dave* gets goose bumps. *Achievement.* Logan still isn't sure what trying things out means, but for now he figures it's camp jargon for spending time together and more kissing. And he can live with that.

The thing that surprises him is, it's easy. Dave makes it easy. Logan teaches swim; Dave teaches canoe. Logan still has his late afternoon power-walk with Sarah. Dave still throws the ball around with the guys. They eat together but don't always sit together. Dave leads the sing-along around the campfire. Logan directs the s'more-making activity and sits with the junior girls, who are slowly becoming his favorite swim class, believe it or not—nothing like a little no-bullshit, *yes you can* attitude from a swim teacher—and Justin.

But when the campers are tucked in, and the campfire and marshmallows are left to the staff, Dave sits down behind Logan and pulls him close with an arm around his waist. Sarah is still in deep thought about the woes of her and Logan's talent show duet, Matt holds her hand and nods his head, and Logan could argue but really just wants to lean back into Dave.

This is a *thing*. His first ever thing. It isn't everything. But it definitely makes him warm all over—it's not just the fire.

Even the scrutiny caused by dating Mr. Man About Camp isn't *that* bad. The swim guys are awesome, actually, mostly for not doing or saying anything at all. Dave sometimes holds his hand, and they don't wince, they don't look or not look; they don't care. It's bliss. And Stuart, well, Stuart told him that he's never seen Dave so happy. Logan admits, that is saying something. Dave is kind of a ray of sunshine.

His junior girls' swim class is another story. They figured it out as a class when Dave walked by, whispered some nothing in Logan's ear and squeezed his hand. It was Leanne who announced it: "Oh my God, there is something happening here, isn't there? You and Dave? Oh my God." He didn't deny it.

And the junior girls are *enamored* of the idea of Mr. Tripper McHotPants—their name, honestly—being "all romantic" with The Marble Angel. They like to make up names. He got "marble" because he's tough in swim class, yet always proudly fashionable, and "angel" because they like him after all and Dave says he sings like one. They'd had a detailed discussion about whether he would sing for them one day during treading water. When Dave happened to walk by, he said, "Make sure he does, girls. Logan sings like an angel." Logan was ready to pull him into the water right then and there for inciting the masses.

These girls are sweet, intelligent, political and well-intentioned, but they are eleven years old. They read *Teen* magazine with appropriate disdain, and sneak in *Cosmo* and talk about sex without having any idea what they're talking about. He doesn't have any idea. Who is he kidding? But man, are they excited that Dave has found a guy! And that it's *him*. They want to talk about it pretty much non-stop.

"So, do you and Dave, like, spend hours talking to each other after we go to sleep?"

"He's a good kisser, right? He is totally a good kisser. I know he is. You have kissed, right?"

Logan just side-eyes the camper and tells her to go get her towel.

"I think it is so great that two guys can find each other here and be open and in love. It just makes me so happy." *Slow down there, Tiger. We kissed five nights ago.*

"You guys are just so cute together. So cute. Oh my God."

"I know we bug you," Leanne says to him at the end of one class. "But seriously, we're happy for you guys."

That's true. So he lets the scrutiny and the overzealousness about his love life roll right off his back because he is happy for himself, too.

FINDING TIME TO BE ALONE IS DIFFICULT. THEY ARE BOTH busy with their own jobs and like to participate in staff evening programs (softball notwithstanding), and Logan absolutely refuses to be that guy who only spends time with one person. He power-walks with Sarah, plays volleyball with the guys, and assists with the junior camper play—*Grease*. Justin is a fantastic

Kenickie. And Leanne is Rizzo. So Logan notices with some amusement and quiet appreciation that Dave tries to make the time they do have together as romantic as a camp filled with rambunctious children will allow.

Like their two-week anniversary.

"Will you come to my cabin? I set up a little something for our anniversary." Dave beams, hands in his pockets, and rocks back and forth on the balls of his feet.

"Anniversary?" Logan side-eyes him. Dave insists on celebrating, but at least he doesn't purchase a mass-produced poem written on a Hallmark card.

"It's been two weeks since we, you know, started this." Dave is shameless. And even though Logan still really isn't sure about the two weeks thing, and is even less sure about what exactly "this" is, he is willing to indulge him.

Logan steps inside a cabin lit by about twenty little battery-operated tea lights and two plastic champagne glasses filled with Dave's mocktail: sparkling water and grapefruit and orange juice, garnished with freshly cut strawberries and blueberries.

On the bed, they cross their legs with their knees touching, sip their drinks and talk about their day: about the Matt and Sarah dynamic, that despite how opposite they are, they do seem to really like each other; and about the junior girls and their newfound interest in Logan's love life. Dave thinks it's adorable. Logan just rolls his eyes.

"But you did tell them that I'm a good kisser, right?" Dave says after Logan recounts some of the many boundary-crossing comments.

"Ha, no," Logan says, "I told her to go get her towel. There are just some secrets I like to keep to myself."

"Mmm." Dave puts his glass down and takes Logan's out of his hand so he can lean over and kiss him.

"Wait," Logan says, breaking the kiss. "How come they never ask you these things?"

Dave laughs. "Actually, they do," he admits as he kisses down Logan's neck.

"Wait, what?" Logan gently pushes him away.

"Junior girls' canoe trip three days ago." Dave shrugs. "They wanted to know *everything*. How we got together, is it the same as with a guy and a girl—"

"Oh my God, who said that?"

"Oh-so-young but well-intentioned Hayley."

"What did you say?"

"I didn't have to say anything. Leanne jumped in with a sassy 'Love is love, Hayley. It feels the same for anyone.'"

"Mmm, smart kid." Logan hums.

"Not that—you know—she just meant—I mean—"

"It's okay." Logan laughs, and pulls Dave down to kiss him again. He really does not need confessions of undying love, but some uninterrupted private kissing would be nice.

They haven't had this chance before—to be alone, on a bed, with time—and Logan, while not being sure exactly where this is going, is sure that he wants it. The strawberries and blueberries and citrus mix with the summer heat and he wants to feel Dave everywhere—fruit-tinged lips on his lips, on his neck, Dave's sun-kissed and camp-tanned body close and hot. The what of it all is a little fuzzy, but he figures Dave knows, and he is definitely interested in finding out. Not *that*, of course not. It's only been two weeks, even on camp time, and he's not in a rush. Just having Dave's body flush against his, and kissing and kissing and kissing is overwhelming.

Before this summer, simply meeting someone was beyond what he let himself think about. He admits, there were those couple of times when he slipped up with Sarah. Like last year, after she went on three dates with Michael Lucas and his curiosity got the better of him. "What's it like to kiss a guy?" She was so happy that he wanted to talk about *that* with her, she grabbed his hands and said, "It's like magic, Logan. Magic strawberry and chocolate perfection. When it's your turn, you're going to melt." He had laughed and tried to hide the bitterness he wouldn't let himself feel and told her that wouldn't happen for a long time. And while he hates to admit when Sarah's right, he did indulge her the morning after he and Dave kissed by saying, "More like raspberries and mint, with a rough tingle left over." The shocked look on her face was totally worth it.

⁂

LOGAN HAS BEEN A BIT TESTY THE LAST FEW DAYS. YES, perhaps he shouldn't have snapped at Dave for finishing the milk at breakfast, and it isn't Dave's fault that the senior girls were late for his class because they canoed out too far during Dave's lesson, but he can't help it. He's irritable. With less than two weeks of camp left, the inevitable end to his summer of bliss whispers in his ear at every turn. And despite at least three pretty steamy evenings in Dave's cabin, Dave still doesn't know that he, too, is a boxer briefs guy. He hasn't even attempted to look. Logan would like him to, but time is running out and he doesn't know how to ask.

"Are you seriously still mad about the swim class thing?" Dave raises his hands helplessly when they meet up after the campers are asleep.

Logan stops in his tracks, faces Dave with his hands on his hips and just blurts out. "Aren't we on a countdown here? Like there are less than two weeks left, and I'd really like to have some kind of—" Logan pauses, takes a breath, and whispers, "*more-than-just-making-out* with you before this thing we have going is over?"

"What?" Dave's jaw drops and he just looks at Logan. "What countdown? And you do—want *that*? Can we back up for a second here? First, who said this is ending?"

"I don't know. I just figured that old adage rings true: 'What happens at arts camp stays at arts camp.'" Logan pauses, feeling guilty because Dave is giving him a *what on earth are you talking about* look.

"Well, considering I've never heard that famous saying," Dave says, crossing his now dark tan arms, "and we both live in Pennsylvania, I think I could handle having a boyfriend just a town away. I mean, I've come to Allentown to go to The Stonewall, of all places, and seeing you would be a far better excuse."

"Wait—so you want this to continue?"

"Yeah." Dave nods. "And I was sort of counting on you feeling the same way?"

"Well." Logan lets out a breath he didn't know he was holding and takes Dave's hands in his. "How do you know I'm not more of a free spirit?" He is being coy and he knows Dave knows it, but he can't let his guard down too easily.

Dave eyes him. "Well, I guess that I'll just have to convince you." And then they're kissing. Which Logan admits is pretty convincing.

"I think it may be worth the drive from Allentown to Lancaster."

"Well, thank you. Glad I'm worth ninety minutes and a quarter tank of gas." Dave seems only slightly exasperated, but also warm. "So, um, what was that other part again?"

"You know what I said."

"Maybe I just want to hear you say it again?" Dave is still in his space, still staring with those puppy eyes. "Or has that changed now that we're Facebook official?"

"No. That hasn't changed. I still want to—" Logan pauses. He already said it once. He really isn't sure he can say it again.

"Get in my pants?"

"*Dave.*" *He is* so *crass.*

"Sorry." But he isn't. "Instead I could ask if you want to *make mad passionate love* to me?" His look is impossibly sweet and wicked.

"Oh my God, no." Logan looks down, trying to control his blush and gather his wits. "Yes, please, Dave. I would like to get in your pants." He bats his eyelashes.

"You're *such* a romantic," Dave says, batting his own long eyelashes right back. "But at the risk of ruining this moment of my incredibly hot *boyfriend* telling me out of nowhere that he wants to, *you know*—can we talk about it?"

"I didn't mean I want to do it right *now*," Logan says, indignant.

Dave laughs. "Well, yes, I figured you would want a slightly more ideal setting than a public beach. I know you didn't mean now. But can we talk about it?"

Logan looks skeptical, as if he's about to hold his nose and jump into a cesspool. "No better time than the present to learn the torrid details of your previous sex life compared to my non-existent one."

"Don't look too intrigued." Dave raises his eyebrows. He takes Logan's hand as they start walking along the beach.

"Ways to make Logan remember that he's a blushing virgin in the face of a sex god—check," Logan mumbles, as they swing their hands and walk.

Dave stops suddenly. "Did you just speak in the third person?"

"It's unforgivable, I know. I take it back." They're both laughing now.

"Okay. But can you please just leave in the part about me being a sex god?"

Logan can't really take it back when it's his impression that it's true. They haven't really done anything *big* yet. Well, it's been big for him, but not, you know, from the perspective of *Cosmo*, which he can't believe he's just mentally cited as an authority. But Dave has this confidence. It can be intimidating. It's also hot.

"So what can I say to convince you that I don't care that you haven't had sex before? I think it's kind of random that I have. I mean, gay boys in Hicksville, Pennsylvania? What are the chances?"

"Tell me about it," Logan agrees. "And I manage to find the one that has." He sighs.

"Oh I promise to make that work to your advantage." Dave is doing that flirty and confident thing again. But he's serious. "So here is my disclaimer. I've had sex with one guy. *One*. And I'm going to be honest here, I like sex—"

"Yes, Casanova. I figured." Logan tries not to be defensive. And fails.

"Buuut, despite everything that happened with Colin, and it *was* good, it was—everything with you, though?" Dave looks at him meaningfully and continues, "I like it more."

Logan closes his eyes. He wants to believe it. "Dave, while that's very nice, we haven't *done it* yet, remember?"

"You know what I mean."

Though they haven't had sex—nothing below the belt, yet—Logan does think that their chemistry is pretty dynamite. At least in his totally inexperienced opinion.

"And I promise that whatever we decide to do, I will do my best to get to you in all the ways that will make you want to drive from Allentown to Lancaster as much as our parents will allow." Dave's shiny eyes belie his attempt to be cutely glib. Well, he is cute. But there's more.

"Yes, okay." Logan nods. Apparently, that's it. It's that simple. "I do have scathing judgment, though. Remember?" And then they're kissing again, so it doesn't really matter.

BECAUSE DAVE INSISTS ON ROMANCE, AND BECAUSE THEY ARE rarely alone at camp, Dave has a plan. It involves a day off "in town;" a dinner at The Burger Joint, the staff favorite; and an overnight at the Best Western. Logan is pretty sure that most staff go to a couple of karaoke bars before crashing, but Dave suggests they skip that part. Dave has the best ideas.

They ride the bus with two arts and crafts staff, both distant but reasonably friendly acquaintances. They banter about tie-dyeing mishaps and water-fearing campers, and Logan is silently lamenting the reality that these two are probably also going to The Burger Joint, when he discovers that, as luck would have it, they're *vegetarians*. Bless the ethical eating movement; he and Dave are soon alone, eating juicy, ketchup-smothered hamburgers and superb fries with malt vinegar at a picnic table at sunset.

It's their first out-of-camp date. They gossip about the latest hookups and breakups at camp, sharply judge the small town summer fashions—if you can call T-shirts with loons on them fashions—and eat the most delicious comfort food available. Then they take a walk along the boardwalk, where Dave stops at a kiosk and buys them matching hemp bracelets.

"I am not wearing a hemp bracelet. Seriously, Dave. Do you know who you're dating?"

"It's a memento of our first official date," Dave insists. "Indulge me, Logan. It's hemp or boondoggle." So Logan reluctantly ties on the bracelet. For tonight. *Only.*

They're in a small town and don't know the scene, so they're being cautious and not holding hands. Instead, they get into each other's space a little too often with gentle touches on the back or arm, or a hand on the elbow to navigate tight aisles in the shops.

Logan turns to point out a kitschy lamp and finds Dave staring at him. "You're hot," Dave whispers. Their eyes lock and Dave reaches up to run a finger along Logan's cheek before remembering where they are and drawing it back. "Oops. Sorry."

"Yeah," Logan responds. "Let's go, okay?"

"Definitely okay."

THERE IS SOMETHING BOTH RIDICULOUSLY LUXURIOUS AND satisfyingly rebellious about having your very own room in a Best Western with your boyfriend and nobody else, at age seventeen. Especially when you're planning to have sex for the first time. It makes Logan feel wild, but also responsible. He *is* sure of how he feels about Dave. Sure of how Dave feels about him. The connection is real and deep and sex will bring them closer. So what if he also wants to know how it feels, wants to see Dave naked, and is nervous. He's allowed all those things too.

For the next ten minutes, they putter around the room awkwardly, opening their overnight bags, folding clothes and unpacking toothbrushes and soaps so they can settle in and choose sides of the bed—Logan on the left, Dave on the right. They're almost like an old married couple on vacation. Except for the jitters and nerves. But Dave just lies down and flicks on the TV. He stops at *The Golden Girls*, of all things.

"Check this out." Dave looks up at him with childish giddiness. "We have access to, like, 230 channels, and this one has all the classic '80s comedies."

Logan stands with his mouth agape. "Seriously, Dave?" He does suspect this is Dave's attempt to make him feel comfortable, but Dave's enthusiasm for pop culture history is pure.

Dave looks up at him, a little bit guilty. "What? How can anyone resist a little Betty White?"

"I'm more of a Bea Arthur man myself," Logan indulges him, sitting on the corner of the bed and folding his hands in his lap. "Dave," Logan says, turning to look at him with the most certain expression he can muster amidst his nerves and excitement, "can we turn off the television?"

IT'S BOTH MORE AND LESS THAN LOGAN HAD IMAGINED. MORE fun and more emotional and more playful, but less intense, less life-changing. It's easy, actually. And he's much less nervous once the TV is off and their clothes are in a pile on the floor and they're wrapped up in each other.

They take their time—all hands and bodies and nakedness, and letting themselves chase that feeling and not pull back or stop. Logan loves looking at Dave. He loves watching Dave touch him. He even loves watching Dave watch him; and he loves all the reactions that embarrass him to think about but apparently not to actually have. It's exhilarating and empowering and the most natural thing he could imagine.

Logan will never understand how one act out of so many has become the only one to be considered "sex," because even though he's not ready for *that* yet, and may not be for a while, he and Dave had sex. That's what it was.

Afterward they lie in bed, sheets tucked around them as they watch '80s family comedies, laughing and talking until they fall asleep with the blankets rumpled messily between them, a pile of sweaty, tangled boyfriends.

⁂

"SHUT UP, YOU TOTALLY DID! OH MY GOD, LOGAN. I CAN SMELL it on you." Sarah is so stunned she practically screams it to the camp. Luckily, they're alone and approximately three minutes into their power-walk the next day when Sarah figures it out.

"Actually, I think you're smelling the beginnings of my workout sweat." Logan smirks at her but he can't *not* tell her—not when he's this excited. "But yes. Did you think Dave and I took our day off together so we could spend the evening playing Scrabble?"

"Oh my God!" she screeches again. "Logan, look at you! I am so happy for you. Was it amazing? Did it feel like the romantic movies tell you it should? Do you feel different?"

Logan side-eyes her. She needs to calm down.

"Seriously, Sarah?"

"Okay, okay. But oh my God, Logan. You are the guy who has told me since day one that there would not even be a romantic kiss in your life until at least college, and then only maybe. Isn't that what you said?"

"Yes, well. Mr. Tripper McHotpants wasn't meant to be part of the story."

"Oh my God! I have never heard you talk this way, Logan. Where is Dave? I want to kiss him."

"Please don't."

"And wait—what about your *what happens at camp stays in camp* theory? You slept with him at the end of your romance? You have lost it, Logan."

"Well," Logan says, "as it turns out, my theory, which I'm sure is generally correct, is not applicable."

"Wait, what? You're staying together?"

"We both live in Pennsylvania," Logan reasons. "Might as well." Logan tries, with everything in him, not to grin like a puppy in love.

"Shut up. You have a boyfriend. A totally not-going-anywhere boyfriend."

"Mmm." They walk in comfortable silence, swishing their arms in sync as the late summer breeze rustles the leaves along the tree-lined path

"So do you feel different? Seriously this time."

"Not really." Logan shrugs. "But also yes? Look, I know this doesn't really make sense, and I'm still kind of in shock—God, I think I'm still in shock about this entire summer. And yeah, I'm kind of desperate to do it again."

"Oh my God, Logan!"

"Shut up," Logan turns to her. He can't help the impish smile spreading across his face, his cheeks now freckled from the summer sun. "And that's all you're getting."

"ME TOO, BY THE WAY." LOGAN JUMPS AT DAVE'S LOW VOICE in his ear. The staff talent show is about to begin, and he is just finishing setting up. He turns around.

"Oh, hello there." Logan smiles at him, giddy for no particular reason. "You too what?"

"Well, Sarah tells me you can't wait to, *you know*, again. Me neither."

Logan turns a burning shade of crimson. He is going to kill Sarah. "She said *what?*"

"Before you decide to kill her, it was actually very sweet."

"Sweet?" Logan sasses. "'*Well done, Dave. Logan has become a sex addict thanks to you.*'"

He's startled by another set of hands grabbing his shoulders from behind. "No worries, bro. Dave was already a sex addict." Stuart smiles coyly behind him before running backstage. "Gotta finish setting up the mikes!" He's gone before Logan can say anything to him and Dave is standing in front of him, hands up defensively.

"I didn't even really tell him anything!" Dave insists. Logan looks at him skeptically. "Well, all I said was that we had a great time and that it was very romantic." Logan can't help but smile before raising his eyebrows. "Fine. And then I winked."

"Oh I see," Logan says and smirks. "The meaningful wink."

"Yes. The meaningful wink."

"Well, Stuart is cooler about these things than Sarah."

Dave laughs and takes his hands. It is really hard to stay furious when Dave does that. "Sarah just congratulated me on cracking the layers of Logan Hart, and she wasn't so subtle about the double entendre."

"Oh she approves, does she?" Logan wants to be so mad, he does, but he can't, because there's Dave. So really, who cares? Besides, Sarah means well, and they have an epic duet to sing tonight, and they are going to kick ass.

Logan and Sarah step onstage with perfect comedic game faces to perform "Master of the House" from Les Miz. Logan loves to sing out their real life combination of teamwork and mockery. And he beams when they get a standing ovation.

In fact, he's flying so high after they take their bows, that he walks up to the microphone, apologizes for interrupting the order of the evening and invites Dave up to the stage for a full circle duet. He figures they could use a second take. The look of surprised glee on Dave's face is totally worth his bit of residual hesitation. As soon as they begin, the entire camp is on its feet, singing along to what will forever be known as "Logan and Dave's 'Summer Nights.'" He feels so alive singing, with Dave beside him. When the summer began, he ran away; now, all he wants to do is stay.

Tomorrow is the last day of camp, and Logan will leave his summer of bliss— he is happy to say that is definitely not hyperbole—and return to Backwardville, Pennsylvania. He is definitely still getting out of Allentown in a year. Definitely still going to San Francisco. It is ironic, though, how far he had to come to find that elusive thing that was so close to him all along. Not a boyfriend—that's just a bonus—but a belief in the present, not just the imaginary future. Sometimes your reflection is clearer on a lake than it is in your bedroom mirror.

In his senior year, he is still going to be the best swimmer. He will also still be the gay kid the rest of the time, even if he's big enough now that tormentors won't come too close. But he may hate it just a little bit less because he can always drive to Lancaster, or Skype Matt or Stuart. And also he gets to have sex with Dave—or at least he'll try to as often as he can when his parents aren't home. It's funny how being the outtest, most totally himself that he's ever been, has made him at least a bit of a teenaged cliché. An ordinary enigma. Well, now he's an oxymoron, and that's pretty much perfect. As long as he never falls into the terrible style vortex of sweatpants and Crocs. He shudders at the thought. He is still way ahead of the fashion curve. Even if he does hide a hemp bracelet under his fabulous layers. ✐

My Best Friend

H.J. Coulter

FIRST OFF, TO BE QUITE HONEST, I AM KIND OF SURPRISED that you agreed to move to Toronto. Sure, it's not like you had much choice—you did marry the woman. And being asked be to an associate with Richardson Langley is a tremendous opportunity for her. But of the two of us, I always figured it would be me that eventually made the move to the big city. It just makes sense, me being a professional photographer and all. And I hate to break it to you, but "driving a tractor since I was old enough to see over the steering wheel" and "milking cows for so long I pretty much do it in my sleep" are not really skills transferable to life in the city.

Plus, you could barely stand the constant noise and the lack of open space during the two years we lived in Winnipeg, and the buses confused the hell out of you. Come to think of it, I would pay good money to see you try and navigate the TTC during rush hour, with your muddy cowboy boots, ripped blue jeans, Winnipeg Blue Bombers jersey, and John Deere hat. So go ahead and move, and make sure you take lots of videos.

I remember the first day we met. I had just finished setting up a photo shoot out behind the barn for all of Anika and Becky's dolls, because the girls refused to pose for me, when you came barreling down the driveway, covered in sweat and dirt, with a big smirk on your face. You were so damn proud of yourself for biking four miles all on your own and couldn't wait to tell Charlie all about it. Of course, knowing your mother, she had already called Charlie in a state of panic when she couldn't find you.

Do you remember how pissed Charlie was when we found him? I felt so sorry for you, because I knew when you got home you were going to get one hell of a spanking. And I think Charlie felt bad too, because he pulled the "responsible big brother" card and somehow convinced your mother he would keep an eye on you for the next couple of hours while he finished up in the shop. And suddenly I had a real, live model—one that was way more fun than my "stupid" sisters anyway. That summer was the first of many we spent attached at the hip.

The other day I heard "I Love A Rainy Night" on retro country and I cranked it up and danced like an idiot out on the deck. Becky and her boyfriend were down by the fire pit and kept giving me looks like "what the fuck is he on?" But I didn't care! I had forgotten how much I LOVE that song. It reminds me of when I was a kid and my only goal was to sleep outside during a thunderstorm. As soon as I heard the first rumble in the distance I would race to my closet; grab my raincoat, rubber boots and camera; and then tiptoe across the hall and down the stairs. I never made it. Every time, somebody was waiting at the door to send me back to bed (and depending on whether it was Dad, Mom, or Great-Aunt Olga, sometimes with a quick spanking). It was almost as if they knew.

The first time I actually got to sleep outside during a storm was on the grade eleven canoe trip. I remember everybody was either freaking out or pissed off. But not me. I was giddier than a kid going to Disneyland. They all thought I was nuts. Except you. I will never forget the look on your face, the one that said, "Yep, that crazy fucker is *my* best friend."

I know that, even though we have serious conversations, you don't really "do" deep shit. But I can't write you a letter talking about all the memories I have with you without bringing this up, because it is really important. I have told you things I haven't even told my journal. Mostly about my dad. About how I love him, and how I know that deep down he loves me too—even if he never shows it. You know my deepest fear: that one day I will become him, and that there is really nothing I can do about it. You have never once told me I am being paranoid—I think you know better. But you have never written me off because of it, either. "We can't pick our genes, Nikki. If we are meant to be fucked up, the least we can do is pray for somebody to be fucked up with." Somebody to be fucked up with. Is that your own twisted way of saying what I should have realized a long time ago—that we are destined to be in each other's lives forever?

The night my dad went to the hospital was the scariest of my life. It's not like we didn't know what was going on; in a way we were all kind of waiting for it to happen. He had been paranoid for weeks, going on and on about how he was certain he was dying from pancreatic cancer, and that it was somehow my Uncle Murray's fault, when Uncle Murray didn't even live in the same city. But still, to walk into the backyard to find your father filling a rain barrel with water and telling everyone he is going to drown the cat because we can't afford to feed him anymore and letting him starve would be cruel—just is not something you can really prepare for. And no matter how many times we told him that it wasn't true, that Muffin was perfectly fine, he never believed us. It's crazy, because besides his family, and maybe his 1949 Ford pickup, that cat was the most important thing in his life.

You hear about crazy shit happening on the news all the time—just last week there was a story about a woman who drowned her kids because she thought they would be better off—but I don't think it really clicks until something happens to you. Sure, technically Muffin was just a house cat. But really, how big a stretch is it to go from wanting to kill the family pet out of mercy to killing your wife and children? Shit. I really shouldn't think such things.

And then there was when I told you I was gay. You had gotten some beer from Charlie. Well, more like you had stolen it, but you were adamant that you really couldn't be held accountable for taking it because "if Charlie didn't want someone to take his beer, then Charlie shouldn't leave it in a cooler on the back of his truck." So we headed out to the fort we had built that year behind your house. It was pretty much a glorified hole covered in branches, but to us it was the coolest damn hole ever covered.

I'm not sure why I was so afraid to tell you. It's not like I thought you wouldn't accept me; I mean, you think Harry and Draco from Harry Potter should be a couple for fuck's sake. Anyway, I think being afraid to tell you had more to do with the fact that, if I told you, I would be admitting it out loud. Sharing it with someone made it real. You didn't even flinch when I told you, just asked if this meant I had the hots for you. That's when I knew for sure that I had picked the right best friend.

I guess I really should thank you for Country Fest, even if I honestly don't remember a good chunk of it. God, looking back, we drank a shitload that weekend. I remember that I really didn't want to go—my upbringing may have made me a redneck, but at least I am a classy one. But as soon as Anika and Jackie said they had bought their tickets, I knew my fate was sealed.

In case you were wondering, his name was Chad—I'm not sure why I never told you that. I mean, I know more details about the first time you made out with a chick (and worse, the first time you had sex, which I REALLY shouldn't know anything about since it was with MY twin sister) than I could ever want to, so it only seems fair that I share just as much with you. I am not even sure why I suddenly have the urge to bring it up. Maybe it's because you just got married, and I'm going through a single and lonely phase, and remembering the first boy I ever made out with reminds me that at least someone found me desirable? Maybe because it's the closest thing I've ever had (and probably ever will have) to a summer fling? I remember being very surprised when he started flirting with me during Lee Brice—that was the last place on earth I expected to meet another gay guy. Cowboys just don't scream gay... I mean, not these kinds of cowboys. Wait, that sounds judgmental. But you know what I mean. Then again, maybe I shouldn't have been so close-minded. If I was there, why couldn't another gay guy be there too? It's not like I'm the only gay guy to grow up in small-town Manitoba.

I was going through my portfolio from that summer class I took between first and second year of university, and you were right—I was one creepy-ass stalker! Do you know how many pictures I have of Alex? And there he is, once again, looking cute as all fuck, with his little headphones and nerdy glasses, drumming on the counter at the laundromat. What if he had been the one, Scottie? THE ONE? But no. And it's not like I didn't have all these opportunities to talk to him, either. After that first day he just seemed to show up everywhere: in the campus bar, at the library. Hell, we ended up having a class together the following semester. But I didn't even have the courage to ask him if I could take his picture, I just followed him for a couple of months. Man, I'm a creeper. Jeez, no wonder I'm single.

And how can we forget the summer your mom decided we were old enough to be responsible for looking after the cows at Morris? You joked that I was jealous because Becky was Brown Swiss Miss that year. And you want to know a secret? I kind of was. She got to hand out ribbons and pose for pictures. I pretty much just shovelled shit.

Everything was going okay until the morning before the show, when I attempted to lead one of the cows to the hose so we could wash her up properly, but she was being a stubborn son of a bitch. No matter how hard I pulled and you pushed, she just wasn't budging. And then you got the crazy idea that you were going to jab her really hard with a pitchfork. I don't think she was expecting that, since she spooked and stepped right on my goddamn toe. I was so pissed off, because hello: A fucking cow stepped on my foot and broke my fucking toe and I had to miss the rodeo, which I really, really wanted to go to because what kind of twin and best friend would I be if I didn't see my two favourite people in the world compete? And then you did something I will never forget—you dropped out of the rodeo and spent the night with me playing Mario Kart in the hotel room. And I think your memory has failed you, because I definitely kicked your sorry ass. I couldn't believe that you would just let all that hard work go to waste, but you insisted that it was not your first rodeo and it wouldn't be your last.

Did you know that your mother called me the other day and said that the Brown Swiss Association wants me to take the pictures at Morris this year? (It will never stop being funny that she puts "BS Ass Meeting" on her calendar every month. And considering that they talk about cows, there is a slight possibility that they could talk about bullshit, which makes it even better.)

Me, taking pictures of cows? I'll probably do it, if only to see the reactions when I show people my portfolio. Can you imagine? "And this is a picture of Oak Point Mission Mary Jane, Grand Champion at Morris Stampede 2015." Oh well, if I have to take pictures of cows, then I am going to make damn sure they are the best pictures of cows you have ever seen.

Speaking of cows, you will never guess what my mother bought the other day. A goddamn Texas Longhorn. And not just a little one, oh no. She had to buy a full-grown one—and then take me out to the pasture to take pictures of it. You know I can't stand those things. Just thinking about them makes me shudder. I mean, come on. What the hell is the purpose of those stupid horns? So they can poke each other's eyes out for fun? And how do they stay standing? Shouldn't they just fall over because they are so top-heavy? And did you know she wants to mount this thing's horns on her living room wall after it dies? Hell, I wouldn't be at all surprised if she decided to use it as her meat for the winter just to get those damn horns. Is she out of her freaking mind? News flash, Mother, we don't actually live in Texas!

Did you know that thirteen years ago today is the day I broke my arm? Boy, I was so mad at you. I don't think I have been ever been that mad at anyone. You and your stupid cousins and my sisters were climbing that fort out behind your parents' barn— you remember, the one we helped our dads make out of square bales—and then jumping off of it. Like any sane person would, I had refused to go up there. But you all kept telling me that I was being a chicken and that everything would be fine. And then I figured that since Becky was jumping and landing on her feet, I might as well do it too. I mean, she was only eight, and I was twelve. Of course, the first time I jumped I landed on my arm funny, and it broke. I don't think I have ever been in more pain in my entire life—it hurt even worse than the time I broke my toe. And everyone just fucking left me there for, like, at least half an hour! You still like to bring up that I didn't talk to you for two weeks. But later on you apologised and even watched *Dawson's Creek* with me, so it's all good. On a side note, if you say you don't have at least a tiny bit of a crush on Pacey Witter, you are lying. Everyone has a crush on Pacey Witter.

Did you know that Lena is coming to visit this summer? God, I haven't seen her in at least six years. We still keep in touch on Facebook and whatnot, but it's not the same. She was by far my favourite of the German exchange students my mother collected over the years. She is just really cool, with her purple hair and comic book collection. She taught me how to develop my own film and even convinced my parents to make that darkroom for me in the basement. She also posed nude for me once—which, judging by the fact that Great-Aunt Olga is excited she is coming, was never discovered by my parents (or hers). And no, you are a married man now, Scott, so I am not going to give copies of those photos to you. Even if you weren't married I wouldn't give them to you. They are art, not pornography.

I am curious to know if she still really wants to see a bear. The whole damn trip we took that August, all she wanted to do was find a bear. What she was going to do after she saw it, I have no idea. But even I will admit that trip was a shitload of fun. I still can't believe we convinced our parents that it was a good idea. If I had been them, there is no way in hell I would have let four seventeen-year-olds—two of whom were dating—pack up a bus they had converted into a camper and wander the countryside for a week. Although I've got to say, if Lena hadn't been there I don't think it would have worked. The whole "but, she's not from here, and she needs to experience as much of Canada as she can," worked to our advantage so many times during the year she stayed with us.

One of my favourite memories is from the second night of that trip. We stayed up all night by the fire, drinking and singing songs and telling stories. It wasn't complicated; nothing crazy happened. It was just four young people, enjoying the simple things in life. That was also the night you told me you loved me, and that if you were gay and weren't dating my sister you would totally do me. I'm going to go out on a limb here and say it was the beer talking, but I appreciate the sentiment. Every once in a while, I do wonder about that moment. What would you have done if I had, say, leaned over and kissed you? Not that I would have betrayed my sister like that, but still, if she had not been in the picture, I might have done it.

I do love you, Scottie. And you are, as you are not ashamed to admit, an attractive guy. It would have been nice to have my first kiss with someone I trusted. But even if we had done something, I don't think it would ever have worked out—whether or not you are gay. Our relationship is more than all that.

That was also the trip when it was confirmed that I just don't fish. I don't care what anyone says, poking a live minnow with a hook is disgusting and cruel. And then on top of that, all you do is sit around for hours waiting for some stupid fish—who is mostly likely too small anyway—to eat the minnow.

We also learned that none of us are the most outdoorsy of people when we parked the bus and attempted to paddle to some island to set up camp for the weekend. I could have told you that would be a disaster. But we had to go anyway, because someone—and I am not pointing fingers here—decided that just because we had all participated in a high school canoe trip, we were "wilderness experts."

I was helping Great-Aunt Olga clean out her closet last week and you will never believe what I found: her infamous marijuana bandana. I can't believe she kept that. Scratch that, I can't believe she bought it in the first place. It's a good thing she already has a reputation for being the crazy old Russian lady, or else who knows what everybody would have thought about this eighty-year-old woman wandering around town sporting a bright yellow bandana with multiple pot leaves on it? "I thought it was a maple leaf, Nicholas." Bullshit. You've been in this country since 1956; there is no way in hell you mistook a pot leaf for a maple leaf. There is just no way. I still can't believe you asked her if this meant she wanted to smoke a joint with you in the basement. As if she needed another reason to be suspicious of you. Seriously, sometimes I wonder why she even lets you visit. I bet she is secretly—or maybe not so secretly, judging by her reaction to Ingrid's job announcement—counting down the days until you move away and aren't over here every second night of the week eating her *kotlety* and borscht.

Speaking of joints, guess who I saw uptown the other day? Stoner Patrick. Do you remember him, the old guitar-playing dude who was perpetually high and pretty much lived in the hotel the summer we worked there? I mean, as you know full well, with my Great-Aunt being the resident drug-dealing granny and all, I have nothing against recreational pot use. But still, I swear I got high every time I cleaned the guy's room. But he wasn't a total waste. He did teach me how to play guitar, mostly some weird random shit like the theme song to *The Care Bears*. Seriously, who plays the theme song to *The Care Bears* on an electric guitar? He couldn't have taught me something that made sense, like, I don't know, "Smoke on the Water"? Regardless, I appreciated the gesture. Although he also tried to hook me up with my twin sister—which, let me tell you, was beyond fucking awkward.

That summer was a hell of a lot of fun. A lot of it had to do with the fact that, because we had that job at the hotel, we had a legit excuse for getting out of working in the fields. As you can attest, my sisters, and Anika in particular, were pissed. I never knew how many people actually came through our little town until I had that job. It sure as hell beat that summer we were chicken catchers. I swear that has to be one of the shittiest jobs I have ever had—which is saying a lot.

I doubt you forget, that was also the summer we "officially" learned to drive. My mother laughed her ass off when she heard you failed your test the first time around. I remember that she had to go pick you up because your mom was sick, and she said you were mumbling and swearing under your breath the whole ride home. I think they failed you on purpose. You can't tell me you didn't go into that test acting like a cocky asshole, assuming you were going to ace it just because you had been driving since you were ten. But don't worry; you were not the only one who had to redo the test. I'm pretty sure Jesse Stevens did too. And didn't your cousin fail as well? I wouldn't really know, because unlike SOME people, I didn't have to retake it.

I remember it was about a week before your seventeenth birthday when you finally did get your license. Charlie thought it would be a cool idea to buy you a truck and had enlisted me to help. Just so you know, I was geared toward getting you a new—well, newer—model. But he insisted he buy you an old clunker so the two of you could bond over fixing it up. Do you remember how against the idea you were? "Why would I waste my time fixing a truck when both my big brother and my best friend's dad are mechanics?" You did kind of have a point, but

I understand why you gave in, because hey, why pass up on a free truck, right? I think I have pictures of you working on it. I should send those to you. (An excuse for you to give me your mailing address, you bastard. Of course I'll hand-deliver this letter to you before you leave.) Although, now that I think about it, I am not sure where they are. Maybe I gave them to Charlie? I will have to ask him.

Anyway, that was the summer of 2007. I don't have to remind you of what else happened that summer. But let me just make something clear—being stuck between you and Anika for two-and-a-half years while you attempted some sort of romantic relationship is not something I ever want to go through again. It was annoying as hell, and kind of awkward. It was always, "Nikki, you go over there right now and tell Scott to get off his lazy ass and come here," and, "Nikki, your sister's taking too long to get ready. Go tell her to hurry up." Jesus, it was like I was a personal messenger boy.

And then after you broke up (the first and the second time) you were both mad at me. As if it was somehow my fault just because technically, you met because of me. Ha—Great-Aunt Olga was convinced that you were going to marry her. Mainly because the two of you reminded her of when she and Uncle Maksim dated, which I am not quite sure is a good thing, because if the stories are to be believed all they did was fight.

And speaking of your wife, I'm still not sure how you convinced her to marry you. Ingrid is one hell of a sophisticated lady; you've seen the price tags on the shoes she buys and the pictures of her when she used to dance ballet. You are... well, you are you. You're like the poster boy for Rednecks Anonymous. Actually, no, your cousin Jim is the poster boy for Rednecks Anonymous. But that's only because he says things like, "Hook me up with that them there tractor, 'cuz it's pretty good, eh?"

Who talks like that? Seriously, if you ever said "that them there" I would disown you. No joke. But back to your marriage. When you were dating my sister, your idea of a date was to buy a shitty-ass truck off some old guy and get it stuck in the mud out in the middle of nowhere. Then you would have to walk like ten miles home, because you had forgotten your cell phone. No wonder Anika dumped you—twice.

I remember the first time you invited Ingrid to hang out with us. I sort of felt sorry for the girl. She really did look so out of place, sitting by the campfire with her cute summer dress on. I bet the mosquitoes ate her alive that night. I thought we would never see her again. But I guess love is blind and all that shit.

Actually, I like Ingrid a lot, and I am going to miss our dinner dates. It's hard to be a self-proclaimed "classy redneck" if you have no one to be classy with. And it's nice to have someone to go to MTC or The Warehouse with, someone to appreciate a good glass of red wine with.

Not to be a big sap, but your wedding really was spectacular. To top it all off everyone was on their best behaviour, including Great-Aunt Olga who, of course, does not drink and was only doing shots of vodka because she could feel a cough coming on.

The pictures from your wedding are some of the best pictures I have ever taken, and I am not just saying that because you are my best friend. Seriously, I often use your photos in my portfolio and I have had many clients comment on them. I think it might have to do with the fact that the groomsmen were not wearing camo. I am telling you right now, I would not have been your best man if I had been forced to wear glorified hunting gear. But I am grateful that you wanted me to both be in your wedding and be the photographer—although it does kind of suck that this means there are no professional pictures of me. Also, I don't think I ever properly thanked you for not having female strippers at your bachelor party. I know you did that for me, and I greatly appreciated it—even if your cousin Jim didn't.

It goes without saying that I am going to miss you a hell of a lot, Scott. You are the most important person in my life. And I would be lying if I said that you moving to a city like Toronto is the greatest idea, because I know you. But I also know that you would do anything for the people that you care about, and that you care about your wife (and best friend :P) very much. And who knows, I may join you sooner than you think, because, honestly, I'm not sure how much more of this country bumpkin lifestyle I can take. (Yes, I know, you are rolling your eyes because we both know I not-so-secretly love it here.)

Giving you the biggest hug, because I know you want it even if you complain,

Love,
Your crazy fucker of a best friend,
Nikki

What The Heart Wants

Naomi Tajedler

"**N**OAM!"

Today, Noam thinks she isn't living up to her name—it is not a day for being pleasant and sweet, especially if she has to wake up and leave the safety of her bed.

"Noam, put on your clothes, it's time to go to school for your summer class!"

Noam buries her nose in her pillow and lets her body slowly awaken within the confines of her well-worn sheets. A smile slowly spreads on her face as she realizes: It's not just any morning.

It is summer, finally. No more boring regular classes, no more giggling girls who point at her when they think she doesn't see them, no more feeling alone whenever her friend is not with her—at least for two months.

"Nomka, I swear to God—" her mother exclaims, simultaneously knocking on and opening the door.

"You don't believe in God, Mamushka," Noam retorts, then throws off her beloved blanket and smirks at her mother.

Myriam Geffen is not a woman to be played with or mocked, and nobody knows this better than her daughters. However, as they've grown, she seems to have accepted the idea that she is raising two sarcastic young women. It's not as though she hasn't entertained the idea of carrying an *"It's called sarcasm"* sign herself.

"Har," she deadpans with a raised eyebrow, "hardy har har, bubby. Now get up and get ready; we're leaving in ten minutes." She points a manicured finger at Noam as she leaves the room. "Whether you are ready or not."

"Aye aye, Captain," Noam calls; her smile softens. "And good morning, fellas," she adds sotto voce as her eyes roam over the posters that cover her bedroom walls: Albert Einstein and her favorite quote of his: "If the facts don't fit the theory, change the facts;" Jackson Pollock captured in the middle of a dripping action; Leonardo da Vinci's self-portrait; Uma Thurman in all of her *Pulp Fiction* glory; and a collage Noam made as a tribute to Natalie Portman.

Noam cracks her neck a couple of times and stretches like a cat until she hears her back pop. Now she can face the day.

In the shower, she goes through the motions as quickly as she can. Her hands cup her breasts in a strictly sanitary fashion—they just get in her way—and she towels herself dry as fast as she can without rubbing the raw patches of skin she scratched in her sleep. She ties her long red hair into a messy bun. One of these days, she's going to cut it all off and be free from its tyranny. It's not that she hates it—or her breasts, now that she thinks about them—but ever since puberty, she's thought her body is no longer her friend. It has become barely more than an acquaintance she's lost touch with, not an enemy per se but not something she can count on either.

Her outfit is waiting for her on her desk chair—a purple T-shirt with wide, reptilian eyes printed on it, her worn denim overalls and her graphic socks and sneakers. She hops around the room as she dresses.

"Noam!"

"Ready, Mother!" she calls back, stomping down the stairs with an angelic smile on her face. She reaches for her bag, which hangs from the handrail.

"Noam, you need to eat something," Myriam says. Her voice carries the weight of the countless times this conversation has been held.

Noam looks away with a wince and is careful to mold her face into a neutral mask when she turns back to face her mother. It's not that she doesn't want to eat, or that she wants to starve herself. But she really dislikes breakfasts. And she knows, deep down, that some of the insults thrown at her by the "Geese Girls"—the girls at school who cluck like a flock of birds—have a factual leg to stand on.

Noam is tall and large, there is no way around it—she is her father's daughter through and through. The only physical trait Noam inherited from her mother's family is her hazel eyes.

"We're late already, Mamushka," Noam says softly, shouldering her messenger bag and clenching her fingers around the strap. "I'll eat twice as much for lunch, promise."

Myriam grimaces and cups her youngest daughter's cheek. "Take a pack of crackers to eat in the car—please?" She pats Noam's lower back as she passes by.

As Noam reaches into the cupboard for one of the dozens of packs of saltines they always stock, Myriam shares a look with her husband, who has just entered the room all sleepy-headed and sporting a frown of concern born from the years of raising his daughters.

"Have fun, munchkin," Alan tells Noam, throwing an apple at her. He claps his hands when she deftly catches it. "*Star Wars* tonight?"

Noam looks at her mother with a raised eyebrow before looking back at her father doubtfully.

Myriam raises her hands in defense. "I am not here tonight," she reminds the pair. "All you'll have to do is manage Dana's disapproval."

Noam dances around the kitchen and snuggles up to her father. "With any luck," she whispers, "Dana will be busy with Jackson." Noam elongates the first vowel of the name in imitation of the affectionate tone her older sister uses when talking about her boyfriend.

"With any luck," Alan repeats softly. "And, if worse comes to worst, she'll fall asleep da moment da credits start anyway." He kisses her forehead, his Chicagoan accent coming at full-force this morning. "Now go, and make us proud."

Noam rolls her eyes but blows him a kiss as she follows Myriam out of the kitchen.

"I'm proud of you no matter what," Alan tells the empty kitchen.

THE CLASSROOM LOOKS DIFFERENT THAN IT DOES DURING the rest of the year—all the tables have been pushed to the side to make room for easels and stools, which are set up in a circle around an empty stage.

"Nomnom, over here!"

Noam waves at her best friend. Charlotte—Charlie, as she prefers to be called—is, in many respects, Noam's complete antithesis. She is dark-skinned where Noam is practically see-through, loud where Noam is quiet, outgoing where Noam keeps to herself and short where Noam is, seemingly, all limbs. The girls are on opposite ends of a spectrum, and yet they had immediately connected, feeling a bond beyond blood, religion or looks.

Noam kisses the top of Charlie's head and grabs the closest stool. "How on earth did you manage to get here before me, Miss Montceau?" she asks and is already pulling pencils and chalks from her bag.

Charlie gives her a look and plays with the one long braid saved from her latest haircut. It's the kind of look Charlie keeps strictly for her best friend, when Noam seems particularly unperceptive.

"The Colo-onel," she replies, and Noam winces in support.

A retired colonel from the French army, Charlie's father applies his military upbringing to the way he and his wife Karen raise Charlie and her three brothers—two of whom have already left for college as far from home and as soon as possible.

"He made Andy drive me here at too-soon-o'clock to make sure I wouldn't be late," Charlie adds with an eye roll so emphatic it nearly gives Noam a migraine.

"Too-soon-o'clock, huh?" Noam doesn't try to hide her laughter. "Is that military lingo, or...?"

Charlie slaps her shoulder. "You're not even funny," Charlie says under her breath, but her dimples show.

The two girls keep up their banter, and Noam starts doodling with chalk on the side of her easel as they wait for their teacher and more students enter the room.

"What do you think we're going to start with?" Charlie asks, rolling a pen between her fingers like a miniature twirling baton.

Noam shrugs. "No clue, dude," she says, with a thoughtful look. "Still life, maybe?"

They slowly turn their heads toward the platform in the middle of the classroom, far from anodyne in Noam's opinion, and Charlie's smile turns predatory.

Noam turns back to her doodles—half abstract patterns, half elaborate phoenix—in an attempt to avoid her best friend's inevitable nosiness.

"Aw, come on, Nom," Charlie whines, standing to wrap her arms around Noam's chest and hook her chin over Noam's shoulder. "Models! Nude! It's going to be fun!"

Noam stays silent and her face warms, and Charlie leans forward. "Better get used to seeing a cock before you have to do anything with it," she whispers. Noam neatly elbows her in the ribs.

Charlie's insistence on talking—lewdly, at that—about Noam's non-existent sex life is her only flaw, as far as Noam is concerned, but it is a discomfiting one, and one that she cannot simply brush under the proverbial carpet as a simple "Charlie-ism." The sharp intake of breath brushing her ear tells her that Charlie knows she's just gone one step too far.

But before Charlie can apologize, their teacher comes in and wins all of Noam's attention.

All year long, Mr. Siski has nurtured and encouraged Noam's love for art and her burgeoning talent. He's given her various contacts in New York to consider for an internship in the summer between graduation and college and college brochures—including some from overseas schools—so she can figure out what type of artistic career she wants to pursue. He has also taken a special interest in her habit of making quick sketches of her classmates. Some students—mostly the Geese Girls—once implied that the bond between the art teacher and his teenage student was not strictly professional. But luckily for him, Alojszy Siski's stellar reputation at New Trier—along with his open gayness—had nipped that rumor in the bud.

Noam smiles warmly at the teacher who commands all seventeen juniors and seniors simply with his presence.

"Good morning, students." Standing on the platform, he greets them in his warm voice. Most of the teenagers reply. "Ready to unleash your inner artists?"

That earns him a couple of laughs, and he smiles benevolently. There's a good reason he's a student favorite.

"Now, this morning, we'll start with some basics," he tells them, "so I can judge your abilities and your strengths."

"Basics?" Charlie calls, her hand raised, and Mr. Siski nods.

"Basics, like the tools," he replies. "Graphite, chalk, charcoal, all on still life for now." As he enumerates various drawing techniques, the tall man pulls apples, oranges and a container of berries from his bag with his long fingers. For not the first time this year, Noam sketches his long, slender silhouette on a corner of her pad, trying to capture the elegance that radiates from her teacher, from his mane of hair to his bushy eyebrows down to his slim torso and the strength of his legs, vowing to come back to his face and to the way his blue eyes shine as he gets more animated.

"And then?" Charlie pushes, tapping her pencil rhythmically against her easel.

"And then, Miss Charlotte," Mr. Siski replies, his voice growing louder, "those of you who can use their pens will start working on models in this room. The others will have a catch-up course next door."

Charlie smiles at him and makes a little whooping sound—and she's not the only one to show enthusiasm for the upcoming portion of the program.

"Perverts," Noam mutters.

"All right, all right, keep your hormones under control." Mr. Siski arranges his fruit on the stage. "Now, do your thing, I'll be walking around if you need help."

They start hesitantly, but after the first twenty minutes, the only sounds in the room are the scratching of pencils on paper and Siski's whispers when a student asks for help.

Noam draws several compositions on the same sheet of paper—just one apple, all the apples, a strawberry with heavy shadows—before trying her hand at the whole composition on a new sheet.

Next to her, Charlie sketches in what Noam can only describe as an art brut style: strong lines crisscrossing and even punching through the paper in Charlie's enthusiasm. Even if this isn't Noam's favorite style, it's not without interest. Art has always been something that the two friends have shared; they first became friends when they reached for the same red crayon in kindergarten. And throughout the more recent years, whenever classes have become too hard to handle, whenever Charlie can't deal with her father's strictness, they have used a common sketchbook to talk via their doodles in a drawn conversation in which one finishes a sketch started by the other.

Thirty minutes fly by before Mr. Siski calls for a break. With a carefree smile, Noam studies the drawings her classmates have produced. Not everything is good, naturally, but everybody has the same sparkle in their eyes from satisfaction at being able to draw to their hearts' content. To know that she shares this feeling with her classmates, to see with her own eyes that other people are just as passionate about it as she is, is a revelation and a relief.

Art classes during the year had not been suffused with the same unity of spirit, nor were Noam's classmates as outgoing about that animating passion as she was. And Charlie, though she loved art, was not consumed by it as Noam was. But from the smiles on their faces now, the relief shown in their slowly relaxing shoulders, Noam realizes that maybe she's not as alone in her love for art as she had thought.

THE MORNING IS OVER BEFORE NOAM KNOWS IT, AND SHE has a dozen drawings on her pad—drawings that she will work on over and over. No matter how much she works on her drawings, lines and colors, she's never satisfied. Noam aspires to be like her idol, Jackson Pollock, and just give in to an action painting, just accept that a first sketch can be her final work, but she also is aware that she needs training first. Pollock went through classical training, didn't he? All in good time, that's her motto.

All in good time.

Charlie has to trot to keep up as they walk to the food trucks near the school entrance to get their lunches. Noam doesn't walk fast, but her long legs definitely give her an advantage.

"Taco Nano?" Noam asks. Charlie nods enthusiastically; tacos are always good, in her book. It is an unspoken rule of their friendship that the Mexican dish is a peace offering.

As they get in line behind most of their classmates and the other students attending different summer classes at the school, Noam turns to look at Charlie.

"Look, nugget," she says softly to keep the conversation between them, "I love you, and I know you mean well. But," she warns, raising a finger before Charlie can open her mouth, "stop trying to embarrass me into punching my V-card."

"Oh Nom," Charlie replies, frowning. "I don't… I don't mean to embarrass you. I just—I think… I only want you to know what it feels like, to love someone and have them love you back."

Noam smiles sadly at her friend. "But love is not necessarily linked to sex, is it?"

They move forward in line and Charlie shrugs. "Of course not," she replies slowly. After a pause she adds, "But it's a damn fine bonus."

Noam rolls her eyes and bumps Charlie's shoulder with her elbow. "You would know."

"Are you calling me a slut?"

"I would never," Noam retorts innocently, hand on her heart.

Charlie frowns before letting out a bark of a laugh. "All right, then. I was afraid for a moment."

They both explode into peals of laughter, which earn them startled looks from the other people in line.

"Hey, chicas," the taco vendor welcomes them with a wide smile. "What can I get you?"

"One hard-shell, carnitas taco for that one," Noam says, pointing her thumb at Charlie, "and one complete breakfast taco for me—please," she adds as an afterthought, smiling with all of her teeth to make amends for her lapse of manners.

"Anything else?"

"A side of rice and beans—extra chili," Charlie calls, "and two apple juices."

"All right, girls. Wait on the side; your order will be coming right up!"

Charlie hip-checks Noam out of the way to pay for them both—"Puh-lease"—and they move aside to wait for their food.

They're not alone. Noam spots their teacher, deep in conversation with a tall man who has his back turned. As he picks up his own lunch, Mr. Siski sees them and gives them a smile.

"Did you enjoy this morning's class?" he asks, passing an avocado-covered taco to his friend.

Noam nods enthusiastically, and Charlie smiles at the stranger. "Well," she says with an angelic smile, "it was fun, but I'm looking forward to this afternoon."

Noam tries to make her stop, but the two men laugh at her attempt to flirt. "We'll see if you're still so emphatic at the end of it," their teacher says, while his companion snorts into his taco. "Noam, Charlotte, this is Gordon Chevrar, our model for the week."

"Gordy, please," Gordon corrects and nods at the two girls.

Charlie beams at him, but Noam's mind jumps to deconstructing the tall man's figure into shapes and lines. His skin is lighter than Charlie's, but a thousand times darker than Noam's, which only serves to make his green eyes even more remarkable. He's built like a swimmer, all shoulders and tiny waist. Noam pictures him as a triangle, as a shape with shadows and lines.

"I, for one, am glad that we're going to see you every day for the next month," Charlie says. "Right, Nom?"

Noam blinks a couple of times. "Right," she replies and smiles at Gordon. He stares at her with a sparkle in his green eyes.

"Sorry to burst your bubbles, ladies," Siski replies, "but Gordon won't be the only model you'll have to work on."

"Charlie, don't you dare," Noam whispers just as her best friend opens her mouth, no doubt to make a lewd comment about the multiple ways she wants to "work" on the man.

"Oh?" Charlie breathes after a moment of hesitation, managing to save face without too much trouble.

"Do you think so little of me?" Mr. Siski replies with a smirk. "Of course I managed to give you more material to unleash your creativity."

"Carnitas and breakfast!" the vendor calls. Charlie skips off to get their tacos.

"What do you mean?" Noam asks.

"Only that you'll have opportunities to discover different kinds of anatomies," Mr. Siski replies.

"Lucky you," Gordy adds. His eyes don't leave Noam until Charlie returns. "Well, ladies, we'll leave you to your lunch—see you later!"

Noam takes her taco from Charlie's hand in a dazed state. Why is Gordy, who looks as if he just stepped out of one of Dana's magazines, paying *her* such pronounced attention?

"God," Charlie groans, as they find a relatively clean bench, "Sisk really knows how to pick them."

"And you will need a roll of paper towels for your drool," Noam says. She takes a picture of her taco to send to her mother as proof that she got a lunch.

"Probably, yeah," Charlie admits with a laugh. "Have you *seen* him?"

Noam takes a bite of her taco and munches while she considers her answer. "I have, yeah—I can't deny that he's aesthetically pleasant," she finally says after sipping some of her drink.

Noam's next bite is more cautious to keep the egg from falling into her lap, which is why she doesn't see Charlie getting ready to slap her on the forehead.

"'Aesthetically pleasant'? Are you insane?" she says, lowering her voice to a whisper. "There are several ways to describe that man, including 'panty-ruiner' and 'drool-worthy.' Aesthetically pleasant doesn't quite cover it, Noam!"

"Well, it does!" Noam replies, batting Charlie's hand away. "Excuse me for not automatically needing a change of underwear at the sight of a pretty face!"

Charlie bats Noam's hand away. "What are you?" she asks. Noam raises an eyebrow in question. For a second, Charlie seems embarrassed. She tears her paper taco wrapper into shreds. Then she scoots closer.

"Nom—you know you can tell me anything, right?"

"Of course." Noam replies. Charlie's behavior is confusing.

"And that there is literally nothing you could do that would make me love you less?" Charlie insists. Noam is more confused.

"Right back atcha, sistah from another mothah," she drawls in an affected accent. "Where are you going with this?"

Charlie clears her throat. "You... you'd tell me if you were—if you loved girls, wouldn't you?"

Noam has to blink more than a couple of times to give herself time and make sense of what Charlie has just asked. And then she has to focus on her breath to keep her anger in check.

"Are you seriously asking me if I'm a lesbian just because I don't show interest in the man who is going to model for us?" she asks slowly, with as much calm as she can muster. "Because I don't flirt with the Neanderthals in our class?"

Her cold tone and lack of expression convey her anger more clearly than a shout or a scream, and Charlie recoils. "It's not just that," she replies just as coolly. "You never show any interest in any boy—it's a legitimate question!"

"First of all," Noam replies, putting the taco on the bench, "it should be my concern, and mine alone, where I stand on the sexuality scale. Second of all, I've never shown any interest in any girl either, as far as I know—that should make you think 'ace' more than anything else!"

Noam says the last sentence louder than the rest, and some heads turn in their direction. She takes a calming breath. "I don't know, all right?" she finally says. "I've never been in a situation where I had to wonder, because I've never been attracted to anybody."

"Not even a crush?" Charlie asks.

Noam shrugs. "Not enough to make me wonder. Maybe it'll come later, but just—let me take it at my own pace, okay?" she asks, voice nearly pleading.

Charlie throws her arms around her. "Of course, Nomnom," she whispers in her ear. "Remember that I'll be here no matter what."

Noam forces herself to smile and pats one of Charlie's forearms. Then she smirks. "Even if my sexual awakening comes because I realize that I've been in love with you all this time?"

Charlie looks up at Noam and bats her eyelashes. "Particularly if that is so," she replies, giggling into Noam's shoulder.

Her laughter ends in a loud snort, and Noam says. "All right, any crush I might have on you in the future just crashed and burned, piggie."

"Jackass."

"Asshole."

AFTER THEIR UNPLANNED HEART-TO-HEART, NOAM AND Charlie have just enough time to finish their tacos and rice and beans before they rush back into the classroom.

As they return to their easels, they see Gordon sitting on the platform; a silky gray kimono with a black, geometrical pattern is wrapped around his frame. He wiggles his fingers at them, even throws a wink at Noam. Then he returns his attention to their teacher, who is standing next to him.

As Mr. Siski waits for the students to settle down, Noam grabs a pencil, turns to a blank page and rushes to sketch the two men. Mr. Siski stands with his hands on his hips, all long shapes and soft curves at his shoulders and midriff, and Gordon sits in front of him with his profile to Noam. Mr. Siski's dark shirt provides a background that strengthens the contours of Gordon's body and creates shadows in the material draped over him. Noam's drawing is just lines—but it's a base, enough for her to work on later and create a new piece for her portfolio.

"All right, people," Mr. Siski calls, "as you may have gathered, this afternoon we'll discover the joy of drawing models."

The class has already shaken whatever digestive slumber had threatened, and all eyes dart from the teacher to Gordon, who preens and basks, presenting himself in the best light.

"I want you to start with simple pencils—like HB and up to 2B, tops," Mr. Siski instructs, and a cacophony fills the room as the students pull out the proper tools. "But no eraser," he adds. "I want you to consider every stroke of graphite carefully. We'll start with two forty-five-minute poses, so you'll have plenty of time. Don't rush anything, and feel free to ask for help. Gordon, whenever you're ready."

Gordon nods, picks up a stool and situates it on the platform. When he's finally satisfied with its placement, his kimono is gone in a flash. Noam has to blink at the sight of his body.

The man looked good dressed, but with nothing to cover his body he is stunning, more regal than she thought at first glance.

Some of the students giggle, more out of embarrassment than anything else, but the sound shakes Noam out of her shock. She picks up her pencil to start measuring the model. Gordon has chosen a simple pose, and is sitting with one leg bent at the knee. She makes a little outline, writing down the proportions. Picking up her HB pen, she focuses on a bigger version of the outline, this time including the stool.

Next to her, Charlie has already drawn an outline that covers her whole page; Noam is just a little envious of her friend's confidence in her own judgment. Noam needs to check and check again before launching herself into a project, but Charlie—Charlie just goes for it, all-in every single time. And if she has to start again, she just picks herself up and does so with the same energy as before.

The first period goes quickly, and, for once, Noam is happy with herself and her work. Gordon's shape fills the sheet of paper, and she has just started outlining the shadows with quick strokes when it is time for a break.

She stands and cracks her neck to get the kinks out—staying hunched over the easel, even for only forty-five minutes, makes her feel as if she's been stuck in a little box—and when she raises her arms, she can sense a drift of air on her skin where her shirt scrunches up just a little bit. She hurries to pull it down, and her eyes find Charlie's.

"You do know that you have nothing to be ashamed about?" Charlie says, trying to play it down as she brushes at the graphite stuck to her fingers.

"Shush, I had one of my rash episodes last night," Noam says. Then she walks away to look at what her classmates have come up with.

Nothing really catches her eye until she reaches the other side of the room and sees a cubist-inspired portrait. Its lines are assertive, wide strokes of pencil that show no doubt and overflow with an energy Noam didn't expect from one of her classmates.

"See something you like?"

Noam turns her head quickly, and then smiles shyly at the young man who snuck up on her. How did she miss the fact that the other bookworm in her core classes is also in this workshop? Peter Zenkov is a quiet boy who always dresses the same way: black shirt, dark jeans, leather boots. He tries hard to stay under everyone's radar—except that he can't hide his talent, and Noam has to tell him so.

"Definitely," she rushes to say. "Peter, it's fantastic. I didn't know—I didn't know you had it in you." Her face heats up, though her embarrassment ebbs when she notices the two spots of pink high on Peter's cheeks. He looks like a porcelain doll, as if someone has applied a paintbrush to his face.

"Thanks," Peter replies. His voice is barely above a whisper, but he has a happy smile. "I've seen yours—it's… very professional."

The generic comment piques Noam's temper. "Gee, control your enthusiasm, Zenkov," she says with a humorless laugh.

Peter's brown eyes widen. "No, no, I didn't—I meant, it's a good drawing, I can't wait to see it finished!"

Before Noam can think of a reply, Gordon comes back. He uses the marks he made on the stool to return to his pose. Mr. Siski claps his hands to tell the students to return to their seats.

"Talk to you later," Noam hurries to tell the blushing boy, before returning to her place beside Charlie.

"What was *that* about?" Charlie whispers as she snatches an oily pen from Noam's table.

Noam focuses on the shadows Gordon's muscles cast over his tanned skin. "What was what?"

"The blushing, Victorian conversation with the bookworm," Charlie says, poking Noam's cheek and no doubt leaving traces of graphite on her skin.

"First of all, if Zenkov is a bookworm, what exactly am I?" Noam replies then throws a pointed look in Charlie's direction and wipes her cheek.

"I'm not going to contradict you on that point," Charlie says with a subdued giggle.

Noam rolls her eyes. "And second of all," she continues, "it was nothing, just an artistic conversation about our sketches."

"And the blushing?"

"An inability to accept a compliment properly on his part, I assume," Noam replies. She leans forward to rub away a smudge of graphite. "And on mine, a propensity for random blushing."

Charlie makes a noncommittal humming sound. "You do have a tendency to blush for the smallest reason."

"I know!" Noam whisper-shouts, instantly feeling her face heat up. "God, why am I friends with you?"

"'Cause I'm awesome, and my awesomeness radiates upon you. Now focus on your drawing."

"Yes, Mom."

THAT EVENING, NOAM EXCITEDLY TALKS ABOUT THE DAY she's had, about the potential this summer class might have for her portfolio and for her college application. True to her word, her mother is not home; but her father is all ears, and asks about the teacher's plan. Noam's sister, meanwhile, looks as if she's about to die of boredom.

Dana sighs loudly in the middle of Noam's recollection of the day and then gives Noam a judgmental look when Noam stops talking to look at her.

"God, you're exhausting," Dana says, prickly as only she knows how to be. "Do you ever temper your enthusiasm?"

"Do you ever show any?" Noam retorts, her voice rising. Alan reaches for Noam's hand.

"At least I know not to let my dreams take over reality." Dana throws her words in Noam's face before she pushes away her plate and storms out, shouting that she's leaving anyway.

Noam sighs and snatches her hand away from her father's, then scratches her wrist and elbow as her nerves light her skin on fire. "Why is it always me who has to keep quiet when she uses me as a punching bag, like a bitch?"

"Language," Alan scolds. "She's in a weird place, right now, Nomchka, you know that. Let's just cut her some slack, all right?"

Noam wants to say that it isn't fair, but she nods—when things get complicated for her, maybe they'll remember it and cut *her* some slack, for a change.

Between the tense situation with her sister, the weird sensation she feels in her gut when she recalls her conversation with Peter and the very newness of being able to draw all day, Noam isn't quite herself the next morning. Charlie is attuned to her conflicted emotions and thoughts and for the time being leaves her alone.

The second day seems a lot like the first; Gordon is still their model, but instead of an hour-and-a-half pose broken into two parts, they switch to shorter time frames. The morning is divided into four different poses of thirty minutes each, which prove to be a much different challenge.

After lunch, Gordon wears a pair of boxers and Mr. Siski has moved the easels. Now, instead of forming a circle around the platform, the easels form two lines, with a path between the two rows.

"Move along, people, you're going to like this," Mr. Siski says loudly, "at least if you like a challenge."

Charlie rubs her hands gleefully, and Noam bites her lower lip to contain her excitement.

Looking across the aisle, she shares a look with Peter, who opens his wide eyes and smiles at her.

"A challenge," Mr. Siski repeats, "because if you thought that this morning's poses were short, well, you ain't seen nothin' yet."

Siski's attempt at slang makes the whole class snicker—including Gordon, who remains silent but can't hide his shaking shoulders—and he gives a little bow in reply.

"Enough joking—as I was saying, shorter poses. First hour, five minutes each." At that, the class stops laughing and gasps. "Second hour, two minutes, third hour, one minute, and last hour, thirty seconds."

By the end of his list, the class is all atwitter—except Charlie and Noam, who remain silent, struck dumb at their easels.

Thirty seconds. That's… yeah, their teacher is right, that *is* a challenge, for Noam in particular. With her need to think things through, letting herself create on impulse, letting the connection between her brain and her fingers run freely without overthinking every scratch of graphite on the paper, the afternoon will definitely be a trial of her adaptability. But it is a good test, one she'll try to accept and get through.

"All right," she says, louder than she had intended. She rolls her sleeves up to her elbows.

"Nom," Charlie whispers, looking pointedly at the constellation of scars and fresh rashes marring the skin of her right forearm. Noam hurries to roll that sleeve down.

"It's not like I'm going to get this arm dirty anyway, right?" she says with a tentative laugh. She mouths a "thank you" that earns her a shrug and a wink from her best friend. Which translates to a combination of "you're welcome" and "anytime" in Charl-ese.

"Ready?" the teacher calls, with his eyes roaming over the class and Gordon. "Set, go!"

TRUTH BE TOLD, THE FIRST POSE OF EACH TIME FRAME IS A train wreck of half-assed drawings and nearly abstract lines, barely managing to catch Gordon as he moves from one stance to another. And don't get Noam started on the first of the thirty-second poses; she is so confused to see Gordon walking around the platform, each movement of his legs and arms exaggerated to fit in the timeframe, that she doesn't even pick up her pencil. The second is just a jumble of messy lines, barely more advanced than the drawings Noam's mother dutifully stuck on the fridge when she was much, much younger.

And then—and then she gets inspired.

Giving up on the third pose, Noam quickly folds one large sheet of paper until she holds a small square of many layers of paper. When the fourth short pose starts, Noam is ready. The smaller format gives her a quicker understanding of the purpose of the pose and lets her fingers and the pen snap the strong lines down just in time for Gordon to move on to a new pose.

The hour flies by, and Noam finds herself feeling disappointed that it is over—even if the prospect of challenging, self-discovering days yet to come makes her smile. She carefully goes through the folded book to look at her quickly realized sketches, selects those she will work on again later and begins to add details from memory or from her imagination. She can already picture this profile in black ink with pastel auras. Or this drawing of Gordon twisting his body to the left, in white pen on black paper—that would help her focus on different aspects of Gordon's body. Or this drawing she didn't think she would be able to complete, because it represents Gordon sitting on the stool, facing her side of the room with his legs spread open. She had managed to keep her hands steady, and that alone is an accomplishment.

"May I have a look at that?"

Peter leans against her easel and nods toward the square of paper in her hand.

"Um..." Noam fiddles with the paper, and Peter pulls his own sketchbook from his bag.

"Show me yours and I show you mine?" he offers, the smile turning slightly crooked.

"Kinky," Charlie comments, smiling at Peter over Noam's shoulder. "Can I get in on that deal?"

Peter turns bright, tomato red, but nods nonetheless. "Sure," he manages to croak and offers the sketchbook to Charlie.

Noam is more than a little surprised to see her friend flutter her eyelashes—and is that a blush darkening her cheeks? Noam can't be sure, but she thinks it is. She places the precious wad of paper in Peter's larger palm, reciprocating his offer.

"Kids, you have to leave the school," Mr. Siski tells them. They're the only students left in the room. "But I'm sure the Mini Beanie will be more than happy to welcome you and your allowances," he adds and winks. He looks pointedly at the folded screen, behind which Gordon is changing, and leaves the room.

"Well, I guess my date awaits me," Gordon tells them as he emerges from behind said screen, fully dressed and with his hair a complete mess. "See you tomorrow, kiddos," he tells them over his shoulder as he struts out of the room.

Charlie, Noam and Peter exchange an incredulous look and start to giggle.

They do go to the Mini Beanie, a coffee shop that is a block away from the school. And if they spend more time than might be considered normal sitting there, with their empty cups and three sketchbooks passing from hand to hand, well, nobody is judging.

⚜

BY THE END OF THE WEEK WITH GORDON, IT SEEMS AS though Peter has been part of their lives for a lot longer.

Noam is convinced that there should be a special word for the platonic soul mate, because the word "friend" doesn't cover the way Peter has completely filled a gap in her life she didn't know was there. The role of best friend was already taken, and "soul mate" carries an underlying sense of romance that doesn't apply.

That said, Noam suspects that "soul mate" is the right term to describe what is cooking between Peter and Charlie. Noam is not one to spread rumors—or, God forbid, gossip—simply because some looks linger maybe a beat too long, but that doesn't make her blind. She can see how those looks between Peter and Charlie walk the line between friendly and flirtatious, just as she notices that Charlie stops wearing her thousand cheap rings when Peter mentions a severe allergy to nickel.

Noam can only nod with a private smile on her face. She's not about to deny herself the pleasure of seeing the two of them make idiots of themselves as they fall head over heels.

She is aware—at least, a part of her is aware—that she should feel jealous; Peter joined their company thanks to her. But jealousy is the furthest thing from her mind. She's mostly happy for them, even if they are still tiptoeing around that leap.

Now, as they sit at their easels, Noam keeps her eyes on the folded screen and waits for the new model to emerge.

Their teacher peeks behind it and smiles at whoever shoos him away. "All right, padawans," he calls loudly, "after a week of studying the male body, it's time for a switch."

A long, curvy leg emerges from behind the screen, and a murmur travels through the classroom.

"Come on, don't play shy," their teacher says.

The new model comes out in all her naked glory, and Noam's heart is trying to jump out of her chest.

"Class, meet my good friend and former student, Amber," Mr. Siski says, as he puts his hand on the woman's shoulder. "Amber, these are my new followers."

Noam tries to smile as Amber looks at them, but she must look like Mowgli smiling at Shanti at the end of Disney's *Jungle Book*, with her mouth twisted in an awkward approximation of her usual smile.

"Are you okay, Nom?" Charlie whispers and bumps their elbows. "You look like you're having a stroke."

175

"She's beautiful," Noam whispers, unblinking. "Like, I can't just—I..."

"Close your mouth, babe. And yeah, she's stunning."

Amber is all curves, from the coppery hair that flows in rivulets escaping her hastily tied bun, to her full lips, to her full breasts and tiny waist, round calves and painted toes. The green varnish is a stark contrast to her caramel skin.

I want to find out if those curves are as soft as they look.

The fleeting thought makes Noam frown at herself.

Amber stands on the podium and puts her hands on her waist, waiting for the teacher's instructions. Her eyes dart around the room; an easy smile is on her face. Her eyes are bluish-gray, and remind Noam of the gem on her mother's wedding ring. Is it lapis? When Amber glances at her, Noam blushes. When her embarrassment becomes unbearable, Noam looks away.

She couldn't say why she's embarrassed. After all, she has done nothing wrong. They *are* asked to look at Amber—but Noam doesn't look at her with her usual objective eye; she is far too flustered by the model, who is still looking at her with her head cocked and a Mona Lisa smile on her lips.

"All right, just like last week," Mr. Siski instructs. Noam shakes her head to focus. "We'll start with a long pose, shortening it as we go and then moving to details. Amber, dear, if you could choose a pose you'll be able to endure for a while."

Amber finally looks away from Noam.

"Do I have something on my face?" Noam whispers to Charlie and Peter; her fingers probe her nose and lips.

Charlie shakes her head, and Peter scrutinizes her before shaking his head, too.

"Then why was she staring at me?" Noam mumbles, more to herself than to her friends, but Charlie shrugs.

"Maybe she thinks you're beautiful, too," she whispers.

Noam scoffs and rolls her eyes, then turns her attention to her easel and the model, who is now lying on her side facing Noam, one hand holding her head up and one leg folded at the knee.

Yeah, no way that… that, that goddess thinks Noam is interesting. Maybe the pattern of freckles on her face interests her.

Noam takes a deep breath and tries to push all these thoughts of attraction and whatnots from her mind, these treacherous thoughts that she doesn't know how to handle, and focus on realizing an accurate portrait of the pose Amber has chosen—.

The first forty-five minutes are fulfilling. Noam manages to draw a rough outline that brings a reversed Grande Odalisque to mind—without the additional vertebra and shortened leg Ingres gave his woman—and she looks up in surprise when Charlie touches her shoulder.

"You want to come out for the break?"

Noam shakes her head. "No, I'm good—have fun."

Most of the students want to use their ten-minute break to soak in some sun. As the room empties, Noam pulls out her "private" sketchbook, the one she uses to rework the various sketches she makes on the run.

"Hey."

Noam looks up and finds herself face to chest, so to speak, with Amber, who has wrapped a black and white robe around her body.

"H-hi." Noam tries to look up. She feels like a pervert; her eyes keep going to Amber's chest.

"Can I look?" Amber asks, and Noam has to hold back a sigh at the velvety quality of her voice.

"Oh, sure," she replies, after maybe a moment too long. "I mean, it's just a preparatory sketch, you know, nothing fancy; it's not good, really. Actually, you don't want to see this—oh, you're already looking, good," she rambles, inwardly smacking her own forehead.

Amber leans forward; her eyes follow the lines on Noam's paper until they find her little doodle with the measurements in the corner. She points at it, and a colorful tattoo on her wrist catches Noam's eye.

"That is really smart of you." Amber crouches so she can get closer to the little sketch. "Really shows an artistic mind."

"I thought artists were supposed to trust their guts and not overthink," Noam replies, twirling her pencil between her fingers.

Amber gives a very unladylike snort. "Impulsive artists don't last long," she says, cocking an eyebrow at Noam. Her gaze is intense and tugs at Noam's heartstrings.

The moment stretches between them, but this time around Noam isn't embarrassed; she is captivated, in the most literal sense of the word, as if Amber's eyes are chains she is voluntarily attaching to herself.

Is this what it is to like someone? Is this what makes so many people act so strangely? Is this the beginning of… attraction?

"You… um, you seem to know a lot about artists," she stammers.

Amber hums in agreement. "Well, I am a freshman at Parsons," Amber replies. "Not bragging, of course."

"Why would it be bragging?" Noam exclaims. "Parsons! That's—that's the dream! Congratulations!"

A light blush appears on Amber's collarbone and creeps up her neck as she beams—literally, it looks as if her face lights up—at Noam. "It's nothing, really."

"Not nothing—Parsons!" Noam cuts her off. Noam's eyes widen. "I'm sorry, that was so rude."

Amber giggles. "It's all right, don't worry—you're passionate, it's… it's endearing," she replies, batting her eyelashes slowly.

Just as Noam wonders what she could possibly say in reply, the students begin to return, guided by their teacher. Amber straightens up and moves back to the podium, after brushing her fingers on Noam's shoulder.

"Had fun?" Charlie asks as she sits down.

"I think so, yeah," Noam replies, dazed.

"At your drawings, people," Mr. Siski instructs.

Amber gets back into the pose; her eyes never leave Noam.

THE WHOLE FAMILY IS SITTING AT THE DINNER TABLE THAT evening, enjoying the cannelloni Alan made—"From scratch, just so you know"—when Dana pokes Noam.

"You're awfully quiet, little duck," she says softly, using a childhood nickname in a rare moment of tenderness. "Not jabbering about your art class and other nonsense as usual," she adds with a snicker, and the moment is gone.

"Dana," Alan says, his voice low in warning. Dana rolls her eyes and pokes at the cannelloni on her plate. "Though she could have phrased that differently, your sister's right." He turns to look at Noam. "You're awfully quiet tonight—is something wrong?"

Noam blushes and looks down, hiding behind her glass of apple juice. "Nothing's wrong. I just—have a lot on my mind."

Myriam pushes her plate away to put her hand on Noam's arm. "Do you want to talk about it, Nomchka?"

Noam shakes her head. "No, not really."

"Shocker," Dana mumbles, just loud enough to be heard. Noam spends the rest of the meal avoiding her sister's gaze.

Noam should have known that her parents wouldn't let it go so easily. Later that evening, just as she closes her laptop to get back to her sketches, a knock gets her attention.

"May I come in?" her mother's voice calls from outside the closed door. Noam sighs, but opens the door nonetheless.

"Mom, I really don't want to talk about it," she says, sitting at her desk while Myriam sits on the bed. "And not because I don't trust you, but because I need to make sense of... of what is on my mind first."

"Maybe saying it out loud would help," Myriam says softly. She takes off her glasses and cleans the lenses.

Noam makes a noise that conveys her doubts, but she puts down the sketchbook and sits on her feet.

"I... may, just maybe," she starts, looking for the right words, "have feelings for the model we have in class."

Her mother nods, clearly waiting for more. When Noam stays silent, she scooches closer to her daughter. "Is he older than you?"

"Yes," Noam replies, biting her lip as the white lie settles.

"Would it be problematic to date him? Because unless he's much older than you or has a swastika tattooed on his forehead—"

"She just has a little rainbow flag tattooed on her wrist, Mom," Noam says all in one breath and waits for her mother's reaction.

While her mother processes what Noam just said, Noam realizes that she just came out to her mother. They have never talked about homosexuality, and if Myriam and Alan have an opinion on it, they have never mentioned it in front of their daughters. What if Myriam is homophobic? What if her mother hates her now? God, what if her parents kick her out? What if...?

"And you want to date her?"

What?

"What?" Noam looks at her mother and lets her jaw fall open.

"Well, if you're attracted to her, honey, you should ask her out, get a coffee or go see a movie—do you need a little extra weekly allowance?"

"Mommy," Noam cries with a dry throat and jumps from her chair into her mother's open arms.

"There, there, sweetheart," her mother whispers as she pets Noam's hair and scratches her scalp in the way she knows Noam loves. "The heart wants what the heart wants. I just want you to be happy, okay?" Her mother gently pushes Noam away to look at her and wipes a stray tear from her cheek.

They cuddle for a little while longer. Noam clears her throat. "Mom?"

"Yes, bubbeleh?"

"I love you."

"I love you too."

"And I'll come to you if I have more questions about love."

"As you should." Myriam kisses the top of Noam's head, then stands up and checks her watch. "Lights out in forty minutes, baby."

Noam sighs and smiles at Myriam as she leaves the room. "Fine."

She returns to sit at her desk, but she leaves the sketchbook where it sits. She feels lighter all of a sudden.

The door opening doesn't surprise her, since she assumes it's her mother coming back to add something, but she smiles when she sees that it's actually her sister.

"Hey, Dana, what's u—" she starts, but her sister's glare silences her.

"So you're a dyke now? Is that the latest trend?"

The use of the slur is a punch to the gut. Noam is not only speechless, but also breathless.

"I—did you listen to my talk with Mom?" she finally replies, enraged at the attack on her privacy.

"The walls are not that thick," Dana sneers. "So?"

"Maybe, I don't know, but even so it's none of your business," Noam says, turning her back on Dana to keep her sister from seeing her eyes fill up with tears.

"I wouldn't wave a rainbow flag just yet," Dana replies between gritted teeth. "I'm sure it's just a phase you'll put behind you when you meet the right guy." She slams the door closed.

Noam closes her fists over her eyes, takes a deep breath and tries to keep her tears at bay. It's too late, though, and the familiar sensation of her nerves lighting up like a bolt of electricity right under her skin slowly spreads through her body.

As tears of anger spill from her eyes, Noam starts scratching the electricity away. Not for the first time, Noam wishes that her sister didn't act as if her purpose in life is to make Noam's life miserable.

"THAT BITCH," CHARLIE GROWLS THE NEXT MORNING DURING their break, when Noam has a chance to explain how Dana has upset her. From her chair, she pulls Noam into a tight hug. "But hurrah for your mom—can I be your mom when I grow up?"

Noam laughs and wipes at the infuriating tears that persist in rolling down her cheeks.

Peter, bless his soul, remains silent and simply offers her an old-fashioned handkerchief and a soft smile.

"What's going on?"

The three look up at their teacher. Mr. Siski's concern is apparent. He puts down his travel mug and sits at Noam's side. "Noam, are you okay?"

"I'm fine, sir," she replies and blows her nose one last time. "My sister is being... mean," she adds, not willing to insult her sister with a stronger word.

"More like being an ass," Charlie mumbles, before Noam can plant an elbow in her ribs.

"All right," Mr. Siski says softly, patting her knee. "My office is always open if you want to talk about it or if I need to talk with your parents about it, okay?"

"Thank you, Mr. Siski," Noam replies. Then she sees Amber approaching and gasps. "Shit, how bad do I look? On a scale from manga cries to Claire Danes cries?" she asks her friends, and Charlie stands up and cocks her head.

"Somewhere around Alice crying in Wonderland?" she offers. She clears her throat and turns to Peter. "Say, I think I need a boost of caffeine—we should get some hot drinks. See you later, Nomnom!" She grabs Peter's hand and practically runs away, waving at Amber as they pass her.

"You all right?" Amber asks, and Noam wants to say that yes, everything is wonderful, but her heart has just decided to set the beat for a rumba and butterflies have apparently grown in her stomach, so all she can do is nod and point at Amber's braids.

"That's cute," she replies, and Amber fidgets, playing with the end of one of her skillfully tied Bohemian side braids.

The gesture looks simultaneously vulnerable and coy, and Noam's lips stretch into a smile against the weight of her heavy mind.

"I think Charlie's suggestion had some merit," Noam rushes to say, willing herself to speak before she can overthink. She stands and straightens her dress. "May I... may I offer you a cup of coffee?" she asks. Her heart beats even faster as she takes the leap of faith.

"Oh—I... I don't drink coffee," Amber replies, and Noam is already berating herself, silently praying for the ground to swallow her now, please—or a giant eagle kidnapping her would work—when Amber touches her shoulder. "But I'd love a hot chocolate?"

Noam blinks at her and leans into her touch without realizing it. "Really?" she murmurs and smiles at Amber.

"Without a doubt—I definitely want a hot chocolate," Amber replies with a teasing smile, and her hand moves from Noam's shoulder to her hand.

Noam doesn't know if she's lesbian, if she's bi, or if she's just Amber-sexual, but she keeps her mother's wisdom at the forefront of her mind. The heart wants what the heart wants, and right now, her heart wants to keep her hands in this girl's. And after that?

After that, she has new poses to draw.

Noam sighs loudly, as she puts her pen behind her ear and looks away from the easel. This gets Mr. Siski's attention.

"Everything all right, Noam?" he asks, his voice soft.

Noam takes a deep breath and presses the heels of her hands against her eyes. "I just... I can't find the right way to get this pose," she admits, wincing at the way her voice breaks at the end of her sentence.

It's not that she's ashamed to admit failure—okay, maybe it is—she's more embarrassed by what is actually throwing her off of the "mojo" she has been building since the class started.

When she worked on Gordon's poses, she would get flustered, sure, but she was still able to find a way to objectify him, translate him into shapes and lines that made sense on paper.

With Amber, this proves to be a lot more complicated. She can't seem to get over the rumba of her heart and the sweat of her palms.

Each look she gives to analyze Amber's body is a second-best option to reaching to touch. Each pass of the graphite on her sheet should be a caress from Noam's fingers on Amber's soft skin.

Mr. Siski's silence stretches for what seems like a century. His bushy eyebrows are drawn together as he looks at the large drawing of Amber's back, at her lifted arms. "I don't see any problem," he says. "Sure, it doesn't have that sense of proportion your drawings showed earlier this week, but it is more vibrant, more um—oh," Siski cuts himself short, his eyes darting from the easel to Amber, who is giving them a pointed look over her shoulder, and back at Noam, who is suddenly very interested in the imprint of her teeth on her pencil. "All right," he says, perhaps a bit louder than he had intended; he clears his throat and lowers his voice. "Maybe you need to change your angle. Go sit on the side; work on the profile."

"You think it will help?" Noam asks, as she gathers her pens and erasers.

"I think you need to change your perspective," he replies with a gentle smile.

Noam nods an apology to the students she's interrupting and takes a seat. She settles down and arranges her materials.

From Noam's new point of view, Amber appears very different: Somehow, her profile is less expressive than her back, and, though Noam can't explain why, she now can stop waxing philosophical about the many ways a human body and face can awake emotions. Noam sends a thankful look in Mr. Siski's direction and starts tracing the rough shape of Amber's profile.

The lines are basic at first, but now, Noam can focus on theories of anatomy: the oval of the face, a polygon for the torso, the two triangles of the legs. She can add circles for the breasts later; they don't play a part in her understanding of the pose itself.

From this side, without the sass of Amber's back, she can concentrate and find the geometry in the body, just as she did with Gordon.

A wave of relief goes through her and she sighs and smiles, tucks one pen behind her ear and picks another, thicker one to start building the actual shapes.

⚜

THE CLASS IS EMPTY SAVE FOR THE TWO OF THEM. AMBER stands on the platform as usual, but Noam is not sitting at her easel at a safe distance from Amber's body.

Instead she stands with her toes against the edge of the platform, clad only in the old, soft denim shirt she usually wears to bed.

Her hands are on Amber's hips, tracing random patterns that make Amber twitch against her, but Amber remains standing, her fingers buried in Noam's unruly locks, tangling them a bit more as she pulls and presses. Her caresses feel divine.

Noam slowly pulls Amber toward her and brushes her nose against Amber's soft belly, then tilts her head to brush her forehead against Amber's breasts as she moves her hands on the small of Amber's back.

Noam wakes up with a start, shocked but somehow still not surprised to find her shorts wet and sticky. This has never happened to her before.

When she arrives at school, it is to an almost empty classroom—just Amber, wearing only a sports bra and tiny shorts, talking with Mr. Siski. Her eyes find Noam's before Noam can look away; and she smiles so brightly at Noam that, for a moment, Noam is convinced that Amber can read her mind.

Noam sits next to Charlie, who is doodling a ribbon on the side of her paper. Avoiding eye contact with Amber, Noam adds her own shapes and shades to the ribbon. By the time the other students have settled down, the ribbon has become the tail of a fantastic creature, half dragon and half phoenix; flames from its head and tail frame the paper completely.

Mr. Siski calls for attention, and Noam rolls her stool to her own easel.

"All right, class," Mr. Siski says, "today we're going to work on something that will be helpful for those of you who intend to study art in the future."

The students are on the edges of their seats when Mr. Siski continues. "Drapery studies on models—today we work with Amber, tomorrow Gordon will be back and the day after tomorrow, we'll welcome a new model."

Amber comes out from behind the folded screen with a wide smile, making a show of turning on her heels on the platform before sitting down. Her body is covered in different fabrics: a stretch of heavily embroidered red silk around her breasts, tied at her back with long fringes; and an off-white sheet draped around her hips in such a way that her legs play with its length to create shadows and shapes. The drapery provides many sketching possibilities.

Mr. Siski gives his instructions. They are to start with a series of short poses, and are expected to focus on details and leave the whole for later.

Noam is preoccupied, in an almost trancelike state. Her body is warm, as if a long-forgotten volcano has suddenly decided to awaken and its lava is now pooling low in her guts.

Every time Amber changes her pose—which is every two and a half minutes—Noam swears she can hear the blood rush from her brain to her breasts and between her legs.

If this is what it's like to have one's hormones agitated, all because of one person, she is almost glad that she has never experienced it before—it is far too distracting. Then again, she's almost eager to go through this—this trial by fire, now; it is beginning to allow her to reach a new level in her art. Now, she's not just drawing what she sees: When she manages to harness her emotions, Noam draws what she feels.

It's not just the way the silk stretches, shimmers and flows down Amber's back that Noam translates onto the paper: it's the sensation of Amber's back under Noam's hand when they hug. It's not just the folds draping over Amber's knee and pooling on the floor that Noam brings to life; with quick strokes of her pencil and red chalks, she draws the butterflies which that same knee—brushing against her leg when they watched a movie together—awakened in her belly.

That's when it hits her: the vision of the roundness of the knee peeking out from under the beige sheet—on her pad, drawn by none other than herself—makes her feel warmth all over, just like the actual knee.

During the break, Noam gently touches the drawings she has made, the different body parts that make Amber. Her fingertips are almost reverent, as hesitant against the paper as they were when she made herself brave enough to reach for Amber's cheek in the moment before she leaned into their first kiss.

Noam picked this particular movie for their second date because she has grown up with it and Amber mentioned never having seen it, which is a great mistake, but one that could easily be corrected. Noam knows it by heart, and soon enough, comfortably seated on her bed with Amber next to her, Noam started singing along under her breath. Her fingers brushed Amber's every now and then.

From the corner of her eye, Noam saw that Amber was not giving the movie her full attention. Instead she turned her head at random times to look at Noam with a fond smile on her lips.

During one of the less important scenes, Noam turned to look at Amber, and there it was, the butterfly swarm that had grown in her body since they met. For the life of her, Noam couldn't look away from the dual curves of Amber's mouth and the little strand of hair that had escaped the tight bun she coiled her hair into after class.

Trying to control the shaking of her fingers, Noam reached to move the lock from Amber's face. The tip of her thumb brushed the soft angle of Amber's cheekbone. Amber tilted her head ever so slightly, leaning into the touch with her eyes wide open and locked on Noam's mouth, making a happy, throaty noise that spurred Noam forward.

It was simultaneously the easiest and the hardest thing in the world to lean closer and brush her lips against Amber's—they're soft, and still carried the taste of the apple gum she had chewed earlier.

Noam had made that first step, but it was Amber who deepened the kiss and sent the butterflies soaring. . .

"Wow, dude, you are seriously hooked."

Noam looks away from the drawing on her easel; her fingers linger over the roundness of Amber's drawn knee. Charlie is looking at her with a mischievous smile; her chin is cupped in her hand.

"Uh?"

"I would ask you if you want me to leave the two of you alone," Charlie continues, sing-song elongating the last vowel as she gestures between Noam and her drawing, "but I don't want to make you, you know, uncomfortable or something."

Noam slides her fingers away from the drawing and gives Charlie a look to convey how little convinced she is by her best friend's "attempt" to keep things from awkwardness.

"But no joke, Nom," Charlie continues, undeterred by Noam's look, "are you two getting, you know... serious?"

"What about *you* two?" Noam nods toward the other side of the room, where Peter is helping Mr. Siski hang crystal garlands from the ceiling.

Charlie's eyes follow Noam's nod, and her whole face goes softer; her dimples show. Noam's feels as if her heart is bursting with happiness, to see this much contentment on her best friend's face.

But then Charlie sighs heavily, looking back at Noam. "I'm not sure," she says softly, fiddling with an eraser that she rolls into a ball only to smash it and stretch it again.

Noam reaches for Charlie's knee. "Is something wrong? Is he—is he pressuring you or something?"

Charlie laughs. The sound is brief and bark-like. "If anything, I'm the one pressuring him."

The lilt of her voice at the end of her admittedly shocking sentence makes it sound like a question; Charlie rolls her stool closer to keep the discussion private. "I... seem to have found myself a hyper-romantic, asexual boyfriend."

Noam's eyes widen and she pats Charlie's leg.

"And as weird as it may sound, I'm fine with it!" Charlie says, blowing her cheeks and letting out a loud puff of air, in annoyance at herself, if Noam knows her as well as she thinks she does. "That's what's bothering me!"

Noam frowns at her. "It bothers you to be happy and fulfilled by a relationship with no... physical interaction?"

"Oh, we kiss, and we cuddle—we're cuddle monsters. But basically, yes."

190

Noam raises her eyebrows at Charlie, and Charlie rolls her eyes. "Oh, shut up," she says, tension slowly leaving her body. "I know I sound cuckoo."

"I didn't say anything."

"Your eyebrows said plenty, jerk," Charlie says, but her smile softens the insult into comfortable, familiar banter. "And don't think I didn't see what you did there, missy," she adds as the other students come into the room. "Or that I'm letting you off the hook."

THE NEXT POSE, LONGER, DEFINITELY CONFIRMS NOAM'S knowledge that what she has in her heart for Amber goes beyond a mere attraction.

The silk scarf and the sheet are gone, replaced by what can only be described as a steampunk ballerina outfit. A metallic-looking corset is laced around Amber's torso, enhancing her small waist and the curve of her hips; coppery ribbons crisscross at her sides. A dark tutu covers her hips and buttocks, but it only serves to make her lace-covered legs look endless.

Using the middle bar of her high stool, Amber finds a comfortable pose that she can hold for an hour as Mr. Siski explains the nature of the exercise. Amber rests her black ballet shoe on the bar and folds her arms over her lap in first position, or "bras bas," if Noam remembers the few ballet lessons she attended with Dana years ago.

Thinking about her sister is not comfortable, and Noam's heart hurts as if it has been squeezed. Ever since the "confrontation," the air around the two has been loaded with electricity and animosity: everything turns into a pretext for Dana to verbally attack Noam, and Noam has decided to act as if she doesn't hear, doesn't see Dana. For Noam, it's the mature thing to do, but obviously her sister doesn't share the feeling. Noam would give almost anything to clear the air, get rid of the tension in the house and erase that deepening line of worry on her father's forehead. But she will not be the one to make apologies. Not this time.

Noam gets her lightest pencil to sketch the general shape of Amber's pose, figure and shades. Then she looks up to start developing the details.

Her eyes meet Amber's and she barely represses a giggle when Amber winks. A sobering thought crosses her mind.

I could draw her my whole life and not get bored.

Noam traces the lines of shiny embroidery on the corset and the reflections of the lights on the ribbons. The installation of crystals Mr. Siski and Peter put on the ceiling makes sense now, the fractal shimmer adding an almost supernatural ambiance to the pose, and some of the other students are already using pastels and colored crayons to capture it.

As far as Noam is concerned, it's too soon to think about backgrounds and lighting effects. For now, she observes the way her pen traces the round knot of Amber's shoulder. Letting her fingers work the lines on muscle memory, her brain goes to the early lessons, and beyond that, to the way she used to draw, the way she used to handle her pen. Oh, she's still a long way from Charlie's confidence or Peter's boundless energy, but Noam is more than what she is *not*, and now she can see it; she only has to let it show.

The Most Handsome

S.J. Martin

I AM PROBABLY THE WORST CAPE COD RESIDENT IN THE history of the world.

I hate seafood. I also hate tourists and the beach. All year long, thousands of people flock to our beaches, fresh ocean bounty and quaint villages. I grew up in one of those quaint villages—Oceanside. Our town is tiny, the kind of place where everyone knows each other and they've all got their noses in your business. I'd love to say that I'm anonymous around there, but the truth is: I'm kind of famous.

Ever since I was a little kid, I've felt like a boy instead of a girl. I came out of the closet as a gay transgender guy when I was a junior in high school, and it was big news. I came out because I couldn't handle hiding it any more. I cut my hair, changed my name from Christina to Carter, and began wearing a binder, which flattens my breasts so I can have a more male-looking chest. Weekly injections of testosterone helped me develop more masculine traits such as facial hair and a deeper voice. What do you think of my fantastic attempt at a goatee, by the way? At the time, not many folks had any idea what the word "transgender" meant, and I had to do a hell of a lot of explaining. My parents were beyond confused—I had to work really hard to get them to understand. I'm sure some of you get that.

It's really simple actually: I was labeled a girl at birth and I don't feel as though that title fits. I feel like a man. My four-year-old sister Hannah understood when I told her, "I was born in a girl's body, but I have a boy's brain."

If only everyone got it as well as she did. It's been okay though; I was lucky and I wasn't bullied very much—my school had a Zero Tolerance policy for bullying. Any kids dumb enough to start trouble with me soon found themselves in deep shit. Through all of the changes, my family and friends stood behind me one hundred percent. Sometimes, I felt kind of lonely though. There weren't any other openly trans people in Oceanside. I wish I'd had another person who identified with me.

I never went out with anyone in high school. All of my friends paired up and did all of the usual things: dances, dating, hooking up and stuff like that. I never did, because I was keeping a secret.

I remember thinking that I should have been born a little boy when I was really young, but I never thought I could tell anyone—I thought I was crazy. How could I explain feeling the way I did? Growing up, I was more of a tomboy and looked pretty masculine naturally. When I was a young teenager, I thought that, because I looked more male, I must be a lesbian, even though I felt more like a boy who liked other boys. Yeah, that's really not the most open-minded thinking—it's more than a bit homophobic, but I was young and uninformed. So, I came out for the first time when I was thirteen—as a lesbian. Yeah, I know. Hard to imagine looking at me now, right?

Surprisingly, I was not the only out kid around. My friend, J.P. Allen came out at around the same time. J.P. is a really handsome guy with lovely green eyes. He's also tall and muscular with a fantastic swimmer's build. I had a huge crush on him and no idea how to explain it. I'd have intense dreams where he and I fell in love and got married. I settled on having him as my best friend instead. And before you ask, yes he's single. No, I won't give you his number.

Today, I can't imagine anything romantic between us—he's been such an amazing support all of these years. He's more like a brother—one who sometimes drives me insane just the way a real brother would. He's a sarcastic guy and loves to tease me.

Back then, we bonded over feeling different from all the other kids. My mom and dad drove us to Provincetown often so we could be exposed to the diversity there. If you haven't heard of it, Provincetown is a small, seaside town at the tip of Cape Cod, and is the gay capital of Massachusetts. I loved sitting on a bench downtown and watching the crowds pass by. Gays, lesbians, bisexuals and straight people—a true rainbow of humanity all mingling in colorful, loud, groups.

Provincetown was where I first became aware that transgender people existed. Oliver's Bookshop sat smack dab in the middle of Commercial Street, right on the main drag. I was always saving my money to buy new books, and one day a book with a shirtless man on the cover caught my eye. I stood on my tiptoes and pulled it down from the high shelf—*Our Emerging Selves: Stories of Transformations and Truth*. If you haven't read it, I totally recommend it.

I sat down on a rickety chair in a corner and flipped through the book. I couldn't tear my eyes away from the pages of photos of young men, but that wasn't the remarkable part. The pictures were accompanied by side-by-side comparisons of those young men as young women. I couldn't believe what I was seeing. Girls who felt as if they were actually boys? People who are open and honest about who they really are? I was shocked. I thought, if they could change, could I change too? I finally had a name for what I was and I remember I was so relieved I almost started to cry.

I looked at the price tag on the book and gathered all my money—I had just enough. As the cashier rang it in, I felt a lump in my throat and my cheeks burning. I wasn't ready to let anyone know my secret, but I was overjoyed knowing I wasn't alone.

Turns out, I wouldn't be ready for four more years, but I really figured out who I was just before I turned eighteen.

The summer before I started at Boston University, I got a job at a snack bar at the beach so I could save as much money as possible. Yep, the snack bar was on the beach. I mentioned that I hate the beach and tourists, right? Every day, I put on my "Dave's Clam Shack" T-shirt and khaki shorts, walked across hot sand and worked behind the counter serving customers all manner of fried foods. The Shack (as we lovingly called it) was built in the fifties and was really run down—probably still is. The wooden building was originally covered in faded shingles; many of them blew away during our famous nor'easters. Even though it's practically falling down, it's still popular with tourists and locals.

I got to work with J.P., and my boss, Joe Cohen, was pretty cool, but by the third week of summer I was already over working with the public. I really looked forward to my days off. J.P. used to laugh at me and say, "You're such a ball of sunshine, dude."

A huge mix of people came through our lines, and we saw more than a few handsome college guys on a daily basis. J.P. and I had a secret code word for when a particularly hot guy came around—"Hot Dog."

One day, J.P. called out, "Hey! Carter—hot dog at two. I need a hot dog at two o'clock."

I followed his gaze and almost choked when I saw the guy. He was compact and trim and he wore swim trunks. He had wavy chestnut hair and striking blue eyes—trust me, this man was gorgeous. I figured he was a little older than me—maybe a junior or senior in college. Out of my league, definitely.

J.P. caught my eye and winked. He said, "Go take his order, hot stuff."

I told J.P. to shut up, cleared my throat and managed to ask the guy what he wanted.

"What do you recommend?" he asked.

When I asked him what he was in the mood for he said, "Something seafood-y."

Considering that I would rather eat cut glass than shrimp, scallops, clams or lobster—I said, "The burgers are pretty good." I know, right? Super suave.

He ordered a cheeseburger and fries, and oh, my, God. His *smile*. It was one of the loveliest smiles I'd seen in a really long time and he was aiming it at me.

I wanted to drop to my knees and ask him to marry me, but instead I just gave him his total and accepted a crisp twenty-dollar bill from his (perfect, veiny and strong-looking) hand.

"Thanks... Carter," he said, reading my nametag.

When I handed him his change all I could think to say was, "Have a good one." Fantastic conversationalist, right? You know when you imagine yourself punching yourself in the face? Yeah, that was me.

As he walked away holding his platter of food, I exhaled a breath I hadn't realized I'd been holding.

J.P. smacked me on the back of the head. "Wake up, lover boy. We've got more people to make happy. You can dream about him later—I know I probably will."

I rolled my eyes at him and sighed dramatically. I wished that Mr. Attractive would come back and sweep me off my feet but resigned myself to the idea that I'd never see him again.

As I pulled into my driveway that night, I saw that both Mom and Dad were home at the same time—a rare occurrence. I love my parents. They're not perfect by any stretch, but they've always been loving and supportive, and I know I'm really lucky. Mom's a teacher, and Dad is a pediatrician. You should see the two of them; they are so mismatched in appearance, it's hilarious. My mom has really curly brunette hair and is tiny. She's only about four foot eleven. My dad is super tall and lanky with stick-straight silver hair. He's about six foot six, and when they walk together they make an entertaining pair.

I was an only child until I was thirteen, when my little sister Hannah was born. She's the greatest little kid. Sure, she drove me crazy when she was really young and I was still getting used to not being the only child. Now, she amuses the hell out of me. I'm her favorite person. As I got out of the car, she flew out of the front door and shouted my name over and over. Her unruly chestnut hair escaped a loose pony tail and stuck out all over the place.

Hannah jumped up and wrapped her arms around my neck for a hug. I used to call her Hanna-Banana—still do sometimes, just to annoy her. I asked her about summer day camp and she said, "It was really, really, good! We made bracelets and I maked you one."

"You did? What color is it?" I asked.

"Purple, your favorite," she said.

I love when my Dad makes dinner. He's obsessed with shows like *Top Chef* and *Chopped* and spends a lot of his spare time making up recipes and trying all sorts of new techniques. Most of the time he's successful, but every blue moon he fails miserably— like the time he made brownies but put in salt instead of sugar.

You should have seen Hannah's face as she tasted them—I don't think she's fully recovered yet.

My dad likes to give me a hard time. When I asked him what we were having for dinner he said, "Hello, Father. How was your day? Did you have a good one? Why, yes, son, I did."

I called him a wiseass.

When Dad asked me about my day, I decided to be honest with him. I know some of you can't do that with your folks, so I'll tell you how that went.

I said, "I met the most handsome man in the entire world at work."

"*The* most handsome?" my dad asked.

When I told him the mystery guy should win an award for "most attractive," my dad laughed and said, "Should he be in the paper?"

Then I laughed because our town paper, *The Enterprise*, is often called "The Emptyprise" due to the supreme lack of interesting things happening in Oceanside.

"He'd definitely earn a place on the front page," I told him. "I keep hoping against hope he'll come back to The Shack, but I don't think he's going to. I guess our love affair was not meant to be."

Dad made a sympathetic face and then called everyone for dinner.

I know families can drive you crazy sometimes, but I am so lucky, mine is pretty great. I felt better just by hanging out with them. After dinner I read Hannah *Where the Wild Things Are*—a book I read to her approximately a million times. When I checked my phone, I noticed J.P. had called nine times. Nine. Times.

I called him back immediately. "What's wrong, man?" I asked.

J.P. said, "I've got intel on your mystery man. Apparently, he's here for the summer."

My heart jumped. Suddenly I had a million questions. "What? What else do you know? What's his name? How old is he? Is he gay?"

He said, "Here's the problem: all I know is, his family rented a house up in the Heights. My friend Sara Fieldman lives next door, and when I told her you were all obsessed about Mr. Hotpants, she told me the house next door was rented and she'd seen a guy who could possibly be the one we're looking for hanging out in the back yard."

And my heart sank.

I said, "You're telling me that the only so-called information we've got is that he looks like a guy some girl has seen hanging out in the yard next to hers? That is ten kinds of not very helpful, J.P."

"Dude, it's more than you knew before—be grateful," he grumbled.

J.P. had a point.

"Okay... I'll take it, thanks," I said

The next day at work, I prayed that my gloriously handsome friend would come back, but he didn't. All week long, I scanned the lines for him, hoping he'd be there. J.P. thought that was the funniest thing he'd ever seen, and kept poking fun at me.

He said, "You've got it hard for this nameless guy, huh? You're at least going to have to know his name before riding off into the sunset."

Joe wasn't as amused. I was distracted and kept screwing up orders and forgetting the most basic things. Customers were also not very enthusiastic. I tried to pay attention, but visions of my dream guy clouded my head.

At the end of that week, I had the worst day yet. I messed up so much that Joe threatened to make me pay for all the food that I wasted. I burned my hand on the grill, accidentally made a little girl cry and was rude to a customer, who then demanded to speak to the manager.

After thinking about it long and hard, I finally decided to stop looking for my guy. It had been over a week, and there was no sign of him. I figured I wasn't going to see him again. I don't know what I was hoping for anyway, it's not as though we would start a relationship or anything, right? It was just fun pretending. I was used to being alone.

After the end of the day cleanup, J.P. grabbed my arm and said, "Remember, tonight. I'll come by and get you at nine—we're taking my car. I'm not about to drive around in your shitbox."

"Thanks, friend," I said.

J.P. said, "You *know* your car is a falling-apart piece of crap, Carter."

"Shut up," I muttered, knowing full well that he was right. My 1992 Toyota Camry had seen better days, but it worked nicely getting me around town. I knew it didn't have much more life in it though, and every time I put the key in the ignition, I crossed my fingers that it would start.

We were going to an LGBT dance at a youth center a couple of towns away. Because I'd spent so long hiding who I really was, I'd never danced with anyone—let alone another boy. I was hoping to change that. It was so difficult explaining to people how it was possible to be a gay trans guy. It took me a long time to figure out that gender identity and sexual identity were separate, so I could see why others might not understand right away either.

I dressed in my nicest pants, a button down shirt, T-shirt and binder. I debated wearing a tie, but that that was probably overkill.

At nine exactly, J.P. pulled into the driveway and honked his horn. J.P.'s boyfriend, Nathan Graham, waved at me from the passenger seat. He's this free-spirited punk rocker with multiple tattoos. He dyes his hair, and that night it was an interesting light blue. Social justice and vegetarianism are two of his favorite topics, and he's known on campus as an activist. J.P. is more conservative, but I think the two of them work really well as a couple; they balance each other nicely.

As I slid into the backseat I told Nathan I was nervous and he said, "You're going to be fine. We're going to find you a cute boy and you are going to dance the night away."

"Yeah, right. I'm sure. I'm such a catch," I said.

"Stop talking shit about yourself, Nathan said. "You're really cute. I'd do you."

I burst out laughing. J.P. turned up the radio and we all sang along to his collection of 80's British new wave mixes as we drove to the dance. When we arrived, the party was in full swing—a lot of dancing in couples and in small groups. Everything was fun and festive, with balloons and streamers all over the place. Whoever had decorated had really gone all out: a giant disco ball rotated over the dance floor.

Of course, I made a beeline for the refreshment table. J.P. and Nathan gave me a "get out here, you loser" look and went out to the dance floor holding hands.

I contemplated the array of food in front of me and grabbed a plate. Chips and salsa seemed like a pretty safe bet—snacks couldn't reject you the way people could. I wasn't the only person lurking near the table—a good number of people had the same idea. As I turned to get a cup of soda, I smacked into someone.

I apologized and then…

"No worries, I didn't even spill my drink. Hey! Carter, right?"

It was him. *Him.* I could barely breathe, let alone think.

I said, "I, um, yeah. Carter. I'm Carter," but all the time I was thinking, *I am the biggest dork in the entire world.*

"Alex," he said and held out his hand. As I shook it, I silently prayed that my hand wasn't too clammy. I truly believed I might have a heart attack.

We made small talk about seafood, and he laughed because I hate it and work at The Shack. You know when you can't stop smiling? That was me. Fortunately, Alex smiled back. Then he said, "Would you like to dance?"

My stomach flipped and my mouth went dry. I didn't know what to say. He looked so amazing in the low light, tanned and smiling.

I said, "I can't dance."

"Can't or won't?" Alex asked.

"I don't know how. I've never..."

"Danced with another boy?"

"Uh, yeah. Never danced with another boy. I'm not sure I know how to either," I said, as heat flooded my face.

Alex laughed. "Wanna try?"

I don't know what came over me. I tossed my plate into the trash and, before I could think it through, grabbed his hand and dragged him out onto the dance floor. He looked so at ease, dressed in a polo shirt and crisp khakis. I prayed that I didn't look too awkward or have food stuck in my teeth or anything embarrassing like that. Loud dance music pumped out of speakers and I was relieved to know the song. Alex began to sway back and forth, and I started to copy him. I really hoped that I didn't look as absolutely stupid as I felt.

Alex grinned at me.

"You look good," he half-shouted over the music.

"You're crazy—you're the one who looks good," I shouted back.

I couldn't believe it—I was actually having fun. If you had told me before that night that I'd *ever* dance with another man, I'd tell you that you were nuts.

Another song came on, and Alex made no attempt to stop. We kept dancing. At one point, I spotted J.P. and Nathan across the room and they both shot me thumbs up. Two songs became five and then we started to get tired. As the latest Lady Gaga song came to an end, Alex motioned for us to leave the dance floor. We made our way back to the snack table where we could talk easily.

"That was fun," Alex said.

"Thanks for a great first time," I replied and blushed when I realized what I'd said.

I'd never had a first kiss, and I couldn't stop imagining us making out. Alex didn't seem to notice my nervousness, thankfully. Somehow, he wasn't sweaty or out of breath from dancing—he still seemed so perfect. I was entranced.

Then Alex asked me if I wanted to go outside and talk. I couldn't think of anything I wanted to do more. When we told J.P. and Nathan where we were going, J.P.'s eyes widened. "Oh, my God." he mouthed to me

"I know," I mouthed back.

I introduced everyone and they all shook hands and said hello. Alex smiled the whole time and seemed to charm the socks off of my friends. When we left, J.P. said, "Have fuuuuuun." I was pretty sure that I might try to kill him at a later date.

We found a large stone bench right near the front entrance. The almost choking humidity of the afternoon had gone, and there was a nippy breeze. Alex motioned for me to sit first, then he sat down beside me.

He said, "So, Carter, I only know your name. Tell me another fact about yourself? It can be really random."

I said, "I play the piano and I'm really good at burping the alphabet. It amuses my little sister endlessly."

Alex laughed. It was a glorious sound. I didn't think I'd ever get tired of hearing it. I had expected the conversation to be awkward, but instead we had this really easy back-and-forth going. It went like this:

"Okay, now I know *three* new facts. Piano, sister, burping. Interesting."

"Your turn. At least one thing—go."

"Um, I'm nineteen, I go to Boston University and I think bologna smells like feet."

"What? That's amazing! I'm going to BU in the fall! How cool is that?" I gushed. "Bologna smells like feet?"

"Yep, total gross feet. And, it *is* cool that you're going to BU in the fall. I'll have to show you all around campus and stuff. I'm taking applications for new friends," Alex joked.

"Is there a paper application or can I apply online?"

Alex grinned. "You're applying right now."

"Oh, sneaky. Jerk," I teased.

Somehow, we ended up with our thighs touching, and I couldn't get over the feeling of the heat of his body pressed up against me. It was the closest to another boy I'd ever been, and my heart fluttered. Suddenly, the sea air didn't seem so chilly.

Then Alex said, "Carter? Would it be too forward of me to tell you that after I met you that one afternoon, I hoped I would be able to see you again? I've been up in Boston doing campus tours all week, but I was planning on going back to the Clam Shack tomorrow just to see if you'd be there."

I stared at him, watching light from the full moon dance across his face.

"You've got to be kidding me," I said.

"Why?"

"It's just... just... I've never had anyone seek me out before. I've never dated anyone. I've never done... anything."

"Carter, you're very cute—it's absurd that nobody's ever told you that. It's a shame you've never dated," Alex said. "I'm not exactly the most experienced guy around, but I do know a thing or two. You are definitely someone worth chasing."

I just shook my head at him. Alex didn't know my secret. He had no idea that I was transgender. He thought I was a cis-male, a guy biologically male and labeled so at birth. I gulped. Did I need to come out to him? What the hell should I say? I watched a group of laughing teenagers head for the parking lot and contemplated my choices.

"Thanks." I responded quietly. "You are too. I told my dad that I met the most handsome man in the world the other day, to be honest."

Alex snorted and laughed out loud. "Me? Stop it."

"No, really. I did."

I couldn't believe what was coming out of my mouth. Had I been secretly abducted by aliens and replaced with a confident robot version of myself?

Alex said, "Okay, so we've established that we each find the other attractive. What do we do next? I propose that we find somewhere to get coffee and go to the beach to talk more. I'll give you a ride home—if that's good for you?"

I texted J.P. to tell him where were going, and we went to the parking lot. For some reason, I'd assumed that he'd have a really nice, fancy car—but it wasn't at all. In fact, it gave my crappy Camry a run for its money. The blue Prizm had to be at least fifteen years old and it was covered in bumper stickers and large patches of rust.

"I saved up for two summers to buy this car." Alex said. "It's not the nicest, but it gets me where I need to go."

I told Alex about my beater car as we drove to Starbucks. As he turned out of the parking lot, I could barely sit still knowing that the boy I liked was driving me around. It felt like a Technicolor dream—one I never wanted to wake up from. I tried not to fidget too much and clasped my hands in my lap. We chatted as we drove, and I learned that Alex was on the Cape for the summer with his family and that he was from Cambridge, about an hour and a half away from Oceanside.

At Starbucks, he opened my door for me.

"How chivalrous of you," I said.

"You know what they said about chivalry not being dead and all."

We placed our drink orders and talked as we waited for them to be made. Alex asked me a few questions about growing up in Oceanside and what I want to be when I grow up. He was so easy to talk to—I was surprised to find my answers coming quickly and my words flowing well. I don't like being the center of attention—I prefer hanging around on the sidelines, listening.

After we left the coffee shop, I came clean about my disdain for beaches and Alex asked me why I disliked them.

"Sand. It gets everywhere—in your hair, ears, under your bathing suit. I hate it." I replied. "Plus tourists. They drive me crazy..."

Alex was a tourist. I had really put my foot in it.

"Er, not *all* tourists are bad, I mean, you are a cool tourist," I said.

Alex just laughed and pulled into a parking lot. "Let's go hang out by the water. I've got a blanket in the trunk. I promise it won't be too bad. I'll try and protect you from the big, bad, sand."

I smiled and got out of the car. I was willing to follow him anywhere—sand or no sand. Alex grabbed the blanket and began to make his way down to the beach. The water was calm, and it was just warm enough to be comfortable in a T-shirt. A slight breeze ruffled the rushes in the dunes near the road. I pulled off my shoes and socks. My sensitive feet protested as I made my way over the rocky foreshore.

"It's so gorgeous here," he said, as he spread out the wooly blanket on fine sand closer to the water. He plopped down in an ungainly heap and motioned for me to join him. I sat down more carefully to avoid getting sand all over the place.

"It *is* pretty," I said.

Alex leaned back on his elbows. "So, you don't like seafood, the beach or tourists. What *do* you like Carter?"

I told myself: *Be brave, Carter.*

"You."

Alex was silent for a moment before he sat up and reached over to me, putting his hands on my face.

"I like you, too," he said. Time seemed to stop as he moved his face closer to me. Suddenly, his lips met mine. Everything was muted and loud at the same time. Alex opened his mouth slightly and his tongue made its way into my mouth. I kept thinking, *I'm kissing a boy. Me. Kissing a boy.* I kissed him back and dared to move my tongue against his. Goosebumps ran up and down my arms. I never wanted it to end, but eventually, Alex pulled away.

"That was amazing—you're really good at that," he said.

I stared at him. "I've never done *that* before."

"Well, you're a quick study."

I sat back and wrapped my arms around my knees. I was going to have to tell him about being trans, especially if things like kissing were going to happen.

Alex looked concerned. "Hey? You okay? Was that too soon?"

"No, it just took me by surprise. It was great."

"Then why do you look so bummed out?" Alex asked.

Shit, shit, shit. I had to reveal my secret—I had to just be brave and blurt it out. I feared that Alex would run away, thinking I was a freak or something. Even though most people know I'm trans in Oceanside, when I meet new people I have to come out all over again. It's frustrating and difficult. Alex was more than just some random person. How he responded really mattered.

I took a deep breath and said, "Alex, I have to tell you something."

He slid over next to me, his side against mine, and asked, "What is it, Carter? I won't judge, no matter what it is."

"I... I, um, I'm transgender," I said quietly.

Alex was silent for a moment—kind of like all of you right now! I figured he was about to get angry or upset. I didn't know if he even knew what the word transgender meant—sometimes people don't.

"It means that I was assigned female at birth..."

"And you don't feel like that fits," he finished for me. "I know what transgender means, Carter."

I stared at him.

"Are you upset with me?"

"No, I'm just a little surprised is all. I had no idea," Alex said. "Give me a second to process?"

"Sure."

We both just sat silently. I stared out into the waves and wondered what he was thinking. I thought about the transgender men pictured in the book at Oliver's Bookshop. Did they find love? What happened when they put themselves out there and told the truth to someone who was interested in them? Were they scared? Were they rejected?

Then Alex said, "I've only been with guys, Carter. Shit, I'm not trying to say you're not a guy. This isn't coming out the way I mean it to—I'm just... this is new for me. I am really attracted to you, and the fact that you have different, um, bits, is just making me feel a little bit weird."

"Alex, you can just take me home or whatever—I'd understand."

Disappointment hit me like a truck. I had always known I'd have to disclose my trans status to potential boyfriends—but I didn't think I'd have a boyfriend for a long time. I didn't think it would be that night.

Alex reached for my hand. "Carter, I don't want to take you home. I want to be here with you."

That was *not* where I thought things were going to go. My stomach swooped.

"You sure?" I asked.

"Absolutely. I want to get to know you. I want to hear your stories and find out what makes you tick. I don't know enough random facts about you yet."

Alex squeezed my hand, and turned to me. "C'mere," Alex murmured, bringing his lips to mine.

His lips were so soft. I moaned softly. Delicious sensations gave me goose bumps as I pressed my mouth to his. Tingles and heat bloomed in my belly.

Alex moved his hands up and cupped my face as we kissed. I put my arms around his waist and leaned into him. Alex moaned too—making me feel less awkward.

When we finally broke apart, we were both breathing heavily.

"That was the best five minutes of my life," I said.

Alex smiled broadly. "I'd have to agree with you—they were most excellent minutes."

Alex turned and lay on his back. I flopped down and rolled onto my back. Alex grabbed my hand.

"Let's lie here and stare at the stars for a few minutes; we can ponder the mysteries of the universe together," Alex said.

I laughed. "Ponder the mysteries, eh?"

So we did. Quiet moments ticked by, and I thought about all that had happened in the last few hours. My mystery man was a mystery no longer. I was still just as intrigued however, and couldn't wait to know more. I'd come out to him and he hadn't run.

"So, what happens now?" I asked.

Alex turned and looked at me. "We stay here for a little while longer, tell each other more stuff about ourselves and maybe kiss some more?"

I had to hand it to him—he sure was a charming guy. I was definitely under his spell. I squeezed his hand.

"So, this plan works for you?" Alex asked.

I grinned at him. "Yeah, it absolutely does—especially the part about maybe kissing some more."

"Well, you'd better get over here then."

I moved into his arms and couldn't remember ever feeling so safe and secure. It was so weird, I'd only just met Alex, but I already could trust him implicitly. As we kissed, the world melted away, and nothing else mattered—it was just the two of us, together.

Unfortunately, reality came crashing down when my phone wouldn't stop buzzing. I grabbed it and checked the screen—five missed messages, two from J.P. and three from my parents, all of them wondering where I was. I checked the time and was amazed to find that it was almost one in the morning. My parents were pretty relaxed about a curfew, but one was pushing it, especially since I had to work the next morning.

"Alex, I've got to go home. I'm sorry, but I've got work early tomorrow," I told him, feeling more disappointed than I had in a long time.

Alex hugged me gently and kissed the top of my head.

"Ok, I get it. It *is* getting late. C'mon Mr. 'Hates The Beach,' let's go."

We shook the blanket free of sand and made for the car. I stopped at the curb to brush off my feet and put my shoes back on.

When I got into the car, Alex was fiddling with the radio. "What's your favorite kind of music?" he asked. "I'm trying to find something good for us to listen to on the way to your house, but I'm not sure what kind of music you like."

"I love me some top forty, but I'm also really into—don't laugh, musicals."

"I will completely not laugh. As a matter of fact, not only do I also love them, but I drive my family nuts singing show tunes in the shower " Alex said.

"I did a ton of singing in school; I made all-state for chorus my senior year."

"Well, let's see what we can find on the radio to sing along with."

Alex found a brand-new Adele song, and soon we were singing at the tops of our voices. More songs came on that we both knew, and it was great belting them out with him. I stopped singing only to give him directions. When we pulled into my driveway, I noticed the living room light was on—meaning at least one of my parents was up waiting for me to get home.

The dashboard clock read almost two a.m.

"Can we talk tomorrow?" I asked.

"Yep, assuming you're going to give me your cell phone number," Alex said, smiling.

God, his smile. I could just stare at it for hours. But, I had to break the spell. We exchanged numbers.

"I'm going to call you after work tomorrow, okay?"

"Definitely," Alex said. "You'd better."

I so didn't want to leave his car. It took all my willpower to open the door.

"Thanks for an awesome night," I said.

"You too."

As I slid out of the car, Alex grabbed my hand and kissed it.

"Thanks for being so honest, Carter—it means a lot. I hope my reaction was okay?"

His reaction couldn't have been better. "No, you were great, Alex—thanks so much for listening and being so accepting."

He blushed. "I'm glad you feel at ease."

I did. It was amazing to know that I didn't have to come out to him—I'd already done it. That he was sticking around even though I'm trans blew me away. I almost cried. For such a long time, dating had been an impossible dream. I've always been proud of who I am, but at that moment, I was even more proud. I had told him the truth, exposed my big secret and things had worked out in my favor. I was no longer too different and weird, I was a person worthy of care and love. I finally got to experience sweaty palms, racing heartbeats, nervousness, first kisses—all the normal teenage stuff.

The front porch light flicked on and off. "Okay, really have to go now."

"Right—that light means business. Just know that I'd be kissing you right now if parents weren't looming."

"Excellent," I said and turned to make way into the house. "Goodnight, my friend."

"Goodnight," Alex called softly.

As Alex pulled out of the driveway, I stared after his car as he drove away, then sighed deeply as I opened the front door.

Mom *and* Dad were up. Super. Mom was on the couch with her feet up and Dad was sitting in the reclining chair.

"Hello, Mister. It's two in the morning," Mom said.

"I know, Mother. I'm sorry it's so late."

"Mother?" she said.

"Well, Mister is so formal," I replied.

"Hardee-har-har," she said.

"What's up with the lateness, Carter?" Dad asked. "You're usually so much better about texting or calling when you're going to be so late."

"I'm sorry, guys. I just… I just had the best night of in the history of nights"

They both stared at me.

"I'm never washing my hand or my lips ever again. I don't care—never again," I said. "Dad, remember I told you about the most handsome man in the world? Well, his name is Alex. He's a sophomore at BU and he likes me. He *like* likes me. Oh, my God, I can't believe it."

Dad and Mom both grinned.

"So, there was kissing involved, I'm guessing." Dad said.

"Yep. Kissing more than one time."

"Oh, Carter, I'm very glad for you," Mom said.

"I met him at the dance; we went out for coffee and then hung out on the beach and talked and… stuff," I said. "I came out to him, too. He was a little taken aback, but he mostly took it in stride. Honestly, he was pretty great about it. I was so freaked out thinking *he* was going to freak out."

"Is he staying down here long?" Dad asked.

"For the whole summer."

"Carter, that's just great!" Dad exclaimed.

I floated up the stairs to my bedroom. I still couldn't believe the amazing night. My mystery man was real—and he wanted to really know me. That was awesome. Even though I had to get up in just a few short hours, I lay in my bed, unable to sleep.

The next morning when I showed up to work, J.P. came rushing over to me.

"Oh. My. God. Carter Stone, you need to tell me everything. *Everything.*"

Joe appeared around the corner. "You can tell him everything after you get over here and help this line of customers." Joe really knew how to ruin a party.

All day long, the lines wouldn't stop—and I didn't have time to tell J.P. anything at all. It was torture waiting to tell my best friend my stories. Finally, a late afternoon thunderstorm drove everyone from the beach and we had a chance to talk.

"So?" J.P. said, sitting on the counter.

"So?"

"Stop it! If you don't spill it, I'm going to kill you," he said, holding up his fists.

I beamed.

"I came out to him! I told him I'm trans. He only took a couple of minutes to get used to the idea. You've listened to me worry about this stuff for forever, and I finally had to just take a deep breath and do it. I thought I was gonna die, but I didn't. He really likes me for me, you know? We kissed more than once. He's great at it!"

J.P. smiled his biggest smile.

"He smells really good, his hands are really soft, his hair is perfect, he held my car door open for me, his laugh is awesome and I still can't believe that he likes *me.* Man, thank you so much for always listening to me. You're the best friend a guy could have."

"Carter, I've been telling you how great you are for years. Can you maybe believe me just a little bit?"

For the first time, I actually did—it was amazing.

I barely remember driving home. I knew that I would talk to Alex soon and I could hardly contain my excitement. I hurried through the kitchen, telling Mom and Dad that I couldn't talk—I needed to make an important phone call. Mom gave me a knowing glance, and Dad gave me a quick high-five.

I sat down on my bed and looked at my phone; my hands were shaking. My stomach flip-flopped. Just as I was going to enter his number, my phone rang. Of course, it was Alex.

"Hey."

"Hey, yourself," Alex said. "How was your day? I know you didn't get much rest last night. Sorry I got you home so late."

"Oh, don't even worry about that, it was *so* worth losing sleep."

"I thought about you all day, just so you know."

I was so relieved to hear that he wasn't the only one.

"Me too," I said and warmth flooded my cheeks. "I couldn't stop thinking about you either."

Alex laughed softly. "Glad to know I'm not alone."

"Alex? I want to know everything about you."

"I want to learn everything about you too, Carter. Where should we start?"

We talked for hours—through dinner, Hannah's bedtime and all the way into the wee hours of the morning. We laughed a lot and cried a couple of times as we shared our stories. We—oh wait. I see Doctor Martinez giving me a one-minute warning so I'll try to wrap things up.

"My First Love" is a great topic and it's been a lot of fun talking to you all today. That terribly lonely and confused fourteen-year old sitting in a rickety chair in Oliver's Bookshop would never believe that, in a few short years, he'd be an out and proud transgender man speaking in front of a group like this one. Look around, there are so many faces in this room—and we all know what it's like being LGBT. I love being a part of this community. I'm not the only trans person around anymore. Life here at BU has been a whirlwind of changes, but I'm enjoying every minute of them.

Speaking of changes, you may be wondering how my summer love story ended? Well, it's not over yet. Our story is just beginning. The slightly shy young man lurking by the door? That's my guy, Alex.

As I sat in our apartment wondering what I should say today, a certain someone came up behind me, hugged me tightly and told me that I should just "go with my heart." And so I have.

Something Like Freedom

Caroline Hanlin

ELIAS MEYER WAS ABSOLUTELY, DEFINITELY, NOT CHECKING out his best friend's cousin. He wasn't even sure how old Hannah's cousin was, so checking him out would have been completely inappropriate. Never mind the fact that, after ten years of friendship, he was pretty sure that her family members were off limits.

No, Eli's staring had nothing to do with how attractive—or not, he really hadn't noticed—Gabe was. Some people might be attracted to redheads with freckles covering every inch of their bodies, but Eli definitely wasn't. It was the mystery of it all that was getting to him. Gabe had appeared out of nowhere while Eli had been traveling in Europe with his parents. Eli had only been away a couple of weeks, but he'd returned home to a message from Hannah inviting him to spend his first day back in the States lounging by her pool. Then she'd casually mentioned that her cousin would be staying with her for a while. Eli hadn't even known Hannah had cousins he hadn't met.

Eli was lounging on a beach chair next to Hannah's pool and pretending not to watch Gabe as he lay on the next chair. After a solid twenty minutes while Gabe did absolutely nothing but nod his head to whatever music was playing on his iPod, Eli officially gave up. If he wanted to know anything, he was going to have to ask.

Eli dragged himself out of his chair and walked around the pool to where Hannah sat with her legs dangling in the water. She didn't look anything like Gabe; she had the same hazel eyes and thick, curly brown hair as her mother. Eli had always thought that she was pretty, but she tended to hide her curves under Mathletes team T-shirts, and she wore glasses because she didn't like having to fuss with contacts in the morning.

"What are you reading?" Eli pulled Hannah's book out of her hands as he sat down next to her. "*The Signal and the Noise.* Sounds thrilling. I can't believe you're reading about math on vacation."

"Statistics, technically," Hannah replied and tried to pull the book out of Eli's hands.

"Watch out." Eli held the book up out of her reach. "If you're not careful, I might drop it in the water."

Hannah crossed her arms and glared at him. "You're terrible. Did you come over here just to bother me?"

"Of course not! I came over here to talk to my best friend, who I haven't seen in weeks," Eli said, leaning backward to put the book on the pool chair behind him. Hannah looked skeptical, but Eli wrapped an arm around her shoulders and said, "So what's new with you, best friend?"

"You're not subtle, you know," Hannah said as she leaned into him.

"Whatever do you mean?" Eli asked. Hannah glared at him. "Okay, but seriously. What's up with your cousin? In two hours, I'm pretty sure the only thing he's said is 'Hi.'"

"He just doesn't need to fill every waking moment with chatter, unlike some people," Hannah replied.

Eli ignored the sting of her words. "Come on, Hannah, seriously. Who is he?"

"He's my father's nephew," Hannah said, then sighed and leaned back on her hands.

For a minute, Eli just gaped at her. Hannah and her parents weren't in contact with her father's family at all. The only time Hannah had met any of them was at her grandfather's funeral. Other than that, none of them had spoken to Hannah's father, Jeremiah, since he married her mother. Jeremiah's family was incredibly religious—as in, no sex before marriage, being gay is an abomination, evolution is a lie conservative Christian—and Hannah's mother, Rebecca, was Jewish.

"Holy shit," Eli said. "What is he doing here?"

"He needed somewhere to go," Hannah said quietly. "His parents found out that he's gay."

Eli closed his eyes and took a deep breath. He didn't need Hannah to explain further. He felt Hannah lay a hand on his back, and he rested his head on her shoulder.

"I don't really know much else, honestly," she said. "He wasn't very chatty at the funeral last year either, but I don't know if he's always this quiet or just when he's upset."

"I can't even imagine," Eli replied, dropping his legs in the water. His parents had been so supportive when he'd come out as bi a few years ago. He didn't know what he would have done if they hadn't been.

Eli heard a scream and then a splash as Gabe went flying into the pool. Hannah rolled her eyes at her boyfriend and wiped the water droplets from her face. "Really, Richie?"

Gabe surfaced a second later, and, once he'd pushed his hair out of his eyes, he crossed his arms and glared up at Richie. Richie was six foot two and solidly built—more like a football player than an engineering student—and Gabe was tiny. Gabe glaring at Richie was like a terrier trying to stare down a Saint Bernard.

"You looked like you needed waking up," Richie said with a winning smile.

Gabe held his glare for a minute, then started giggling. Eli hadn't seen Gabe laugh before, and there was something about it that made it impossible for him to look away. Gabe shook his head at Richie and then dived underwater to start swimming laps.

When Eli finally looked at Hannah, she was giving him a knowing look. "So, have you seen Melinda?" Hannah asked.

"No, I haven't seen my ex-girlfriend in the day and a half I've been home," Eli snapped. He knew exactly what she was trying to do, and it was a low blow. Melinda, Eli's high school girlfriend, had waited until they were both home from their freshman year of college to break up with him over ice cream sundaes. After dating for nearly two years, Eli had thought he deserved more than that. He'd left for Europe only a week later, thrilled to have something to take his mind off her and her new boyfriend.

Hannah laced their fingers together and gave Eli's hand a quick squeeze. "We're going to have an amazing summer, okay?"

"We always have amazing summers," Eli replied, squeezing back and smiling at her. Summers were their time. No matter who else might join them, the "Eli and Hannah show" was the center of the universe for those months. When they were kids, they'd played make-believe, crawling around Hannah's back yard and Eli's attic. Once Hannah got her driver's license, they had taken advantage of the ability to go wherever they wanted.

🦅

THE NEXT NIGHT, THEY HAD THEIR FIRST SLEEPOVER OF THE summer. Sleepovers at Hannah's always involved pitching her parents' giant tent in the back yard, filling it with blankets and talking until they fell asleep.

Hannah and Eli always forgot how to set up the tent. Even though they'd been doing it for years, Eli ended up shouting that the stupid diagrams didn't make any sense, and Hannah insisted that the problem was that they were missing a pole.

This year, Richie helped by flopping down across the tent where it was spread out on the ground. "Wake me when you guys stop arguing."

Eli and Hannah were just starting to get into the swing of debating whether the stakes went in first or last when the directions were tugged out of Eli's hands.

Gabe studied the diagrams. "Aren't you supposed to be the engineer?" he asked Hannah, gesturing at her Rochester Institute of Technology T-shirt.

"Good point!" Eli said, shooting a quick smile at Gabe, who blushed and wandered in Richie's direction. "What's the point of those fancy degrees you guys are getting if you can't even put up a tent?"

"I'm an electrical engineering major. It's totally unrelated." Richie got to his feet when Gabe tugged on his arm.

Hannah rolled her eyes. "Do you really think chemical engineering is more useful?"

"More useful than my music ed major? Yeah, I think so," Eli replied. That caught Gabe's attention, and Eli wondered why.

After a minute, Gabe grabbed the longest poles and started showing Richie what to do with them. It only took a few minutes for them to set up the tent. "Now you stake it down." Gabe handed the stakes to Eli and winked.

Eli stared after Gabe as he headed back to the house with Hannah. Apparently Gabe was capable of speaking in complete sentences if he wanted to, and he had a nice voice, even if it was quiet. He didn't know what to think about being winked at by someone who'd barely spoken to him.

By the time Eli and Richie got back inside, Hannah and Gabe were engaged in a serious popcorn fight. When Hannah saw them, she grabbed Richie to use him as a human shield.

"What on earth are you two doing?" Eli asked, looking at the popcorn-littered kitchen.

Gabe shrugged and smiled. "She started it."

On his way back from the bathroom, Eli caught sight of the clock on the microwave; it was past four o'clock in the morning. He was almost back to the tent when a shadow moved by the fire pit. He spun around, one hand pressed to his chest. "Jesus Christ!"

"Gabriel, actually," Gabe said, with a hint of a smile illuminated by the dying embers.

"Did you just make a Bible joke?" Eli wandered over to stand next to where Gabe was sitting in a folding chair. Gabe just grinned.

Eli deliberated about whether or not he should sit down. If he'd found Hannah or Richie sitting up this late at night, he'd have known that they would want to talk, but he didn't know anything about Gabe. Nevertheless, he dropped himself into the chair next to Gabe's.

"I hope I didn't wake you," Eli said.

"It's difficult," Gabe replied, leaving Eli totally flummoxed. He couldn't figure out what was difficult. Waking Gabe up? Or something else?

The two of them sat in silence while Eli tried to control his need to say something, anything at all. Gabe picked up a stick lying by the fire and started to move the coals around. Eli watched his hand; the steady motion was soothing, and it relaxed him until he could have fallen back to sleep in the chair.

"So, music ed?" Gabe asked, startling Eli from his reverie.

"Yep," Eli said and sat up straight in his chair. "At the University of Connecticut, but it's really just the backup plan." Gabe raised an eyebrow. "My band is working on recording an EP."

Gabe leaned toward him. "What do you play?"

"Guitar usually, and I sing lead," Eli replied. If Gabe was interested in music, Eli would happily talk about it forever. "I started on the piano when I was a kid, but I'm a much better guitar player."

"Must be nice," Gabe said and sighed.

"What must be nice?"

"Having a plan. I keep trying to figure out what I'm going to do with my life now. I haven't been able to think about much else since I left."

"Can I ask you something?" Gabe shrugged, so Eli said, "How did you end up here?"

Gabe nodded and pulled his feet up onto the chair so that he could wrap his arms around his legs. He looked so small and scared that Eli wished he knew Gabe well enough to hug him.

When Gabe finally spoke, Eli had to lean over to hear him. "There was this guy," Gabe explained. "He was in my church youth group and a lot of my classes, so I'd known him forever, and I didn't even know he wasn't straight. I usually miss these things."

Eli gave Gabe what he hoped was an encouraging nod. "He came over to study for our last final—history—and, right in the middle of the French Revolution, he kissed me." Gabe blushed and stared at his knees. "I don't think he knew my father was home."

"Oh, shit," Eli said, closing his eyes.

"Yep, and then my parents spent the next few days arguing about what to do with me and saying terrible things..." Gabe trailed off into a sniffle and used the sleeve of his oversized hoodie to wipe his eyes.

The tears broke what little restraint Eli had left; he knew he often annoyed people with his questions, but he didn't usually make them cry. He pulled his chair next to Gabe's. "I'm sorry. You don't have to keep telling me." Eli said, tentatively resting a hand on Gabe's back. Gabe relaxed a little under his touch, so Eli figured he'd gotten it right.

"I want you to know," Gabe said. "I'm just not very good at this."

Eli nodded and rubbed slow circles over Gabe's back while he pulled himself together. As the silence dragged on, he started to worry about what he was doing. Should he stop touching Gabe? Move farther away?

Just when Eli was starting to wonder if Gabe had changed his mind about telling the story, he started to speak again. "My parents eventually decided that I should go to one of those places that are supposed to cure you. I don't really want to be cured, so after graduation, I got on a bus. Everyone I was close to went to the same church as my family. Hannah was the only person I could think of to ask for help."

Eli could picture the whole thing, and the images made his heart hurt. He shifted to wrap his arm around Gabe, and Gabe rested his head on Eli's shoulder. For once, Eli was comfortable with the silence. He wanted to ask Gabe when he'd realized he was gay, whether he'd known his parents were going to react the way they did, if he'd talked to his parents at all, if they even knew where he was. Probably a bit selfishly, he also wanted to ask if that had been Gabe's first kiss or just the first time he'd been caught. But he was content just to sit and stare at the trees.

Eli was wondering why he could see everything so well when Gabe spoke again. "I was supposed to go to this evangelist college about an hour from home. Obviously I'm not doing that anymore. But I didn't really know what I was going to do there, either."

"There's nothing wrong with not knowing yet. You're only, what? Eighteen?"

"Seventeen," Gabe replied. "Until August. I'd just like to have a plan for September."

"That makes sense. It sucks not knowing where you're going next." Eli winced at how idiotic he must sound. He was distracted from contemplating why he always said stupidly obvious things when he looked down at Gabe and realized that he could make out the plaid pattern on Gabe's navy blue pajamas. "I think if we stay out here any longer we're going to catch the sunrise."

Gabe nodded and pulled away from Eli. "Guess we should sleep," he said and smiled.

Just as Eli turned to head back into the tent, Gabe grabbed his hand and pulled him into a tight hug. "Thank you," Gabe whispered.

Eli slipped back into his sleeping bag and closed his eyes, but he couldn't stop replaying his conversation with Gabe in his mind. Every time he did, the knot in his stomach grew. He kept picturing Gabe curled up in his folding chair crying and, even though he didn't know Gabe's parents, he was furious at them.

Every time Eli learned something about Gabe, he wanted to know more. Gabe was a puzzle, and Eli desperately wanted to understand him.

✍

"There isn't a snowball's chance in hell I'm going on that roller coaster, Hannah Collins, and you know it," Eli said, crossing his arms and glaring at her. For some reason, every time he and Hannah went to Six Flags, she tried to convince him to get on one of the theme park's several giant roller coasters. This year, her target was a ride that went upside down not once, but twice. Eli didn't like heights very much, but going upside down was even worse.

"Be adventurous for once! I hate abandoning you while we go stand in an hour-long line," Hannah replied, returning his glare.

"But you don't mind badgering me into doing something that I'll hate?" They were starting to make a scene, but Eli was too hot to care. Normally, he was willing to go a few rounds with Hannah, but it was already three o'clock and he'd been baking in the hot sun since nine in the morning. His shirt was sticking to him with sweat, and he was pretty sure the back of his neck was starting to burn

Hannah rolled her eyes. "How do you know you'll hate it? You've never been on it."

Gabe rested a hand on Eli's shoulder. "He won't be alone. I don't want to go, either."

"Fine!" Hannah said, throwing her hands in the air. "You two be lame together. Come on, Richie."

As soon as she was out of sight, Eli shot Gabe a grateful smile. "Thanks. It usually takes Hannah much longer to give up. Are you afraid of heights?"

"Something like that," Gabe replied. "What now?"

"Usually, I just get some ice cream and hang out. Where do you want to go?"

"How do you feel about getting wet?" Gabe grinned. The two of them headed to the line for one of the water rides, although they stopped to grab ice cream on the way.

"You know, you never told me what kind of music your band plays," Gabe said, after a few minutes of waiting in line.

"Oh, it's sort of folk rock inspired." It occurred to Eli that he should probably stop being so surprised every time Gabe started a conversation. Over the last couple of weeks, the two of them had begun to figure out how to talk to each other.

"Folk rock is still a thing?" Gabe asked innocently.

"Oh my God." Eli blinked at him. "I can't believe I just got burned by a guy who barely even talks."

"It's about quality, not quantity," Gabe replied, seeming incredibly pleased with himself for a moment before he burst into giggles.

Once they regained their composure, Eli said, "Seriously though, we're playing a gig next week in Hartford. I know Hannah's going to be out of town, but I'd love it if you came to see us."

Gabe's smile dimmed, and Eli couldn't figure out why. "So you'll still hang out with me while she's not here?" he asked and then bit his lip.

"Of course I will," Eli said, surprised that Gabe had to ask. Hannah and her parents were going to Costa Rica for a week. He knew they'd tried to include Gabe in the trip, but Gabe had convinced them that he'd be fine alone.

Now Eli wondered if that was really true. "You know you don't have to stay there by yourself if you don't want to, right?"

"I'm not asking them to cancel their vacation for me," Gabe replied, staring at the ground somewhere behind Eli's feet.

"I'm not suggesting you do." Eli stepped closer to Gabe. "You could stay with me. There's plenty of room."

Gabe's eyes snapped up to meet his. "Really?"

"Of course really. We're friends, right?"

Gabe nodded, then leaned close and ran his thumb over the tip of Eli's nose. "Ice cream," he said, then blushed and backed away. Gabe followed the line as it started to move, leaving Eli standing there, stunned, and getting strange looks. He pulled himself back together and hurried to catch up with Gabe.

On the ride home, they were all a little sun-drunk and sleepy. Eli was driving, and Hannah and Gabe had taken the back seat so they could sprawl out, leaving Richie riding shotgun. After a few miles, both occupants of the back seat had been lulled to sleep.

Richie looked over his shoulder to make absolutely sure that they were asleep and then said, "You know he's not afraid of roller coasters, right?"

"What?" Eli asked.

"Gabe," Richie said slowly, as if Eli were being especially dense. "I asked him what rides were his favorite last night, and he told me that he loves everything. So whatever reason he had for staying on the ground today, it wasn't about the roller coaster." Then Richie turned up the volume on the radio and left Eli to ponder that revelation.

Richie was implying that Gabe hadn't gone on the roller coaster because he'd wanted to stay with Eli. That thought made Eli a little giddy, but he didn't want to let himself get carried away. Still, there had been the moment with the ice cream, and that wasn't the only time in the past couple of weeks that Eli had thought Gabe might be flirting with him.

Eli glanced in the rear view mirror at Gabe sleeping with his feet in Hannah's lap and his head against the window. He didn't look as though he could possibly be comfortable, the way the seatbelt was twined around him, but that hadn't stopped him from falling asleep. The picture was so adorable that Eli couldn't help but smile.

⤛

ELI LOVED HIS PARENTS' HOUSE. IT WASN'T BIG AND BRIGHT and impeccably decorated the way Hannah's was, but it felt more like a home. Now that Gabe was coming to visit, though, he was hyper aware of what the place might look like to someone who had never seen it before.

It tended to be what his mother, Lorraine, called "pleasantly lived in." The furniture was a little bit worn, especially the armchair in the living room that was covered in golden retriever fur to the point where humans could no longer sit on it. His father, Joe, kept a rack of gardening magazines in the bathroom and was fond of explaining to anyone foolish enough to ask that they were there in case he had to be in there long enough to get comfortable. Eli was pretty sure he'd die if his father said that to Gabe.

Lorraine was perpetually in the middle of a scrapbook project, so she'd left piles of photos, albums, old ticket stubs and other mementos everywhere. She'd been trying to finish the scrapbooks since Eli's freshman year of high school and never made much progress, but she had managed to make the den into an Eli shrine. Several collages lined the walls, documenting Eli from the day he was born all the way through his high school graduation. The last one featured pictures of Eli's proms, so both of his exes, Melinda and Jason, were on display.

When Gabe texted on Saturday morning to say that he was headed over, Eli was struck with the urge to redecorate the whole house in the five minutes that it would take Gabe to get there. He had to settle for washing the sink-full of dishes that his mother had left after breakfast.

Eli gave Gabe the grand tour, even though it made him nervous. He started with the second floor, showing Gabe which room he'd be staying in and which room was Eli's, in case he needed anything. Gabe took everything in quietly, which left Eli to wonder what he might be thinking.

On the ground floor, Eli showed Gabe the kitchen and started telling him about the weird things they'd found in there when they'd renovated a few years before, but he trailed off when he realized that he'd lost Gabe's attention entirely.

Gabe stood in the doorway between the kitchen and the living room, one hand holding onto the door frame, staring at the black baby grand piano in the corner.

"Do you play?" Eli asked.

"A little," Gabe replied.

"Go ahead and play it if you want to."

Gabe crossed the room to the piano as if he was being pulled and settled himself on the bench. Eli followed him and hovered until Gabe said, "You can sit."

Eli perched on the edge of the bench. Gabe lowered his hands over the keys and took a deep breath before touching them. Then he began to play through scales.

Even though he'd done nothing more complicated than warm-ups, it was clear that Gabe loved playing. His long fingers glided across the keys, and he seemed more content than Eli had ever seen him.

Gabe turned to Eli with a smile and asked, "Any requests?"

"I wouldn't know where to start."

Gabe thought for a moment and then began to play. The music was familiar to Eli, but it took a few bars for him to figure out that it was Beethoven's "Moonlight Sonata."

Eli had thought that he was starting to get to know Gabe, but now it was clear that he hadn't even come close. Eli didn't know the music well enough to be sure that Gabe was playing every note perfectly, but he could see that Gabe played as if the instrument was an extension of himself. He was so clearly lost in the slow, somber melody. "Moonlight Sonata" had always seemed like a lonely piece to Eli, and the choice told him more about how Gabe had been feeling these last few weeks than any conversation they'd had. It was as if Eli had only seen the black and white version of Gabe. All of a sudden, he was seeing Gabe in color. Eli could have left, and Gabe wouldn't have noticed for hours. Eli could tell, because he was the same way when he was writing music.

When the first movement was finished, Eli said, "I don't think that was only playing the piano a little."

Gabe shrugged and—as if he couldn't stand to have his hands off the keys for even a minute—he began to play something slow and gentle. "I started playing when I was five," he said. "I used to play for church services."

That jogged Eli's memory, and he realized that the song was a hymn. Eli listened to Gabe play and then asked, "Do you believe in God?"

Gabe's hands stopped, but then he started playing again. Finally he said, "I've been trying to figure that out for years. I'm sure that I don't believe what my parents believe, but there are a lot of Christians in the world, and a lot of them wouldn't agree with my parents."

"That's true," Eli replied.

"It took me a long time to really accept that being gay isn't what's wrong with me," Gabe said, barely audible.

"I don't think there's anything wrong with you." Eli rested a hand on Gabe's back.

"There's something wrong with everyone," Gabe said stiffly, not looking at Eli.

Eli drew his hand back, stung. "Sorry. I shouldn't have interrupted you. I know I talk too much."

Gabe's eyes widened, and he took his hands off the piano so that he could turn and look at Eli. He let one hand drop to rest on top of Eli's on the bench. "I don't always say much, but that doesn't mean I want you to stop talking. I like listening to you."

Eli's breath caught in his throat, and he flipped his hand over so that he could lace his fingers with Gabe's. Everyone had always said that Eli talked too much, even his friends; it was overwhelming to hear someone say the opposite. When Gabe squeezed his hand back and smiled at him, Eli leaned close and pressed their lips together.

Eli realized what he'd done and pulled back, wrenching his hand away and scooting back to the end of the bench. "I'm sorry!" he said; he felt guilty when he saw Gabe's hurt look. "I didn't mean to, like, ambush you. I don't want to make you feel weird about staying here or anything. And I'm sure you don't need anyone else kissing you out of nowhere—"

"Please don't apologize for kissing me." Gabe cut him off. "Unless you don't want to do it again, I guess."

Eli took a moment to figure out what that meant, then he cupped Gabe's chin and kissed him again. Gabe pressed his hand to the small of Eli's back and urged him closer. Eli's heart was racing by the time he pulled away and smiled at Gabe. Part of him wanted to keep kissing and see how much further this would go, but he didn't want to mess up by going too fast.

Gabe turned back to face the piano, which made Eli laugh. "Well, at least I got your attention away from that thing for a few minutes."

"What should I play?" Gabe asked, then smiled and nudged Eli's shoulder with his own.

"Play something I'll know the words to," Eli replied.

Gabe rolled his eyes, but he started to play "Someone to Watch Over Me."

Eli started to sing along. Gabe let him sing alone for a verse and then, to Eli's surprise, he started singing harmony. It was a sweet song, if a little old fashioned, and Eli felt a bit giddy that Gabe had chosen a song about wanting to fall in love.

When the song was over, Eli raised his eyebrows and said, "I didn't know you could sing."

Before Gabe could say anything, Eli heard the front door slam open, and his mother shouted, "I wonder if my ungrateful child is going to help me unload all these groceries!"

Eli pressed one more quick kiss to Gabe's lips before he headed to the front door to help his mother. When he turned back, he saw Gabe still sitting on the piano bench staring at him in surprise. "You won't win any points with her if you don't help," he teased, and Gabe got up to join him.

"ELIAS JONATHAN MEYER, WHAT ON EARTH DO YOU THINK you're doing?" Hannah nearly shouted as soon as Eli answered the door. She'd gotten home from Costa Rica late last night, and this was the first time he'd talked to her in more than a week.

"I was going to make myself a sandwich," Eli replied, heading into the kitchen.

Hannah huffed and trailed after him. "You know that's not what I'm asking. What are you doing with Gabe?"

"Why, whatever do you mean?" Eli pulled his fridge open to see the options. He was used to Hannah's freak-outs.

"Don't play innocent with me! When I asked him if he had a good time with you, he blushed. Blushed!" It was hard to take her seriously when her sunburn made her look like an angry lobster.

"Gabe's a redhead," Eli pointed out and pulled a pair of tomatoes out of the fridge. "He blushes very easily."

Hannah walked around the kitchen island and smacked him on the arm. "Ouch!" he exclaimed, rubbing the spot, even though she hadn't really hit him hard enough to hurt. "See if I make you a sandwich now."

"Come on Eli. Cut the act and just tell me," Hannah said and pulled herself up onto the counter so she was at eye level with him.

Eli sighed and met her eyes. "Okay, fine. Gabe and I are dating."

"Do you really think that's a good idea?" Hannah asked. "You just got out of a two-year relationship. And Gabe's been through so much this summer. I don't want to see either of you get hurt."

Part of Eli wanted to tell her that they weren't going to hurt each other, but he knew better than to promise that. "Did you know he plays the piano?"

"He does?"

"Yeah, it turns out he's pretty brilliant. You should hear him." Eli closed his eyes and remembered all the hours Gabe had spent at the piano over the last week. "He's special, Hannah. I don't want to lose the chance to be with him because I was waiting for the right time."

Hannah's expression softened, and she said, "What am I going to do with you?"

"Continue to put up with me, I guess," Eli replied and then leaned over to give her a quick hug.

When she pulled back, she said, "Just remember, I've got my eye on you."

🐢

ELI WOKE SLOWLY. THE SOUND OF THE OCEAN ONLY A FEW yards from the Collins's beach house was so soothing that it was hard to get out of bed, even after nine hours of sleep. He wondered if Gabe would want to laze in bed for a while longer. Six weeks into their relationship, all he and Gabe did was fall asleep together, but Eli was still thrilled with the arrangement.

The two of them hadn't done a very good job keeping their relationship low key. Eli had meant to try—he knew that Gabe's life was still completely up in the air, and he didn't want to be one more thing that Gabe had to try to figure out—but he hadn't been able to keep things from getting intense. After being together all the time for the first week, neither of them had been content with only seeing each other every few days.

They were together almost every day now, at one house or the other. Eli would have spent most of his summer hanging out by the side of Hannah's pool anyway, and as soon as Eli's mother had heard Gabe play the piano, she'd issued him an open invitation to come over whenever he wanted to practice. Eli had spent countless hours listing to Gabe play while he pretended to be busy at his computer.

Eli had even worked up the courage to talk about composing with Gabe. Richie and Gabe had gone to see Eli's band, Decaf Coffee, play, and Gabe had stopped by a few practices. But Eli hadn't mentioned to Gabe that he'd written most of their original songs until Gabe found him in his bedroom a few weeks later, trying to fix a song that wasn't working. Writing music had become one more thing that they could do together.

Eli had figured out that everything Gabe didn't say was in his facial expressions, his gestures and his music. He was so accustomed to his world being loud, to filling empty spaces with idle chatter and laughter and music, that it was surprising how easily Gabe had slipped into his life. But, even if it was too soon, he knew that he was dangerously close to falling in love with Gabe's gentle silence.

It took Eli a minute to process the fact that Gabe wasn't next to him. He rolled over and found a sticky note on the pillow: *beach*. He put on swim trunks and went to look for his boyfriend.

Eli found Gabe in his blue plaid pajamas staring out at the ocean, running his fingers through the sand. Eli took a moment just to watch him. It had only been two months since they'd met, but he still thought that Gabe looked older. Hannah and Eli had taken Gabe shopping for new clothes a few weeks ago, at Mrs. Collins's insistence, because Gabe hadn't brought much with him. That definitely had an effect, but the real difference was in the way he held himself. As Gabe had gotten more comfortable, he'd stopped looking as though he was trying to be as small and unobtrusive as possible. It was as if he'd figured out that it was okay with everyone if he took up some space.

Eli sat down next to Gabe and bumped their shoulders together. "What are you thinking about?"

Gabe was quiet for another minute and then he took Eli's hand. "I miss them sometimes," he said quietly. "But I feel like I shouldn't."

"Your family?" Gabe nodded, so Eli said, "I don't think you shouldn't. I think it's totally understandable."

"I've been thinking about my future again."

Eli probably should have guessed that. It was what had occupied Gabe's thoughts ever since he'd come to Connecticut. He'd registered for some classes at the local community college, and he planned to apply to four-year colleges for the spring or next fall, but he still hadn't figured out what he wanted to study.

"Did you come up with anything?" Eli asked.

Gabe finally turned to Eli with an unreadable expression. "Did you know I've never seen the ocean before?"

"No, I guess I didn't," Eli said, wondering how on earth that was an answer to his question.

"It's hard to get very far with eight kids, and Minnesota is pretty landlocked," Gabe replied. "It's like I've spent the entire summer thinking that I was lost. My whole life, I'd planned on doing exactly what my family expected of me. But this morning, I woke up and all I wanted to do was play the piano, and really that's all I want to do for the rest of my life."

Eli gave Gabe an encouraging smile and squeezed his hand when he trailed off. Gabe was making the right choice—every time he touched a piano, it was clear that music was what he should be doing with his life, but Eli knew better than to interrupt. It wasn't always easy for Gabe to put complicated things into words, but he did it to keep Eli in the loop. Eli just needed to be patient.

"My first thought was that my father would never let me," Gabe continued, "and then I realized that he doesn't get a say."

"He sure as hell doesn't," Eli said, grinning at him.

Gabe stood up resolutely. "I can do whatever I want," he said, as Eli stood to join him, and then he wrapped his arms around Eli's neck. "I can go see the ocean, and be with you, and play the fucking piano and I don't have to ask anyone's permission."

"And you can swear!" Eli added.

"Damn straight," Gabe replied, giggling until Eli cut him off with a kiss. Gabe ran his fingers into Eli's hair and pulled him even closer.

After a few moments, Eli broke the kiss and rested his forehead against Gabe's. "So what do you want to do, now that you can do anything?" he whispered.

Gabe pulled away. "Go swimming?"

"You're wearing pajamas!"

"Who's going to stop me?" Gabe asked and then turned and ran towards the water.

Eli was completely floored, but if Gabe was happy, he wasn't going to complain. He pulled off his shirt and followed his boyfriend into the ocean.　🐾

On the Shore

Rachel Blackburn

S ALT WATER HEALS EVERYTHING—THAT'S WHAT POPPY Carter had been told. She couldn't remember the first time her mother had said it; it was always a family mantra. It was the reason they had a beach house, a place to escape to during the summer where the grime and unfortunate moments of everyday life could be soothed and washed away by the salt water, by the waves lapping against the sand and pulling whatever they could into the ocean.

It was why she yearned to head for the shore anytime something even remotely bad happened in her life. Saltwater had always healed her, and there was no better place to find saltwater than the beach she considered her second home.

Poppy's parents usually took a trip down for at least a few weeks in the summer, but she hadn't wanted to wait for them. A rough spring semester at college had begun with her heart being broken, and she'd needed to run to the sand and waves much sooner than planned. Being on her own was what she'd wanted anyway and the freedom to spend her time without obligation to anyone else, not even the obligation of polite conversation. Her parents were good people, and she loved them dearly, but there were some things about her they didn't completely understand.

It had been years since Poppy showed any interest in boys, and the first time she'd shown interest in a girl her parents had displayed mixed reactions: confusion from her mom, concern from her dad, disbelief from both. They'd had more than enough time to get used to it, but, while Poppy knew they accepted her, she hadn't wanted them to come with her to the beach house. Not after things had ended so roughly with a person they'd come to know. She could still sometimes see a glimmer in their eyes that told her they hoped she would try dating some guy again. This was not an intentional hope, but a subconscious one, and she didn't hold it against them. They tried, and she was grateful for that.

She just didn't want them near while she tried to feel better.

Even driving to the beach was different, a solitary road trip as opposed to her usual ritual of settling into the backseat, reading a book and paying no attention to where they were. Now, on her own, Poppy noticed each and every landmark that meant she was getting closer to crossing the bridge. The neighborhood seemed even more welcoming than usual. And then she saw the sign she'd been waiting for, tacked up on one of the back balcony's support beams: *Ocean Break*.

Poppy felt the salt in the air as soon as she opened the car door and heard the rush of the waves hitting the shore on the other side of the house. She heard the sound of people too, their voices washed out by the waves and seagulls. It only took seconds of standing there, taking it all in, for the tension she'd been holding in her shoulders to ease away. It made her smile to know that she already felt better and more relaxed, though she had just parked her car.

It took only two trips to get all her things to the room she'd always claimed as her own. The house seemed abnormally quiet after the dormitory, but Poppy couldn't imagine anything better. It was clean, and all hers, and as soon as she found one of her swimsuits in a suitcase, she changed, leaving the rest of the unpacking for later. After checking her reflection to make sure she looked all right with her dark hair tickling against her skin below her shoulder blades and her blue eyes protected by sunglasses, she grabbed a towel and headed out the front door, down the wooden pathway and onto the beach.

The sand was soft beneath her feet. Poppy let her toes sink in as she walked and, after she found a clear spot to set her things, she kept going, feeling the transition from soft, dry sand to the place where it became wet and dense. The water rushed up over her feet and pulled back into the ocean as she approached the shore. It felt wonderful, and even better as she walked into the ocean until she was deep enough to push off the bottom and dive under, letting the salt water cover her entire body and start to work its magic.

"LOOK OUT!"

The quiet of the past few days had been wonderful, especially combined with the lack of a schedule. Waking up whenever and not having to worry about anyone noticing how long she slept was especially great. It wasn't as though she was wasting time; she had nothing *but* time. All that greeted her in the morning was an empty house, all her own.

It had been days since she'd spoken to someone, or been spoken to. The brief pleasantries exchanged with a cashier when she'd gone to the grocery store didn't count. She hadn't even called her parents to let them know she'd made it, just sent a text. Three days into her vacation she was feeling settled, as if she never wanted to leave. It felt right to be in a place of such calm and warmth.

Her cycle had been simple: sleeping, swimming, lying on the beach and reading as she let the sun dry her, more swimming, more relaxing and then eating whatever food she managed to throw together. She had spent days on her own, glorious days of quiet and calm—which was probably why she didn't realize that those two rather important words were directed at her.

"Look out!"

Poppy could also blame the fact that she'd been lying there, letting the sun do its job of drying the salt water on her body, and the warmth had been lulling her into a half-sleep. She knew better than to fall asleep, even if she was careful with sunscreen, but that halfway point was such a nice place. She'd been listening to the waves, letting them break through the chatter of people around her with their rhythmic crash against the shore.

It was peaceful, wonderful, right up until the moment something hard smacked her in the forehead.

Her eyes flew open, and she blinked a few times to readjust to the bright sun. The haze of drowsiness faded and she shifted to prop up on her elbows. *What* had hit her? She barely had time to register the culprit—a Frisbee—before her attention was drawn to a person running toward her.

"Oh my God, I'm so sorry!"

Sand pushed against the edge of her towel as a girl dropped to her knees beside Poppy, and Poppy had barely parted her lips to say she was fine before the girl took Poppy's face lightly in her hands. This was almost as startling as being hit by the Frisbee in the first place. Poppy stared up at the girl, whose gaze flitted back and forth between Poppy's forehead and her eyes as though she might be able to see if something was wrong below the surface.

"I'm so sorry," the girl repeated. "Are you okay?"

Her voice was much softer now that she wasn't yelling from across the beach, as soft as her hands where they cradled Poppy's face. Poppy hadn't felt this kind of touch for weeks, months, not since before her breakup, and the long absence of contact only resonated more deeply when the girl's thumb brushed over her cheek. The girl's touch was so gentle, her gaze so intent, Poppy almost didn't register that she'd been asked a question.

"I'm fine," Poppy replied, clearing her throat when the words came out rough. Days of not using her voice had combined with her almost-nap to leave her throat dry and scratchy. "It was more startling than painful."

"Are you sure?" The girl's fingertips, feather-light, traced the spot on Poppy's forehead where the Frisbee had hit. Poppy nodded in confirmation. "I'm still sorry, it got thrown way past me, and there was just *no way* I could have caught it."

"It's all right, it happens," Poppy said, sitting up a little more as the girl pulled her hands away.

"I'm Ava, by the way. Ava Laurent."

Ava had been at the beach for at least a few days, if her tan was anything to go by. It was easier to see her once she wasn't leaning so close, and Poppy was glad to have a chance to take her in. She was tall and lean, and her dark blonde hair hung past her shoulders and covered the straps of her blue bikini. She was gorgeous—that much Poppy had known from the moment she saw her.

"Poppy."

"You know, we have some beer in a cooler over by our stuff if you want something cold to put on it, just in case," Ava said. She added, "Or if you wanted one to drink. That would probably help too."

"What time is it?" Poppy asked, furrowing her brow and pushing her hair out of her face with her sunglasses.

"Five o'clock somewhere," Ava replied with a soft smile. She rocked back onto her heels, stood up and brushed the sand off her knees, then extended a hand and wiggled her fingers. "Come on."

Poppy took Ava's hand and got to her feet. Even if Ava weren't pretty—it was a bonus that she was—Poppy would have gone with her. It was refreshing to have a conversation, even if because of a rogue Frisbee, even though Poppy had gone to the beach for solitude. After several days of being on her own, it felt good to join a group of people, to be taken into their fold with a simple introduction, as Ava threw the Frisbee toward one of the guys.

"Everyone, this is Poppy," Ava announced. "Poppy, this is everyone. Now, no one else hit her with a Frisbee, or anything else for that matter, or she might not be our friend!"

The eight people in the group were evenly split between boys and girls, all of whom replied with some sort of greeting amid the laughter. Poppy offered a small wave and smile before Ava's hand found hers again. With a little tug, Ava pulled her over to the cooler.

"How long are you guys here?" Poppy asked, pulling her sunglasses down out of her hair and sliding them into their proper place again.

"Through the end of the week," Ava replied. She flipped open the cooler, pulled out two bottles and passed one to Poppy. "Cheers! You're here by yourself, aren't you?"

"Right." Poppy took a sip. The coolness of the liquid in her mouth and the chill of the bottle in her hand were more than welcome after so much time in the sun. She knew she should have water instead, but she *had* had a bottle, which was now sitting empty by her towel. And, the beer was a welcome burst of flavor. "Were you just guessing that, or..."

"Sort of..." It would have been difficult to miss the sheepish look that spread across Ava's features, even if the sun could have explained away her barely there blush. "It's just... I've seen you out here before and you're always by yourself, so I figured... either that, or whoever came with you really hates the beach. I swear I'm not creepy!"

"I didn't think you were creepy," Poppy said with a soft laugh. She shook her head and absently tapped her finger against the bottle. "Yes, I'm here by myself. Which sounds more pathetic than it is—I chose to be, I didn't get stuck with it."

"I didn't think it was pathetic," Ava replied and furrowed her brow. She shifted a step closer. "I think it would be nice to be someplace like this without having to worry about anyone else. Don't get me wrong, I love being here with my friends and we had fun planning this trip together, but waking up to nothing but quiet and not having to worry about whether someone's already in the shower, or if I made enough coffee for everyone or need to start another pot..." She trailed off with a shrug and a gentle smile. "It sounds peaceful."

"It is."

The peacefulness was Poppy's favorite part. She hadn't had it for the longest time. In the dorm there were always doors slamming, voices carrying through the halls, any number of disturbances.

"I didn't mean to disrupt that." Ava bit her lip and shifted her weight from side to side. "By bringing you over here, I mean. I just thought maybe you'd like to have fun with us? But if you want to be by yourself, that's totally fine! No hard feelings or anything."

"No, you're fine," Poppy said, to quell whatever hesitation or regret seemed to be reflected in Ava's words. "You didn't disrupt anything—well, other than the Frisbee part. I promise. I'd love to have fun with you."

"Really?"

Even if Poppy wasn't quite sure she'd meant it, the hopeful look in Ava's eyes, paired with the brightening of her smile, would have been enough to convince Poppy of her own sincerity. Something about Ava produced a swoop in Poppy's stomach, slightly terrifying but uplifting at the same time. The swoop was familiar; she knew exactly what it was. She hadn't been sure if or when she would ever feel it again, not after how things ended the last time—but there it was. She gave a smile in return, nodded and clinked the neck of her beer bottle with Ava's. "Really."

"Yay!" Ava hopped onto the balls of her feet, grinned and brushed the pad of her thumb over Poppy's forehead with her free hand. "Let's try to keep you away from flying objects, though, okay?"

As much as Poppy had looked forward to solitude and quiet at the beach, she was taken aback by how glorious it felt to be drawn into an established group that treated her with familiarity. Ava had been serious about keeping her away from Frisbees, but they played bocce and helped one of the other girls with the huge, elaborate sandcastle she'd been working on for at least an hour; and when Poppy felt a nudge from one of the guys, who yelled "Tag!" and ran in the opposite direction, she sprinted after him without hesitation.

Poppy had forgotten it was possible to feel pure, carefree *fun,* with nothing behind it to make her think twice. She'd been missing that for a while, since she'd been with her ex-girlfriend, Elizabeth, who had been the perfect example of a Type A personality, and who hadn't done well with spontaneity. It was refreshing and wonderful to run around on the sand with people who were practically strangers, but seemed like old friends, and laugh so hard and so long that she thought she might cry. Everything that happened after being hit by that Frisbee was far more of an escape than any of the books she'd brought, or watching movies at night by herself in the house or even swimming.

And then there was Ava, who seemed to be the queen of everything light and cheerful. As if it weren't sunny enough on the beach, Ava seemed to make it even more so, with beaming smiles and laughter so full it made Poppy breathless. She couldn't recall the last time she had been around someone so energetic and bright. And she felt a pull between them; no matter what Poppy was doing, she found Ava close by—and Poppy lingered near Ava, as if being close to her might transfer some of that bright energy.

Poppy lost all track of time. It was only when someone mentioned wanting to go back to their house to rinse off that she realized it was probably time for her to do the same. As fun as the afternoon had been, it had also been tiring in the heat. The thought of showering off the sticky sweat and sand clinging to her body was blissful. Yet she didn't want to say goodbye to the feeling of weightlessness and pure happiness and she definitely didn't want to say goodbye to Ava.

"Thanks for letting me hang out with you guys," Poppy started, touching Ava's arm. She'd been arranging the bocce balls in their case. "Maybe I'll see you out here tomorrow?"

"What are you doing later?" Ava asked, biting her lip.

Poppy shook her head. "Nothing?" The question caught her off guard, but she would be lying if she said it didn't make her heart race. "I don't have any plans."

"We're having a bonfire; you should come!"

"I wouldn't want to intrude..." These words weren't the ones Poppy wanted to say; she wanted to accept the invitation with a "Yes, I'd love to," but they slipped out automatically, the product of her polite upbringing.

"Are you kidding?" Ava pushed her sunglasses up into her hair and gave her a playful look. "Don't be silly, Poppy, I want you to come!"

"All right," Poppy replied. A smile tugged at the corners of her mouth as she watched Ava grin. "Can I bring anything?"

"If you want, but we have *so* much," Ava said, rolling her eyes. "We made the mistake of taking too many people shopping when we went for food, so—"

A shout interrupted them, and both girls looked over to the rest of the group, which had started to their house. They had already gathered everything but the bocce set, leaving Poppy and Ava. Ava's eyes widened as she realized what they were shouting about.

"Oh, I have the key!"

Ava tugged a keychain out of the bocce case, then quickly zipped up the case and picked it up. She offered Poppy a smile and took a step toward her and rested her hand, with the keychain dangling from it, against Poppy's arm. Ava's touch was soft, soft as her hands had felt against Poppy's face. Poppy closed her eyes slowly and opened them again. Ava looked at her intently, and her smile seemed to be just for Poppy.

"We'll probably be out around sunset; I'm sure you'll be able to find us pretty easy. Don't worry about bringing anything but your pretty self, all right?"

And just like that, with a light squeeze to Poppy's arm, Ava turned on her heel and ran to catch up with her friends. Her smile growing, Poppy watched Ava go. She made herself walk back to retrieve her towel.

With a bonfire to look forward to, Poppy made her way along the path to her house. She would be glad to shower and then linger in the coolness of the air conditioning before it was time to head out to the beach again. It would give her time to think, too, to reflect on the turn her afternoon had taken. Ava was a breath of fresh air—so different from the personalities Poppy had grown used to. Poppy had had a semester to realize how, working so hard to keep things together with her ex, she'd lost herself in their relationship.

It had been so long since she'd thought she could be fully herself, but Ava had made her believe she could, and in just one afternoon of running around and having fun. That was enough to make Poppy nervous but hopeful, so she looked forward to the evening.

It seemed the sunset was slow to come.

Ava had been right, though, because when sunset finally did roll around and Poppy walked down the wooden path to the beach, she couldn't miss Ava and her friends for the brightness of their fire. Poppy felt the wind coming off the water on her arms and legs; she hadn't been out on the beach at night or in anything but a swimsuit yet this trip, but for the bonfire she wore a light dress with a flowing skirt that blew easily against her legs and fit closely in the bodice.

The now-familiar voices of the group grew clearer as she approached, and to be able to pick out and identify individual laughs made her smile. Still, her steps slowed; despite having been invited, she was unsure how to join them. Poppy barely had a chance to think about this before Ava glanced in her direction and lifted her hand in a wave.

It was both amazing and slightly scary how just that small gesture was enough to put Poppy at ease, but she tried to focus on the ease as opposed to the way her stomach swooped.

"I saved you a seat!" Ava proclaimed with a smile, patting the spot next to her on a cooler covered with a towel. Flicking her hair back from her face, Poppy held out the six-pack of beer she'd brought.

"I said you didn't have to bring anything!"

"I know you said that, but I felt bad coming empty-handed," Poppy replied with a grin. "Plus, you guys shared with me earlier, so it's only right I share with you."

"Tricky," Ava said, with a shake of her head. Then she stood to put the beer in the cooler, and asked "Anyone else want something while it's open?"

Drinks were passed around and the cooler was shut again. The crackling of the fire was so lovely, with the waves crashing in the background and just enough breeze to make the warmth of the flames welcome. Clearly it wasn't the first time someone in the group had built a fire like this: the perfect size and neatly contained. Poppy felt so comfortable, she might want to stay for hours.

"Thanks for inviting me," she said just loud enough for Ava to hear.

Ava smiled, so genuinely, as though she had all the time in the world to spend with the person she directed it toward. It was silly to read so much into a smile, Poppy knew, but she had been dealing with those bright smiles for much of the day. She'd spent a fair amount of time already thinking about what it was, exactly, that made her feel the way she did when Ava smiled.

"Of course! I would have been sad if you didn't come." Ava shifted toward Poppy and tilted her head. "How's your head?"

"My head?" Poppy raised her hand to her forehead; her fingers ghosted over the place where the Frisbee had hit her. "Oh, it's fine. There's not even a mark to use to get sympathy."

"Aw, well that's good, I suppose," Ava said with a sigh. She grinned. "I was going to offer to kiss it better, otherwise."

"I would have said it hurt if I'd known that."

The words were out before Poppy realized she was saying them. She'd said them in a teasing tone, for which she was instantly glad, but still, the few seconds after she spoke froze, and the words hung in the air between them, waiting. Ava didn't look put off; her grin turned into a smile, and she brought her hand up to rest gently against Poppy's cheek. She sat up straighter, leaned over and tilted Poppy's head down slightly. As Ava pressed a kiss to Poppy's forehead, Poppy's eyes closed.

The swooping feeling Poppy had felt in her stomach was nothing compared to what she felt then. Ava's lips were soft and warm and they lingered long enough to make Poppy wonder if time had stopped, but the sound in the background—waves, the fire, conversations—proved otherwise. She rested her hand over Ava's hand on her cheek, fighting the way her breath threatened to catch in her throat. When Ava started to pull away, the loss of the gentle pressure against her forehead caused Poppy's eyes to flutter open.

"There," Ava whispered; the corners of her mouth quirked up in a smile again as she pulled back enough for them to see each other. "Now you have that saved up, if starts to hurt later."

"Thank you," Poppy murmured. Her fingers flexed slightly where they rested over Ava's. Ava laced their fingers together and then pulled her hand away from Poppy's cheek.

"Of course," she said. She nudged Poppy's shoulder with her own, keeping her body angled toward Poppy's but letting her attention flicker to the others around the fire.

Even though she was on the fringe, Poppy felt welcome watching Ava's friends interact. As they shared stories and inside jokes around the fire, Poppy could see how close they were and how well they knew each other.

Music from portable speakers was a pleasant distraction, something to listen to when so many words were flying around. It ranged from pop songs to music Poppy wasn't familiar with, loud enough for her to hear but soft enough to keep her from being able to take it in. A few more logs were thrown on the fire, and Poppy sank into a warm sense of comfort.

Then the song changed just at a lull in conversation, and Poppy recognized a song she hadn't listened to for months, a song that had been a particular favorite of her and her ex-girlfriend. It was a song she'd managed to forget. She sat up straight, frozen in her seat, staring into the fire.

"Poppy?" Ava's voice, too soft to be heard by anyone else, broke through the music. Poppy glanced away from the flames to look at her. "You okay?"

Seeing so much concern in Ava's eyes, Poppy realized she'd overreacted, even though her response was involuntary. The thing was, it wasn't even a romantic song. It had always made her want to get up on her feet and jump around as if she didn't have a care in the world; it was a song she'd loved before it became something meaningful between her and her ex.

Just thinking of that made annoyance flare up. It was a *song*. Sure, it had been *theirs*, but she hated that it might make her feel this way every time she heard it. She'd enjoyed it before and she wanted to enjoy it again. The easiest way to do that was to find it a new context.

"Yeah," she replied, and cleared her throat. "This song always makes me want to dance."

"Then dance!"

"It wouldn't feel right dancing by myself," Poppy said, and she couldn't help but smile when the other girl's eyes seemed to light up.

"I would *never* make you do that," Ava replied with mock seriousness. She squeezed Poppy's hand as she got to her feet. "Let's dance."

When Poppy and Ava stepped out from the circle of make-shift seats and started to move, someone turned up the music. It was freeing to let loose and flow with the music. They weren't alone for long—many of the others joined them—but, with Ava holding her hand, it still seemed to be just the two of them. It was blissful to make new memories to be triggered by the same song, memories to take the place of those from the past.

The waves were still audible through the music and the voices mingling as they sang along in parts of the song. The breeze grew stronger and tousled Poppy's hair; it picked up the fabric of her dress and blew through it as if trying to carry her away—she thought she could fly, if she wanted to.

Ava danced as though she didn't care if the whole world was watching. Her hand hadn't left Poppy's since they'd stood up. Their fingers hooked together to keep them from drifting too far apart. Poppy thrilled at the touch of Ava's fingers, and the way their eyes kept meeting in the low light from the fire.

Song after song, the dancing continued. Finally, Poppy felt breathless and took a step back as another song faded out. She pushed her hair back from her face and glanced at the fire, which didn't seem nearly so inviting now that she had been moving enough to break a sweat.

"I think I'm going to walk a little," she said, stepping close enough for Ava to hear. "Just by the water."

"Want some company?" Ava glanced at the shoreline and turned back to Poppy, her eyes slightly widened. "Unless you meant to go by yourself... sorry. I thought it sounded like a good idea, get a chance to cool off."

"Company sounds perfect."

Ava grinned and let go of Poppy's hand to move over to the few people still sitting by the fire and tell them where she was going. Then she hooked her own arm into the crook of Poppy's. "To the water!"

The closer they got to the water, the darker it got; but the lights from the houses along the beach kept them from being too blind. Every few seconds the water rushed up over their feet and then pulled back out to the ocean, taking wet sand from beneath them and tickling the soles of their feet. Poppy let their arms untangle as Ava leaned down to pick up a seashell, and then felt slightly disappointed that they didn't hook arms again. But Poppy didn't want to care too much about that. She already felt beyond lucky.

"I'm glad you invited me," she said between waves and glanced at Ava. Poppy didn't mind taking the brunt of each wave; none of them splashed higher than her calves. "To hang out with you guys this afternoon, and then tonight."

"Of course," Ava murmured. She paused and then went on, speaking less softly. "I mean, we hit you with a Frisbee! I'd been wanting to talk to you anyway, though."

"So the Frisbee was a ploy—"

"No!" Ava laughed, shook her head and scrunched her nose. "It wasn't a ploy, it got thrown too hard, and I couldn't get it. Believe me, none of us have good enough aim to hit you on purpose."

"Why'd you want to talk to me?"

"It's like I told you before, I noticed you," Ava went on, giving a little shrug. "You were always by yourself, and I know some people like being by themselves sometimes, but you were *always* on your own, and I thought you might be lonely. So I was going to invite you to come play with us if you wanted, but I never got up the courage. And then the Frisbee happened."

Poppy glanced at Ava and furrowed her brow. "Courage? I'm not *that* intimidating—"

"No, but you're beautiful."

They both stopped in their tracks—Poppy first, her feet settling in the wet sand as the water rushed over them, then Ava a few steps later, when she realized she was walking on her own. Her eyes wide, she turned back to face Poppy; she took a step closer. The silence hanging between them was soon broken by the next wave coming up over their feet and the distant sounds of laughter and music from a nearby house—too soft to be disruptive, but still loud enough to hear. Loud enough to make Poppy close her eyes for a long moment. She extended a hand toward Ava.

"Dance with me?"

Ava wordlessly slipped her hand into Poppy's; her fingertips grazed Poppy's palm and sent tingles all the way down to Poppy's toes. They laced their fingers together and Ava took another step toward Poppy. The song was slow, timeless, so different from the fast-paced pop that had blasted from the speakers by the campfire. Poppy's arm moved around Ava's waist as though it was always meant to be there, and Ava's arm circled Poppy's shoulders. By the time the next wave splashed their legs, they were pressed close, swaying with the music as they rested their temples together.

One word Ava had used stuck in Poppy's mind: lonely. She'd always taken time away from other people to recharge, decompress, settle back into herself, and that's what she'd anticipated her vacation would be about. Going places on her own had always been an adventure, an escape from obligations or having to stick to a schedule. Usually, she didn't feel lonely.

She hadn't been wallowing; she hadn't let herself linger over memories or feelings that had come and gone dozens of times since one bad day turned into several and then into weeks. No, this vacation had been *peaceful,* and maybe that should have been a sign to her earlier on that she was already over it, already moving on.

But she hadn't realized that until Ava. Until she saw that smile, until she felt a swoop in her stomach instead of a pang in her chest. She had the same swooping feeling now, with her fingers laced in Ava's as they held each other close and slowly danced to the barely audible music. It wasn't until Ava's hands had touched her face that she'd realized how much she'd been missing human contact.

Yes, she'd been lonely.

Being with Ava felt right, with the water moving over her feet and the wet sand covering her toes, with the ends of Ava's hair tickling her arm where it rested against Ava's back. The soft sound of Ava's breathing, so close to Poppy's ear, was not lost in the vast roar of the ocean. A light sprinkle of rainfall had begun, and the music had faded out, but that wasn't enough cause for them to stop. Ava's arm left Poppy's shoulders just long enough for her to drop the seashell and let her fingers trail through Poppy's hair. Ava's fingernails scratched Poppy's scalp luxuriantly, then started their descent. Poppy's eyes slowly closed; her breath caught.

"Now *I'm* the one who needs to get up the courage," she murmured. Ava's fingers paused before moving back up through her hair.

"Why's that?" Ava asked, her voice nearly soft enough to be drowned out by the waves.

"Because I want to kiss you."

To be honest with herself, Poppy knew she'd thought about kissing Ava ever since that first moment when Ava held her face, so gently, and checked to make sure Poppy wasn't hurt. The thought had grown in frequency as Poppy had become more familiar with the way Ava laughed, the way her hair fell into her eyes on the right side of her face more often than on the left, the way she rubbed her thumb against the back of Poppy's hand almost habitually, and the way she tilted her head to rest her temple against Poppy's.

"You don't need courage for that," Ava whispered, her mouth so close to Poppy's ear her lips brushed the skin. The touch was barely there, but it was enough to send a shiver all the way through Poppy and make her toes curl in the sand.

They pulled back. Poppy took in the small raindrops clinging to Ava's eyelashes and slipped her hand out of Ava's to gently cup Ava's jaw as she pressed a soft kiss against Ava's lips. As she let her lips part, Ava's fingers ran up into Poppy's hair and cradled the back of Poppy's head, and her lips caught lightly against Poppy's as she pulled away, only to kiss her again a split second later. Poppy felt her whole body tingle; each little kiss sent her senses into overdrive and made her want more. She felt as if a fire had flared up inside of her, one that had been dormant for too long. Ava had sparked it, and not even the waves from the ocean rushing up against Poppy's legs or the rain falling down on her from the skies posed a threat of putting it out.

It seemed that neither of them wanted the moment to end—Poppy knew it for herself, and Ava did not pull away except to take a breath. Poppy felt lost in the best way, lost in Ava and the way her lips felt against Poppy's own, the way her fingertips pressed gently into her hair, the way everything felt as if it were happening so quickly and so slowly at the same time. Poppy had no idea how long they'd been away from the fire, how long they'd been standing in this exact spot.

A loud, long clap of thunder made them jump and finally broke the spell. Poppy looked at Ava and then tilted her head back to peer up at the sky. At some time the rain had gone from a mere sprinkle to a full-fledged shower, but she hadn't noticed. Lightning lit the sky.

Ava let her hand slide from Poppy's hair and down, her fingertips tracing Poppy's arm. She reached for Poppy's hand. "We should get under cover!"

Poppy pushed her wet hair out of her face; she scrunched her nose at the sensation of her hair clinging to her skin and gave a nod of agreement. She squeezed Ava's hand softly and glanced back; she didn't want to leave the spot where they were standing or the close proximity to Ava's body, or lose the lingering phantom of Ava's kiss on her lips, and she absently nipped her lower lip. More thunder rumbled, and she took it as a sign to stop wasting time. The rain was a downpour already, and there was no sign of it letting up.

They started back down the beach holding hands, walking as fast as they could without starting to run. With no sign of anyone else on the beach, it was clear that the rest of the group had had the sense to get inside when the rain started. It was eerie, traipsing through the sand on an empty beach in the rain, finding their way back to someplace familiar.

"I'm sure they took everything back to the house already," Ava said, giving Poppy's hand a tug. "No use being out by a fire when it's raining and all."

Poppy nodded and turned to walk backward, facing Ava, so she could see her as she spoke. She remembered part of a conversation they'd had so much earlier in the day that she'd almost forgotten it. "House full of people all raucous and trapped inside because of the weather... want to go somewhere quieter?"

Poppy's house was closer; even if it hadn't been, she wasn't ready for the night to be over. It had all felt so easy and right—no way their time together should be cut short just because of some rain. It was worth being soaked to the skin to walk slowly backward and to see the way Ava's eyes lit up and how quickly the smile spread across her features.

"I'd love to," Ava replied, taking a quick few steps and getting close enough to kiss the corner of Poppy's mouth. She nudged Poppy's cheek with the tip of her nose. "Take me home."

Poppy couldn't recall a combination of six words that had ever sounded so sweet. She tugged Ava's hand, and they started to run across the sand, all stumbling giddiness and laughter as they made their way toward Ocean Break with the rain pouring down. Poppy's mom had been right—salt water heals everything.

By the time they got to the house—both soaked to the skin, neither ready to let go of the other's hand—Poppy was confident that rainwater could too. 🐚

About the Authors

Rachel Davidson Leigh, "Beautiful Monsters"
Rachel Davidson Leigh is a writer, educator, and small town native who tells stories she wishes she could have read as a teen. Beautiful Monsters is her first published work of fiction. She lives in Wisconsin with her family and two dogs, who are spoiled out of their tiny minds.

Suzey Ingold, "The Willow Weeps for Us"
Suzey Ingold is a writer, linguist and coffee addict, currently based in Edinburgh, Scotland. Brought up in a household where children's books are quoted over the dinner table, literature has always had a strong influence on her life. She enjoys travelling, scented candles and brunch.

Amy Stilgenbauer, "The Fire Eater's Daughter"
Amy is a writer and aspiring archivist currently based in southeast Michigan. She is the author of the novelette series, *Season of the Witch*, as well as the Young Adult novel, *The Legend of League Park*. When she isn't writing, Amy enjoys all things bergamot and tries to keep her cats away from her knitting.

Ella J. Ash, "Surface Tension"
Ella J. Ash is a lawyer by day and an author by night. She has been a writer in online fan communities wince 2006. She also enjoys dance parties with her family and cooking experimental vegetarian cuisine. She lives in Toronto with her partner, three daughters and four tropical fish.

H.J. Coulter, "My Best Friend"
H.J. Coulter lives in Winnepeg, Canada, where she works as a respite worker and studies music, in hopes of one day becoming a musical therapist. "My Best Friend" is her professional writing debut.

Naomi Tajedler, "What the Heart Wants"
Bio: Born and raised in Paris, art has always been in Naomi Tajedler's life—including painting, restoring books, and working in auctions. She started writing in online fan communities in 2009.

S.J. Martin, "The Most Handsome"
S.J. Martin lives with his partner and their cranky, rotund, cat in Washington D.C. He's a barista by day and a writer by night. He makes a mean cappuccino and lives for good coffee, good books, and good company. "The Most Handsome" is his first published story.

Caroline Hanlin, "Something Like Freedom"
Caroline Hanlin is a full time statistician, a part time stage manager, and an avid sports fan. She currently resides in Boston, where she enjoys writing during her commute. "Something Like Freedom" is her first published short story.

Rachel Blackburn, "On the Shore"
Rachel Blackburn is a writer, musician and librarian based in central Ohio. When free from work, she enjoys cuddling with her cats, drinking tea, and baking more cupcakes than necessary. On the Shore is her professional writing debut.

Say hello to

an imprint of interlude **press**

Also from
duet

duetbooks.com
the **young adult** imprint of interlude**press**

CPSIA information can be obtained at www.ICGtesting.com
Printed in the USA
LVOW06s1453191115

463342LV00003B/543/P